BUTTERFLY
STORIES

Also by William T. Vollmann

You Bright and Risen Angels

The Rainbow Stories

The Ice-Shirt

Thirteen Stories and Thirteen Epitaphs

Whores for Gloria

Fathers and Crows

An Afghanistan Picture Show

William T. Vollmann

BUTTERFLY STORIES

A NOVEL

GROVE PRESS

NEW YORK

This book is for

Ben and Charlotte

First published in Great Britain in 1993 by André Deutsch Limited
First Grove Press edition, November 1993

Published simultaneously in Canada
Printed in the United States of America

FIRST PAPERBACK EDITION

Library of Congress Cataloging-in-Publication Data
Vollmann, William T.
    Butterfly stories: a novel / William T. Vollmann.—1st ed.
    I. Title.
    PS3572.0395B88   1993
    813'.54—dc20   93-2489

ISBN 0-8021-3400-9 (pbk.)

Grove Press
841 Broadway
New York, NY 10003

10 9 8 7 6 5 4 3 2 1

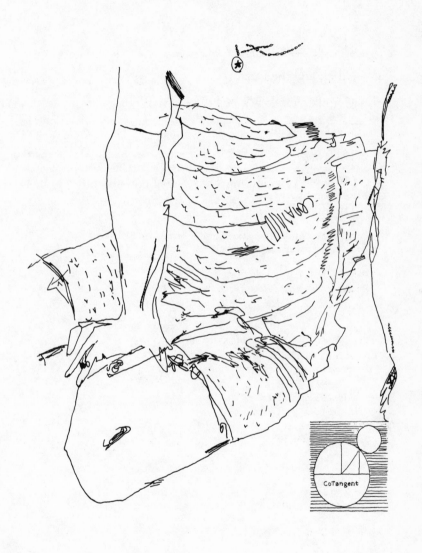

CoTangent

Contents

In case any of you readers happens to be a member of the Public, that mysterious organization that rules the world through shadow-terrors, I beg you not to pull censorious strings merely because this book, like one or two others of mine, is partly about that most honest form of love called prostitution – a subject which the righteous might think exhausted with a single thought – or, better yet, no thought at all – but the truth is that there are at least thirteen times as many different sorts of whores as there are members of the Public (and I think you know what I mean by members). Shall we pause to admire them all (the adults, I mean, the ones with the ambitiously long-tubed mouthparts)? Looking under the trees I spy billions of species, most of whom fly only during the night, unlike the insects after whom they're named; the pupa stage is often enclosed in a cocoon of brightly colored silk. And yet some are alive and some are dead and some find money to be the least of their worries! – Oh, my prismatic Nymphalidæ, my cross-veined Psychidæ, my Sesiidæ with the delicious anal veins, how could cruelly unimaginative lepidopterists have pinned you to a common corkboard of classification, when after all the world is so shadily large? I'll not commit that crime! So fear repetition not; there remain many seas of blood and cream to be traversed. If this advertisement be not sufficient, I can only protrude my wormlike tendrils of apology, craving forbearance on the grounds that a writer must write about what he knows, and since I know nothing about any subject it scarcely matters where I dabble.

Your friend,

The consequences beasts draw are just like those of simple empirics, who claim that what has happened will happen again in a case [that] strikes them [as] similar, without being able to determine whether the same reasons are at work. This is what makes it so easy to capture beasts . . .

G. W. LEIBNIZ, Preface to *The New Essays* (1703–5)

1

U nder the leaning plant-tumuli were galleries of wet dirt in which the escapees hid, panting like animals, naked and trembling, gazing up at the flared leaves whose stalks, paler than beansprouts, wove each other's signatures. Not everybody was caught again. Their families had to be bulldozed into the American bomb craters without them. Wormy dirt pressed down on bloodstained dirt until everything stopped moving, and the slaves were forbidden to work there for a month, until the mound had settled. The slaves had no desire to go there anyway. Water buffaloes rooted and splashed slowly in the rice paddies. They were valuable. As for the slaves, there was a slogan: *Alive you are no gain; dead you are no loss.* So the slaves obeyed the rule of absolute silence. After a month, they were sent to plant the grave with cassava. Meanwhile, the

8

ones who had gotten away lived hour by hour beneath the roof of maculed leaves swarming with darkness as they crept toward Thailand, ducking through green-fringed purple leaves, dodging golden berries as hard as copper. Sometimes a land mine got them, and sometimes a snake did. It did not matter whether the land mines were Russian or Chinese because they rended people with the same sudden clap of smokepetaled flame. But the snakes came in so many varieties as to guarantee an interesting death. One kind let you live a day after you were bitten. Another kind killed in an hour. There was a kind that let you walk two steps before you fell down dead. The people who survived the snakes fled on toward Thailand, where if they were lucky they might win admittance to a barbed wire cage. As they ran, they gasped in the strong wet smell of ferns. Fallen flower-bowls, red and yellow, lay in the knee-deep carpet of ferns. In the very humid places, moss grew out of the tree trunks and mounded itself upon itself in clusters like raspberries. From these places ferns burst out, and spiderwebs grew on the ferns, and within the webs the spiders waited. Some were poisonous and some were not. Sometimes the people who survived the spiders became lost and came out into a clearing where their executioners were already conveniently waiting. Around the lip of the bomb crater, generous grass bowed under its own wet weight, the dark star-leaved trees meeting it in a terrifying horizon. The people would begin to scream. The order was given to approach the grave in single file. Sometimes the executioners cut open their bellies or wombs with the razor-sharp leaf-edges of sugarpalm trees. Sometimes they smashed their skulls in with pickaxes. The executioners who were especially skilled at this enjoyed practicing what they called "the top." When you stand behind someone and smash his skull in in just the right way, he will whirl around as he falls and gaze up at you with his dying eyes. Sometimes they beat them to death with gun butts. Sometimes they pushed them off cliffs. Sometimes they crucified them in trees. Sometimes they injected them with poison. Sometimes they peeled back their skins and ate their livers while the victims were still screaming. Sometimes they wrapped up their heads in wet towels and slowly suffocated them. Sometimes they chopped them into pieces.

2

The butterfly boy knew nothing about this, firstly because he was only seven years old and in another country, and secondly because it hadn't happened yet. It would be two more years before he even saw a dead person.

3

The butterfly boy was not popular in second grade because he knew how to spell "bacteria" in the spelling bee, and so the other boys beat him up. Also, he liked girls. Boys are supposed to hate girls in second grade, but he never did, so the other boys despised him.

4

There was a jungle, and there was murder by torture, but the butterfly boy did not know about it. But he knew the school bully, who beat him up every day. Very quickly, the butterfly boy realized that there was nothing he could do to defend himself. The school bully was stronger and faster than he was. The butterfly boy did not know how to fight. When the school bully punched him, it never occurred to him to punch back. He used his arms to protect his face and belly as best he could, and he tried not to cry. If it had been just him and the school bully, he probably would have cried, because he regarded the school bully as a titanic implacable force in comparison to which he was so helpless that he was as a sacrifice to an evil god, so there was no shame in crying before him. But since the other boys loved to gather in a circle and watch the butterfly boy being beaten up, he would not cry; they were his peers – not, of course, that *they* thought so. To every other boy in the school, the butterfly boy was so low and vile that he was not a human being.

5

The school bully was retarded. He had failed fourth grade three times. He was therefore much bigger and stronger than any other boy in the elementary school. In the winter time the custodian shoveled all the snow in the playground into a great heap in one corner, and the pile froze into a mountain of ice that almost topped the fence by February or March. The school bully claimed this mountain as his kingdom. He stood on the summit of that dirty blue pile of frozen slush and picked out his victim, following a sorting algorithm which may have been similar to the butterfly boy's once he grew up and had to decide which whore to fall in love with. The bully, however, appeared to have studied at the school of the eagles. He turned his hunched head in a series of alert jerks, his eyes rarely blinked, and when he had spotted someone he could torture he shrieked like a bird and brought his arms up into wings. The way a boy walked, the color of his shoes, these and other unknown criteria were scanned by his hard little eyes, until he had searched out a rodent worthy of his malice. It was always the butterfly boy first, but sometimes it was someone else, too. You might think that that someone else and the butterfly boy would become allies, but it never happened. Whomever the school bully hurt was so

11

disgraced and humiliated that he was no good for anything. He had become so despicable by virtue of being hurt that not even other despicable people could stand him.

6

So the only playmates that the butterfly boy had were girls. He loved girls. Sometimes he kissed them, and sometimes they kissed him. Occasionally the stronger girls would even defend him from the bully. But this only made the butterfly boy even more miserable. He would rather have gone home with another bloody nose than endure the additional odium of being defended by girls.

7

So the butterfly boy's pleasures were of a solitary kind. One evening a huge monarch butterfly landed on the top step of his house and he watched it for an hour. It squatted on the welcome mat, moving its gorgeous wings slowly. It seemed very happy. Then it rose into the air and he never saw it again. He remembered that butterfly for the rest of his life.

8

The last bell had rung. The children rushed into the wet and muddy hallway in a happy rage of shouts and clattering lunch-boxes. As the butterfly boy reached the halfway mark with his galoshes buckles, a girl came to help him. Some of the buckles were crooked or a little rusty. Every day this girl did up the most difficult ones for him. The outer door kept banging open and closed as children ran into the snow. Through it the butterfly boy caught stroboscopic glimpses of the waiting steaming school-buses, not as yellow as they would be in the spring rains when their gorgeous new yellowness shouted itself even more brightly than the No. 2 pencils given out for penmanship; the sticky snowflakes paled and frosted the buses into something coy and lemon-gold, more fit now to swim through blizzards illuminated by their pale yellow eyes.

Want to come to my house? the girl said.

When? said the butterfly boy, startled.

Now.

The butterfly boy smiled down shyly as the girl fastened the last buckle for him. – Yeah, he said.

When he got into her bus with her, he had a sense of doing something deliciously wrong. Her bus had a different black number stenciled on it, and a different driver. The black vinyl seats smelled different. There was chewing gum stuck in different places. The children who got on the bus were different. They seemed quieter and happier and more perfect to him. They left him alone.

The bus that he usually rode drove away first, and when he saw it go he felt nervous for a moment. His parents might be angry.

The girl was taking him somewhere he'd never been. They sat warmly together with their lunchboxes on their laps, passing white winter hills and farmhouses and horses shaking snow off themselves. Some of the trees were only dusted with snow, as a cake might be with sugar, while others below, onto which they had discharged their loads, resembled snowmen or plump downy birds. They passed a little evergreen heavily lobed with it like a brain stood on its end, and by its agency the light passing into the bus window was whitened, so that when the girl turned suddenly toward him her face resembled a marble angel, and then the tree was past, and her features obeyed the vibrations of a rosier light. Without knowing what he was doing or why, he

13

suddenly plunged his face into her warm hair. The girl looked at
him with great seriousness. The snow was getting deeper the
farther they rode into this unknown land, and it had begun to
get dark. He was entirely happy by the girl's side. The bus
stopped more frequently now to let the pupils off. It was almost
empty. Then they traveled for another long interval along the
edges of snowy fields. The butterfly boy saw a low pond in the
direction of the setting sun. A wavy black channel had formed
between its plates of ice. – Our dog likes to play there, the
girl said. – A great rolling hill caught the sunset in the distance.
Below it was another wide field of steep-roofed farm sheds and
half-frozen ponds and trees becoming successively more frosted
in the distance. They drew closer to the base of the hill, and the
girl pointed to a white house. – That's where I live, she said.

It was late twilight, and getting cold when the bus let them
off. – Now we have to walk a minute, the girl said. – She took
him up a wide road that swiveled through the bare and spacious
forest. The road was irresistibly blank and creamy with snow
like the notebook-paper that they used at school. The butterfly
boy drew loops and circles with his mittened hand. – Come
on, the girl said. I want to show you my things. – The road
had steepened as it curved them up through snowy shade.
Whitened limbs hung over their heads, and then they turned
one more bend, and came to a field again and they saw the girl's
house. – I'm sad, the girl said. 'Cause I wanted to show you
the footprints I made in the morning. But the snow's covered
them up.

The butterfly boy realized that the girl liked him very much.
Without looking at her, he followed her inside, glowing with a
soft warm joy.

Who's this? said the girl's mother in surprise.

He's coming for dinner, the girl explained.

She took him up to her room, and, giggling, opened her chest
of drawers to show him her folded white underpants. He had
never seen girls' underpants before. He was as happy as when
he'd seen the butterfly: a special secret had now been revealed
to him.

After that, he and the girl read storybooks together until dinnertime. There was one book about five Chinese brothers who couldn't be killed. One was condemned to be drowned, but he drank up all the sea. The page showed a night scene, glowing with the rich pigments of children's books like some lantern-lit stand of fruits in bowls. People were diving in the stagnant pond, their ploughs parked under the trees. They were bringing up armloads of skulls. Across the brown river's bridge, a white monument rose like a Khmer tombstone. Here the executioners, skinny serious men in black pajamas, were trying to drown the Chinese brother. They had tied his hands behind his back with wire and forced his head down into the water, but he was drinking it all up with bulging cheeks; they couldn't hurt him even there at the foot of the lion's gape where white teeth blared. Making a festivity of the event, little kids were beating a drum and leaping barefoot down the dirty street lit by a single orange-shaped lamp held to a power pole. They didn't see the man in black pajamas who was coming with an iron bar to smash the lamp. The Chinese brother was still drinking; the water got lower and lower. On the bridge, a one-legged boy leaned on his crutch in astonishment. There was a golden temple in the background, with snarling stone figures carved on the pillars; other winged figures were about to swoop. Skinny boys in black pajamas were smashing it down with pickaxes. There were dark gratings in front of which people sat under lightless awnings and the girls laughed. They were eating at a table crowded by bowls of string beans, limes, yellow flowers, peppers, a bowl of red chili powder, chopsticks, the people putting everything in their soup, sitting down on little square stools with other big bowls of soup steaming at their back. Their backs were turned, so they didn't see the men in black pajamas coming toward them with machine guns. The butterfly boy had never seen anybody who wasn't white. He wondered if all Chinese people possessed these supernatural capabilities.

This is my favorite picture, said the girl, turning to a page which showed another unkillable Chinese brother being pushed

15

off a precipice. The cliff was walled with dark green palms that glistened as if dipped in wax, and there was glossy darkness between them down which children scrambled barefoot, their shirts fluttering bright and clean in the hot breeze; palm-heads swung like pendulums. Men in black pajamas were waiting for them. Banana leaves made green awnings; then other multi-rayed green stars and bushes with dewy leaves that sparkled like constellations held the middle place; below them, rust-red compound blooms topped lacy mazes of dark greyish-green leaves, everything slanting down to the dark water, white-foamed, that came from the wide white waterfall towards which the Chinese brother screamed smiling down.

The butterfly boy looked at this picture with her for a long time. Then he hung his head. – Can I see your underpants again?

9

The next year the school districts changed, so he didn't see the girl anymore. Another girl invited him over to make Creepy Crawlers. He only had the Plastic Goop, but she had the other kind that you could bake into rubbery candy. They made candy ants and beetles and spiders and ate them and he was very happy. But he was afraid to invite her over because he didn't know what his parents would think about his playing with girls, so she never invited him again.

10

The school bully roared, ran down from his mountain of snow and ice, and charged the butterfly boy with outstretched arms. The bully's parka was the same every year. His parents never seemed to wash it, so it was very grimy; and it had become too small for him. The bully had thick hairy arms like a monster and a reddish-purple face full of yellow teeth. He knocked the butterfly boy down and sat on his stomach. Then he began to spit into his face. He spat and spat, while the other boys cheered. Then he took the butterfly boy's glasses off and broke them. He punched the butterfly boy in the nose until blood came out. Then he stood up. He jumped on the butterfly boy's stomach, and the butterfly boy puked. Everybody laughed. He let the butterfly boy go. The butterfly boy staggered into the far corner of the chain-link fence and tried to clean the blood and vomit off himself.

11

You fell down *again?*   said the butterfly boy's mother in amazement.

Yes.

What happened this time?

I don't know. I just fell.

Maybe he needs his glasses changed,   she said to his father.

12

I don't want to go outside for recess anymore,   the butterfly boy said.

You have to go out,   the teacher said.

Why?

Because if you stay in here with me you'll never learn how to take care of yourself.

What can I do? Every time I go out there I get beaten up. He's waiting for me right now.

The teacher sipped her coffee, trying to think of some miracle strategy that would make the butterfly boy grow out of his subhumanhood. But she couldn't think of anything.

You can stay in with me today,   she said.   But only today.

Thank you,   the butterfly boy said gratefully.

She let him look through the schoolbook that the grade above him was reading, *People from Foreign Lands*, so he got to peer down a page of partly shaded bystreet, drivers resting in their cyclos under the trees, sun hot on their toes, stacks of hollow-cored building bricks on the street corners, and he was contented, but then the second hand of the big clock made a ticking sound and he found himself already beginning to dread tomorrow's recess.

13

High up upon his filthy crag, the school bully crouched, flapping his arms like an eagle and muttering to himself. His head jerked back and forth as he scanned the playground, searching for victims. The substance that his soul was composed of was pain. Since the most basic pleasure of substance is to see or dream or replicate itself, the bully fulfilled himself by causing pain in others. This proves that he could perceive and interpret, since otherwise how could the agonies of others enchant him? However, if we allow what certain philosophers do, namely, that memory is a necessary component of consciousness, then we cannot say for certain that he was conscious. He always attacked in the same way, and seemed to derive exactly the same joy from the butterfly boy's anguish. Conscious pleasure, on the contrary, seems to require a steady and continual augmentation of the stimulus, since comparison of the pleasing sensation with the ingrained memory of that sensation will gradually devalue it. This explains why the higher order connoisseurs must inevitably shuck their rubbers after their beginning years, and hence contract sexual diseases.

The butterfly boy took as long as he could in buckling his galoshes. (He could do all the buckles now.) The other boys were shouting: Come on out! Don't be a sissypants! – When he came out, they started to clap and shout. Their heads swiveled expectantly toward the pile of ice where the bully lived. The bully began to gnaw very rapidly on his lower lip. His eyes rolled. Then he screeched, raised his arms, and rushed down upon the butterfly boy like death.

Don't you dare hurt him! a big girl shouted. She ran up to the bully and punched him as hard as she could. The bully cowered away. He began to sob hoarsely. Instantly the other boys forgot the butterfly boy. They threw delighted snowballs at the bully and called him a nasty stupid retard. The bully sat down. A steaming yellow stain began to form in the snow around him. The boys laughed and the girls whispered.

The butterfly boy did not join in the attack upon his enemy. He went to the part of the playground where the girls played, and stood timidly beside the big girl.

You can't play here, the big girl said. But I wish you were a girl, so I could play with you. You're so cute.

The butterfly boy was silent. He went slowly back to the other boys.

14

The boys had declared war against the girls. Girls were ugly. Girls were sissies. Girls polluted the playground just by being there. It was an outrage that the boys should have to breathe the same air that girls did. They ran them down, shouting and knocking them to the icy asphalt and pulling their hair. Yowling, the girls scratched back. It was not a precisely coordinated campaign of gun butts and pickaxes because these were boys who soon would be upstanding Eagle Scouts, lighting fires, prancing about in jungle-green uniforms, holding lighted torches aloft to conduct smoke-signaled conversations with one another about the sizes of various girls' boobs, stealing each other's neckerchief rings, farting into each other's faces, striding through the woods without ever getting lost; thus to the teacher who sat sipping her coffee indoors and very occasionally glancing out the window, it seemed as if her pupils were playing exactly as usual, a bit more boisterously, perhaps; the girls were not jumping rope, which was odd or maybe not so odd since they had been doing that every day; they appeared to be mingling with the boys most energetically, which was all to the good, the teacher thought, and maybe she was right because when the bell did ring and the pupils came in they bore no wounds more serious than bruises, from which it follows that it had all been in fun. So they captured the big girl and tried to figure out what to do with her. Then they remembered the butterfly boy. − Make him kiss her! a boy shouted.

What they wanted was to degrade and brutalize. The girl would be tortured by being kissed, because it was a universal truth that kissing was disgusting, and because everyone would be watching. The butterfly boy would be likewise raped by the procedure, although it was unfortunately possible that he might rise a little in their esteem by becoming their instrument. All in all, the scheme was as elegant as it was practical. One must admire such cleverness.

For precisely the same reason that they did not subject one of their own to this humiliation, they did not lay hands on the butterfly boy. He was not one of them. His closest kinship was with the bully. He was an untouchable, a prostitute, an eater of dirt. There was thus no need to force him. Because what they demanded of him was disgusting and he was disgusting, he would do it of his own accord. That way there could certainly be no trouble, for if any crime were about to be committed, it was not theirs, but his. − Another point for cleverness.

And weren't they right? No free will, bravery, or self-confidence could be attributed to this creature. He came when they called them.

It was always possible that the end-of-recess bell might strike if he stalled them, but he could not walk too slowly or something worse would be done, so he watched the glossy black tips of his galoshes crunch down upon the white snow with spurious deliberation. With every step, the playground contracted, tightening the ritual bond between himself and the other victim. The crowd of boys had pulled in close. They had been shouting and then they had been quiet and the girl had screamed and

21

then they had shouted again. Now they parted silently to let him through. He did not look into their eyes. He gazed only at the crouching girl, who no longer screamed or struggled. One of the big boys yanked her hair hard.

He was almost upon her now, and had no knowledge of what he was going to do. But it was not up to him to know what to do. His act would rise up red like a pepper, a penis, a pistil of a tropical orchid. Of course he did not think in those terms. He did not think. The world was now no larger than the slanting plane between the toes of his galoshes and her straining face, teeth clenched in fear and hate, neck corded like a tree trunk down to the collar of her sweater; she was jerking and gasping like an animal in the boys' unescapable hands, her nostrils drawn almost flat as she sucked in breath to face him and the butterfly boy took one more step and one more step and now there were no more steps left to take. The boys' hands fell away from her as the circle tightened about them both like an anus. They wanted to see her go mad, no doubt, running about, kicking and scratching and clawing at the butterfly boy (no danger of her escape). Her eyes slammed themselves down to slits. She didn't recognize or remember him. He reached slowly toward her and she stood stock still as he pulled the hood of her parka back up over her head because he knew only that she was shivering, and she glared at him for a moment and shook the hood back down just as a dog shakes itself dry and he embraced her.

He kissed her the only way he knew how, as he would have kissed his mother's cheek or his aunt's cheek or the cheek of any of the nice ladies who came to visit. (The other boys made loud noises of revulsion.) He felt something happening to her but he did not understand what it was. He said: I love you.

Then she was squeezing him back in tight defiance.   – I love you, too,   she said.

The boys made barely feigned vomiting sounds. They raised their fists in horror.

Teacher's looking!   a boy shouted.

Get the bully! Get the bully!

The bully stormed bellowing down from his hillock, and they dropped back to form a line that would protect them from implication but insure that the girl and the butterfly boy could not escape their punishment. What a horrible spectacle it had been to see them enjoying themselves! – Beat 'em up, retard! a boy shrieked, and the bully snorted like an ox and was just about to fall upon them with feet and fists when he recognized the girl who had beaten him, stopped, and slunk away.

Teacher's coming, teacher's coming!

The boys exploded into individual atoms, fleeing everywhere, circling the other girls like maddened sharks (what the girls had been doing the butterfly boy would never know), and the girl and the butterfly boy were by themselves.

Are we going to get married? she said.

This eventuality had not occurred to the butterfly boy before, but now that she had said it, it became the only conceivable choice. He nodded.

For the rest of the school year he considered them engaged, but in the fall he learned that her family also had moved away –

In reality, the *permanent wound cavity* . . .
obviously has more effect on matters than the
temporary cavity, since the temporary cavity
*collapses almost instantly from the resilient effect
of the human paste.*

CHUCK TAYLOR, *The Complete
Book of Combat Handgunning*
(1982)

1

On the morning after what was supposed to be his last
night on earth, the boy who wanted to be a journalist
dreamed that we were falling toward Jupiter. Other people had
no conception of how horrible it was going to be, but he did
because he was an expert on atmospheres. First they'd see the
Great Red Spot getting huger by the hour, tinting everything
red and baleful, driving animals to madness. The oceans would
rear into thousand-foot tides, smashing cities with cold dark
fishy blows, drowning Asia and Africa, exterminating all but the
rich and flabby elite in their mountain bunkers. Their time
would run out, too. Gales of methane and mothball-smelling
gases would rip the air away so that everyone would die in
convulsions of unspeakable pain, kicking like bugs in a killing
jar. The boy who wanted to be a journalist decided not to wait.
He drank paint stripper and swallowed pain killers. The gentle

girl found out and asked why he wanted to worry enough to do that, since he'd die anyway when they got to Jupiter; when he strove to explain, his skeleton overpowered him, and he began to weep in helpless spasms. The gentle girl drew him into her arms. He tried to jerk away, but she held him all the more tightly and he felt better. Instead of crying much harder as he usually did, he vomited poison all over her. She'd saved him.

He was awakened by a pounding at the door. He heard the door handle turning futilely. Last night for the first time he'd locked himself in.

He put his underwear on and went to the door. It was the boy who believed in praxis. He'd known of his plan, and came by early to learn what had happened to him.   – Congratulations! he said.   You're alive!

Yeah,   said the boy who wanted to be a journalist.

He stood there for awhile in his underwear, and then he began to feel that he needed to justify being alive, so that the boy who believed in praxis wouldn't feel that he'd come for nothing.

I decided to flip a coin,   he said.   Heads would be life, and tails would be the other. I went and flipped the coin, and it came up tails. But I figured I'd released it sooner than I meant to, so I flipped it again, and it came up tails. I decided to try one more time. I flipped it, and it came up tails. So I decided the coin was wrong.

2

A couple of weeks later he started slitting his wrists. He never cut deep enough to do any harm, however. A Band-Aid lengthwise seemed to do the trick.

3

He'd found a nice stuffy attic with an archives room that had an inner bolt on the door. Sometimes he'd go up there and stand on a chair and take a good length of parachute cord, throw it over a beam and tie it, put the noose around his neck and then slowly draw his knees up to his chest so that he was suspended. The novelty of it tended to take his mind off things, although his throat really hurt afterward.

4

Once he began to combine cutting his wrists and half-asphyxiating himself he believed that he'd found the ideal. Afterwards he'd dream of mummy sex with the gentle girl, by which he meant her body being suspended ropelessly above him, then slowly drifting down; when her knee touched his leg he jerked and then went limp there; her hands reached his hands, which died; her breasts rolled softly upon his heart, which fibrillated and stopped; finally she lay on top of him, quite docile and still and soft . . . He knew that the others didn't like mummy sex, but that was because they didn't understand it; they thought that it must be cold; they thought that she must paint her mouth with something to make it look black and smell horrible and soften like something rotten . . . He wanted to open her up until the pelvis snapped like breaking a wishbone. Would that be mummy sex?

5

After the gentle girl got married (which happened in the same week that mail service to the People's Democratic Republic of Kampuchea was suspended), he transferred his unclean attentions to a girl who wanted to be a linguist. The girl who wanted to be a linguist wrote him:

> You had virtually always, by your remarks to me, given me the sense that you were not being straightforward with me, that you impregnated your words with a significance I did not grasp and was not sure I wanted to, and that you analyzed me, perhaps attempted, very subtly, to manipulate me. When I got your letter my first reaction was that I did not know what was going on but you no doubt did; no doubt you would carefully watch my reaction; perhaps you were in a way testing me. I realized later that you were not a low creature, that is to say you were not the sort of being that ought to be humiliated. But while I do wish to help you, or to be capable of helping you, or to help you if I knew how, I am deeply skeptical of my ability to do so. If I were like the gentle girl I might be someone who could help. But I am not like the gentle girl. I do not think you would want me to behave in whatever contrived manner. To whatever extent you are dissatisfied with me you want me to be different. But I am not what you want. I wish you would realize that, and stop loving me as you say you do. I do not understand why you do, for I do not and did not feel that I had solicited your love or given you any reason to love me.

He went to bed and cried. Then he fell in love with a lesbian.

6

They were now sitting in their own private compartment, chugging away from Sion into the pink snowy dusk. The lesbian sat reading a tour book beside him. Turning away as if to cough, he palmed the antipsychotic pill and swallowed it dry. Now he was safe for the night. The lesbian nodded at something that the tour book said. The bracelet seemed to be cutting into her plump arm. He wondered how she could stand it. The more he looked at the bracelet, the more gruesome it seemed. He kept expecting her fingers to start turning blue and falling off. But the lesbian did not seem to be uncomfortable. They passed a station full of red lights and funny glass windows.

7

They had seen Dubrovnik and they had seen Split. The lesbian closed her guidebook.

Check our backpacks and I'll save a seat,   the lesbian said.

Save two,   he said, for he was beginning to know her.

He made certain that the packs were loaded into the luggage compartment and got onto the bus.

I couldn't save two,   she said.   I think there's one in the back.

Well, I can sit next to you. That seat's empty, isn't it?

I want two seats to stretch out in,   the lesbian explained.

Fine,   he said.

Oh, by the way,   said the lesbian with the sweetest of smiles, you'll have to pay for my ticket.

He went to the back and took a pill.

8

They arrived in Titograd at five in the morning. It was so cold that the water had frozen in hanging arches from the fountain. The boy who wanted to be a journalist used his German to ask the way to the railroad. They came to what they thought was the waiting room, but when he opened the door it turned out to be the signalmen's office. The signalmen stared at the lesbian and licked their lips. The boy who wanted to be a journalist pulled out a bottle of slivovitz and they shared it around; after that they were friends. They showed him dirty cartoons (they wouldn't let her see) and stuffed them insistently with dried pork, bread drippings, and a tin of mackerel and vegetables. The two Americans amused them. When the lesbian shook hands with them like a man, they laughed so hard a glass jumped off

the table. Curling up in the most comfortable chair, the lesbian slept, and then the signalmen asked the boy if she were his sister (they knew that English word). He said no. One man pointed at them, moved two fingers into intersecting courses, and continued the motion with the fingers attached to each other. – *Ja, ja?* he said. – The boy who wanted to be a journalist nodded and thumped his heart vigorously. The signalman put an imaginary ring on his finger and looked at the boy. The boy made clockwise movements with his forefinger on the face of his watch to indicate "in due time," nodded, and thumped his heart again, so that the lesbian would be protected. That satisfied them all.

They never did much work, just made long phone calls all night, bellowing and laughing alternately, and kissed some new arrival on both cheeks. They seemed very happy. In the morning, when their uniforms came back from the cleaners, they tried each other's on, put two on at a time, pulled the sleeves up, and threw their official caps all around.

The boy thought: I'd give anything to have what they have, and they'd probably give anything to have what I have.

9

In Saloniki they checked into a hotel for the night, and the clerk said: One bed or two?

The boy who wanted to be a journalist began to hope. Maybe she wasn't really a lesbian. Maybe she loved him enough that being a lesbian didn't matter. He waited.

The lesbian was looking at him and the clerk was looking at him and finally the lesbian said: Two beds.

A deep flush overpowered the boy's stoic face.

10

The train from Saloniki to Istanbul was supposed to take two days, but sometimes it took three or four. It all depended. When the Greek soldiers heard where the boy and the lesbian were bound, they shook their heads and made fierce throat-slitting motions. Before the border the soldiers got off, giving them fresh goat cheese and shaking their heads again. The lesbian laughed.

This time it looked like the train was going to take three days at least. It had broken down twice. They were at the Turkish border, just inside the wire. They were all starting to wear thin on each other. There were five of them in the compartment: the boy who wanted to be a journalist, the lesbian who didn't want to be anything, a sad boy from England, Ulrich and the doctor. The doctor had been expelled from Saudi Arabia for seducing a nurse. – The girls in Saudi Arabia may be clean in the sense that they're virgins, he said with a bitter wink at the lesbian, – but I don't like a virgin who stinks!

Your brain stinks, said Ulrich. Your heart stinks. Your soul stinks.

Ulrich was the son of an SS officer. He was an alcoholic tramp. He and the boy who wanted to be a journalist got on quite well. – Oh, you poor little American, he'd chuckle every now and then. The boy smiled back grimly . . .

11

The sad boy from England liked to read aloud from the lesbian's guidebook. She was becoming fond of him, as it seemed. He read the same passages over and over, and she leaned back against his shoulder smiling with closed eyes. Sometimes the boy who wanted to be a journalist got so jealous and miserable at the sight of them that he went out and stood in the corridor, or got off the train to trudge back and forth in the snow beside the dark-shawled Turkish women who squatted round a fire. Ulrich never went with him for these walks, but sometimes the boy felt an eerie feeling in the back of his neck and would turn to see the German watching him from behind the half-dark window, waving ironically.

12

I know a man in France . . .   began the sad English boy.

Oh, *good,*   said Ulrich sarcastically, having another slug of brandy.

The train sat in the sunny snow.

It snows pretty good in Frankfurt, doesn't it?   said the doctor, trying to be friendly.

No,   said Ulrich.

He and the doctor had already had a fistfight.

Brigitte, Brigitte, Brigitte . . .   droned the English boy.

No, my name is Bridget,   said the lesbian.   Brigitte is French.

The boy who wanted to be a journalist got up and went into the corridor so that he could take his pill where no one would see. Just after he had unscrewed the top from the vial, a giant grimy palm shot silently down onto his wrist and the grey scarred fingers wrapped instantaneously around his wrist, and then the other grey hand reached and took the vial away.

What is this?   said the grey hands' owner.   Why?

Antipsychotics,   said the boy who wanted to be a journalist. They said I have to take these. They said if I don't take these maybe I'll kill myself.

Kill?   said the German in astonishment.   Why not kill?

He gave back the vial. The boy who wanted to be a journalist took his pill, and then they both went back into the compartment.

Not only Germans kill,   said Ulrich presently,   but they do it more thorough. Only Germans are the peak, you know.

Crazy bastard,   said the doctor, opening a black portmanteau to get at his very own bottle of Scotch.

13

So I cracked that little nurse's legs open, and what do you think I saw? said the doctor.

No one else was much interested, but the boy who wanted to be a journalist was fascinated. – What? he said. What did you see?

Maggots, said the doctor. That little pink tomato of hers was white with crawlers. Now when I say maggots I'm using the vernacular, you understand; I can't vouch for their being the larvae of dipterous insects –

Without warning, Ulrich punched the doctor in the face, cracking his head smartly against the wall. The doctor's mouth fell open, and his nose began to bleed. No one said anything, and for a moment the doctor just sat there breathing heavily. Then he lunged at Ulrich, who grinned and flung up a grey bar of a forearm with automatic precision to slam against the doctor's chest and throw him back.

The doctor sat down moaning. He wiped his nose on his sleeve and stared at the blood. He touched his nose again. His hand came away crimson as if he were a murderer. He pinched his nostrils shut. Then he stood up. He looked piercingly into everyone's eyes. Then he got his portmanteau and went out of the compartment. The boy who wanted to be a journalist heard him going up the corridor sliding open the doors of all the compartments to look for a vacant seat. After awhile he heard him come back and go down the other way. When he ducked outside to take his pill, he saw splashes of blood in the hall. Presently the doctor came back again. There were no compartments free. The doctor stood in the corridor with his nose pressed angrily against the window all that day and into the night when the train began to move again and into the next morning when they got to Istanbul. Then he stomped off to the airport. He was flying around the world, he'd said. It was his fifth time.

14

Ulrich, the lesbian, the English boy and the boy who wanted to be a journalist were sharing a room in the Hotel Gungor. The lesbian had read about it in her guidebook. They didn't have a map of the Sultanhamet district, so the boy who wanted to be a journalist went with the lesbian for directions to the office of police. A thug in a black uniform directed them to the inspector, who got up and offered the lesbian his armchair. He kissed her wrist and shook the boy's hand warmly. When all was understood, the thug showed them out to where Ulrich and the English boy were waiting. The English boy looked scared. Ulrich kept making punching motions and shouting: I am fighting machine!

Is anybody hungry?   asked the lesbian, who had taken charge.

They all were, so after they'd checked into the hotel they went and found the Pudding Shop, an enclave of the sixties whose jukebox played "Revolution," "Strawberry Fields Forever" and "Penny Lane" over and over. Ulrich, who was not used to being with people who could stand him, was so delighted with them all that he bought the dinner. All the journalist wanted was vanilla pudding.

You want hashish sir I excuse me?   said a Turkish boy.

Get out now or I kill you,   said Ulrich.

His life is probably very difficult,   said the lesbian.

I kill him!   shouted Ulrich.

Don't you think that life is inherently difficult?   the lesbian persisted.

I don't think it's inherently difficult,   said the boy who wanted to be a journalist.   I only think some people make it difficult for themselves.

What are you talking about?   said the lesbian scornfully. You take pills to keep alive!

You do what?   said the English boy.

The boy who wanted to be a journalist didn't say anything. Ulrich laughed and had another shot of brandy. – You – you poor little American,   he said, laying a hand on his shoulder.

15

The lesbian wore tall white socks up over her nylons. She had very big breasts, and the nipples usually showed through the purple or black blouses she wore over her skirt. The English boy was wild about her. As for the boy who wanted to be a journalist, he could no longer care less. Maybe that was why he suddenly seemed to be less thanatophilic. His unhappiness (which was probably biochemical, since he could find no reason for it) seemed irrelevant. One of his best friends, a boy who wanted to be a revolutionary, had written him:

> I've stopped taking suicide seriously in recent years as a possibility for myself, because there's a perspective that radically transcends the neutrality that forms the basis of most of my criticism of living. The perspective is in fact entirely mundane in its operation, which consists of a commonsensical and humble interpretation of the pain one experiences in living – an unwillingness to generalize to extremes on the basis of one's failures, an assumption regardless of particular experiences that pain is transitory. Obviously I can't plead with you on the basis of a perspective which you may not share. I mention this simply from the hope that it may come as a bit of a reminder to you because (after all) you do live and may have done so on a basis similar to this. I use the past tense because I imagine that considering suicide as seriously as you are there's already quite a distance between you and such a perspective.

Was this what he'd felt? The snow had almost melted, and the sky was pale blue. They went sightseeing at the Hagia Sophia and the Blue Mosque. After lunch they went to the Royal Treasury. The lesbian loved the Chamber of Emerald Objects. By the time they got to the Chamber of Jade Objects, she was bored, but the English boy read every caption aloud just the same. When they got to the Chamber of Weapons, Ulrich tried to take a mace down from the wall, but the attendant smiled and shook a finger.

The lesbian wanted a snack. The boy who wanted to be a journalist got baklava and mineral water. The English boy read the menu aloud. – Shut up, said Ulrich.

Ulrich sat buttering a big piece of bread and the lesbian was eating her soup but the English boy wasn't eating anything. Suddenly his face twitched and he started to stutter.

Ulrich leaped up, slapped his cheek with a noise like a gunshot, and walked out. When the others returned to the hotel that night his pack was gone.

16

The next day the lesbian and the English boy and the boy who wanted to be a journalist went to the underground bazaar. The English boy's jaw was still numb where Ulrich's hand had struck him, but he hadn't lost any teeth. In fact the incident had significantly benefited him, since Ulrich was gone and the lesbian had been very sympathetic. The boy who wanted to be a journalist permitted his jealousy to construct a proof of almost geometric rigor that the English boy had planned it. It was true that the English boy's thoughts, at least as he had expressed them, seemed to possess little shape or divisibility, but that might well be simply a manifestation of the English boy's cunning. In short, the lesbian and the English boy were now holding hands. Maybe the lesbian wasn't a lesbian after all.

17

Nonetheless, he felt a very strange sense of well-being. The lesbian and the English boy were away at the Turkish baths. He went to visit the hotel clerk, a dark-skinned boy who always smiled. Since the trip was almost over, and the boy who wanted to be a journalist could not possibly use up all his Swiss cereal, he gave the clerk some. The clerk didn't know what it was at first, but when the boy who wanted to be a journalist ate a handful as a demonstration of its gustatory powers, the clerk also tried a taste. His eyes widened. Then he got out his flute and played a song for glee. He beckoned the other boy to the counter and pointed to his lips to show that he had something he wanted to say. He patted his cheek. Then he got out his Turkish–English dictionary. He searched for the words for a long time. Finally he frowned, mouthed something to himself as though he were rehearsing it, and then his forehead smoothed and he patted the boy who wanted to be a journalist's shoulder and smiled delightedly and said:

I – love – you . . .

18

He went outside to take his pill, and Ulrich found him. Ulrich's palms were lacerated and gritty with fragments of glass. Ulrich said: Because I kill my father, you know. In 1972. That doctor you cry for, he was just a little bastard. But my father was SS. He was the peak. He was good enough to die at my hands . . .

Do you love your father? said the boy who wanted to be a journalist. I need to know what love means.

Love? said Ulrich. Why not love? You tell me this now, you want to know what love means. Who do you love?

Nobody.

Ah, then no more pills for you, my poor American. You love no one? No one? Good! You are the peak. You and I, we know what love means . . .

And he began to applaud, slamming his great grey hands together until the blood and glass shivered out –

more BENADRYL,
WHINED THE JOURNALIST

William T. Vollmann

One obvious question concerning the ultimate reproductive success of males is whether it is better for a male to invest all of his sperm in a single female or else to copulate with several females.

BERT HÖLLDOBLER and EDWARD O. WILSON, *The Ants* (1990)

1

Once upon a time a journalist and a photographer set out to whore their way across Asia. They got a New York magazine to pay for it. They each armed themselves with a tube of cool soft K-Y jelly and a box of Trojans. The photographer, who knew such essential Thai phrases as: *very beautiful!*, *how much?*, *thank you* and *I'm gonna knock you around!* (topsa-lopsa-lei), preferred the extra-strength lubricated, while the journalist selected the non-lubricated with special receptacle end. The journalist never tried the photographer's condoms because he didn't even use his own as much as (to be honest) he should have; but the photographer, who tried both, decided that the journalist had really made the right decision from a standpoint of friction and hence sensation; so that is the real moral of this story, and those who don't want anything but morals need read no further. – Now that we've gotten good and evil out of the way, let's spirit ourselves down (shall we?) to the two rakes' room at the Hotel Metro, Bangkok, where the photographer always put on sandals before walking on the sodden blue carpet to avoid fungus. As for the journalist, he filtered the tap water (the photographer drank bottled water; they both got sick). There was a giant beetle on the dresser. The journalist asked the bellboy if beetles made good pets. – Yes, he grinned. It was his answer to every question. – Good thing for him he doesn't have a pussy, said the photographer, untying his black combat boots with a sigh, putting foot powder on; and the journalist stretched out on his squeaking bed, waiting for the first bedbug. The room reminded him of the snow-filled abandoned weather station where he'd once eked out a miserable couple of weeks at the North Magnetic Pole; everything had a more or less normal appearance, but was deadly dangerous, the danger here being not cold but disease; that was how he thought, at least, on that first sweaty super-cautious night when he still expected to use rubbers. The photographer had already bought a young lady from Soy Cowboy. In the morning she lay on the bed with parted purple-painted lips; she put her legs up restlessly.

Last night *tuk-tuk* fifty bhat, she said.* Come back Soy Cowboy, thirty bhat.

So you want some more money for the *tuk-tuk* ride, is that what you're trying to tell me? said the photographer in disgust. Man, I don't fucking believe it. You know she only let me do her once. And then she wanted a thousand bhat – that's why I had to get that five hundred from you.

The woman's teeth shone. She slapped her thigh, yawned, walked around staring with bright black eyes.

Where do you come from, sweetheart? asked the journalist, flossing his teeth.

Me Kambuja.

Cambodia?

Yes. Kambuja.

We go Kambuja, said the journalist. You come Kambuja?

* In 1991 a US dollar was worth about 25 Thai bhat, or 1,000 Cambodian riels.

No.

Why?

She grimaced in terror. — Bang, bang! she whispered.

Outside, the *tuk-tuks* made puffs of smog. Men huddled over a newspaper by the Honey Hotel. — You want Thai food I wait for you, she said.

Oh, that's all right, said the photographer. You go on back to Soy Cowboy. We'll find our way around.

You come Soy Cowboy me tonight?

Sure. Sure, honey. You just go back to Soy Cowboy and sit there and hold your breath.

You like? You like me?

Sure. Now beat it.

You come tonight I have friend she go hotel with you, the girl said to the journalist.

OK, he said. He smiled at her. She smiled and darted into a *tuk-tuk*.

Well, I guess we go get her and her friend tonight, right? said the journalist.

45

Are you crazy? said the photographer. There are thousands like her, twice as nice for half the price. She had the nerve to ask me for a thousand bhat! I've *never* paid more than five hundred before. You don't have to give 'em anything after you buy 'em out. I remember one time this bitch kept pestering me for money; I sent her away with *nothing*, man. She was *crying*; it was GREAT!

So what did you pick her up for?

Her? She really stuck out – her long hair, her shorts up the crack of her ass; I really liked that. But next time I want a big girl, man. Not one of these fucking little babies that don't know what the hell they're doing.

But later he said: I felt sorry for her. Next time I pick up a girl, I won't screw her.

2

On the slightly tippy table visited by flies, there were four jars: one with salt, one with capers and vinegar and other things like aquarium plants, one with curry powder, and one with pickled peppers. The photographer and the journalist sat there having lunch, in the alley with colored striped sheets for awnings, and colored umbrellas over the tables. They had noodle soup with vegetables. Roof-water dripped slowly into pools on dirty glazed trestles. It was monsoon season. Motorcycles passed slowly between the tables. The young smooth-faced vendeuses turned and scraped the meat in their woks, looking patient behind their glass bulwarks stacked with eggs, tomatoes, bok choy, sprouts, noodles of all kinds. The vendeuse squirted new oil into the wok, then strolled to a grating, where she reached into her apron and gave someone money; then she made her easy way back, just in time for the oil to bubble. A policeman came by, took out his wallet and bought ice. Water dripped onto mossy benches.

The journalist kept thinking of the hurt look in the Cambodian girl's eyes. What to do? Nothing to do.

3

At half past four in the afternoon, the sticky feeling of sweat between his fingers felt like fungus growing. There was an American detective video on: gunfire and smashing glass and roaring cars at maximum volume. He sat reading the *Bangkok Post:* **'Big Five' see eye-to-eye on Khmer arms cuts.** Two girls were sitting at the bar where it curved, playing a game like tic-tac-toe with poker chips in a wooden frame. Their cigarette smoke ascended the darkness of the long mirror. When a man was tortured on TV the girls looked up with interested smiles. Then they clicked the chips back into the board. More girls drifted in, filling out forms, making business calls. The whirling circles of light began to go around. A girl watched a fistfight on TV, her forefingers meeting in a steeple on her nose. A girl came in to refill the journalist's beer glass so that the bottle could be taken away and then she could sell him the next; the web of skin between his fingers continued to stick more with each passing moment. Another gunfight. The girls saw him grinning and grinned back. Bored with their game, they peered through the holes in the gameboard which stood on its end like a grating between them.

A white man came in, rubbing his mouth, checking his wallet, resting his arm on the table.

The smokers raised their hands to their mouths like buglers. One of the girls was playing the game of plastic counters with a white boy, and she smiled much more when she won or lost now than she had when playing the other girl. The boy put a cigarette in his mouth, and two girls' hands reached to light it for him.

Slowly, the beer receipts piled up in the journalist's ringed teakwood cup. When a girl refilled his beer, she exhibited the utmost concentration, holding it critically to eye level.

Straight-eyebrowed faces, arch-eyebrowed faces, all gold and oval and framed by straight black hair, watched the gameboard or the TV or themselves in the pink-bordered mirror. Whenever something violent happened on TV, they looked up with calm interest.

Traffic crept outside. A police whistle shrilled steadily, then there came a sound of faraway singing or screaming; a *tuk-tuk* passed slowly enough for the passengers to watch the TV. At a quarter to six, when the next white man came in, they switched on the music for a minute, and a girl started dancing, leaning on the bar, clapping her hands. Outside, the lights were turning red and the girls were standing everywhere in sexy skirts. A middle-aged midget in a double-breasted suit came down the alley, walked under one girl's dress, reached up to pull it over him like a roof, and began to suck. The girl stood looking at nothing. When the midget was finished, he slid her panties back up and spat onto the sidewalk. Then he reached into his wallet. The music was getting louder everywhere; girls grinned gently in every doorway as the businessmen passed, sometimes hand in hand; a girl leaned against a vegetable cart smoothing her long hair as the motorbikes passed.

The long-haired girl in the burgundy shirt looked up from her calculator and came to put ice in the journalist's beer.

4

There was a bar aching with loud American music, pulsing with phosphorescent bathing suits. He picked number fourteen in blue and asked her to come with him but she thought he wanted her to dance, so she got up laughing with the other girls and turned herself lazily, awkwardly, very sweetly; she was a little plump.

You come with me? he said when he'd tipped her.

She shook her head. – I have accident, she said, pointing to her crotch.

She sat with him, nursing the drink he'd bought her; she snuggled against him very attentively, holding his hand. Whenever he looked into her face, she ducked and giggled.

You choose friend for me?   he said.   Anyone you want.

When you go Kambuja?

Three days.

She hesitated, but finally called over another lady.   – This my friend Oy. My name Toy.

You come to hotel with me?   he said to Oy.

She looked him up and down.   – You want all night or short time?

All night.

No all night me. Only short time.

OK.

5

In the back of the taxi he whispered in her ear that he was shy, and she snuggled against him just as Toy had done. She smelled like shampoo. She was very hot and gentle against him. Knowing already that if he ever glimpsed her soul it would be in just the same way that in the National Museum one can view the gold treasures only through a thick-barred cabinet, he tried to kiss her, and she turned away.

Please?

She smiled, embarrassed, and turned away.

No?

She shook her head quickly.

6

He reached over her to turn out the light, and she cuddled him. He sucked her little nipples and she moaned. He kissed her belly, and eased his hand in between her legs. She'd shaved her pubic hair into a narrow mohawk, probably so that she could dance in the bathing suit. He stuck his mouth into her like the midget had, wondering if she'd push him away, but she let him. He had to suck a long time before he got the cunt taste. She started moaning again and moving up and down until he could almost believe in it. He did that for awhile until she pushed his face gently away. He got up and opened her with two fingers to see how wet she was because he didn't want to hurt her. Not surprisingly, she wasn't very wet. He reached under the bed and got the tube of K-Y jelly. He squirted some in his hand and smeared it inside her.

What's that?   she said.

To make you juicy,   he said.

When push came to shove, he didn't use a rubber. She felt like a virgin. When he was only halfway in she got very tight and he could see that she was in pain. He did it as slowly and considerately as he could, trying not to put it in too far. It was one of the best he'd ever had. Soon he was going faster and the pleasure was better and better; she was so sweet and clean and young. He stroked her hair and said: Thank you very much.

Thank you,   she said dully.

He got up and put on his underwear. Then he turned on the light and brought her some toilet paper.

She was squatting on the floor in pain.

Look,   she said.

Blood was coming out of her.

I'm sorry,   he said.   I'm really sorry.

No problem,   she smiled . . .

I'm sorry!

Maybe I call doctor.

He got her some bandages and ointment. She prayed her hands together and said   Thank you.

He gave her one thousand bhat. She hadn't asked for anything.   – Thank you, sir,   she smiled.

Enough for doctor?

This for taxi. This for *tuk-tuk*.

He gave her another five hundred and she prayed her hands together again and whispered: thank you.

He gave her some ointment and she turned away from him and rubbed it inside her. When they finished getting dressed she hugged him very tightly. She turned her face up to let him kiss her if he wanted. He kissed her forehead.

She hugged him again and again. When he'd shown her out to the *tuk-tuk,* she shook his hand.

Well,   he said to himself,   I certainly deserve to get AIDS.

7

I can't help but feel it's wrong,   he said.

Well, we're giving 'em money, aren't we?   said the photographer, very reasonably.   How else they gonna eat? That's their job. That's what they do. What's more, we're payin' 'em real well, a lot better than most guys would.

8

What did the journalist really want? No one thing, it seemed, would make him happy. He was life's dilettante. Whatever path he chose, he left, because he was lonely for other paths. No excuse, no excuse! When the photographer led him down the long narrow tunnels of Kong Toi (they had to buy mosquito netting for Cambodia), he got bewildered by all the different means and ways, but everyone else seemed to know, whether they were carrying boxes on their shoulders or hunting down cans of condensed milk, dresses, teapots, toys; it was so crowded under the hot archways of girders that people rubbed against each other as they passed, babies crying, people talking low and calm, nothing stopping. How badly had he hurt Oy? He had to see her. Lost, the two vampires wandered among framed portraits of the King, greasy little blood-red sausages, boiled corn, fried packets of green things, oil-roasted nuts that smelled like burned tires, hammerheads without the handles . . . But it was equally true that the vampires felt on top of everything because they were fucking whores in an air-conditioned hotel.

9

In the bar after the rain, the girl leaned brightly forward over her rum and coke with a throaty giggle; everyone was watching the gameboard, smoking cigarettes while the TV said: Jesus Christ, where are you? and the girl said to the photographer: Tell me, when you birthday?

She said to the journalist: You smoke cigarette? so he bit down on his straw and pretended to smoke it, to make her laugh . . .

The girls leaned and lounged. The photographer's girl was named Joy. She kept saying: Hi, darling! Hi, darling! – Her friend's name was Pukki.

Come here, darling, said Pukki. What you writing?

I wish I knew. Then I'd know how it would turn out, said the journalist.

He likes to write long letters to his mother, said the photographer.

The girls had brought the photographer a steak. He didn't want the rest of it, so he asked Joy if she wanted to eat it. Pukki cut pieces for her, nice and fat; she screamed teasingly because it was hard to cut.

You buy me out please, Pukki cried to the journalist.

I love Oy, he said. Tonight I buy Oy.

(That's real good, said the photographer admiringly. That's the way to show 'em!)

The journalist got a little loaded and made the bar-checks into paper airplanes and shot them all over the room. Patiently one of the girls gathered them all up; she smoothed them and put them back in his cup and he said: You boxing me? and she giggled no. More girls swarmed around, cadging drinks (he bought them whatever they asked for), sliding their arms round him, snuggling their heads on him, stroking his money pouch slyly.

The photographer squeezed Joy's butt and Pukki's tits and all the other girls cried in disgust real or feigned: You butterfly man! – He bought Joy out, and Pukki screamed at the journalist: *Please* you no buy me out *whaiiiiieee?*

I'm sorry, he said. I promised Oy. I'm really sorry.

He slipped her a hundred bhat and she brightened . . .

10

So they went to Oy's bar, the photographer, the journalist and Joy. Toy said: She no work today.

Is she OK? said the journalist. I worry about her. I hurt her pussy. I'm sorry, I'm sorry . . .

She no work today, Toy smiled.

11

The manager came and said: Oy? Which Oy?   – Evidently there were so many Oys . . .

The photographer went and looked (he was very good at picking people out), but he couldn't find her.

12

Racing the unhappy accelerator in stalled traffic, the taxi driver ignored the tree leaves wilted down into balls in the air that smelled like a black fart. The journalist sat up in front with him so that the photographer and Joy could fondle privately. The letters on the bus beside him swirled in white flame. Wet noises came from the back seat. The driver stared from the righthand window, disapproving, envious, appalled, or indifferent.

He say me where you go I say Metro Hotel,   Joy announced.

Finally the light changed, the driver shifted gears so that his weird mobile of shells tinkled as the taxi sped past dogs and corn-stands. A big canvas-covered truck loomed in the darkness. The driver looked ahead when they stopped again: his lips were wide and rounded. Raindrops shone like dust on the other cars' windshields. A foreigner made chewing motions in back of a *tuk-tuk* and then he was gone forever as the taxi driver made a roundabout and rushed between twisted pillars, honking his horn in the fog. He took them down secret-arrowed alleyways to the hotel . . .

13

All night the TV went   aah!   and   oi!   to dubbed movies while the prostitute lay wide-eyed in the photographer's bed, bored and lonely, snuggling her sleeping meal ticket while the journal-

ist, unable to sleep on account of the TV and therefore likewise bored and lonely, could not ask her to come even though the photographer had offered because he didn't feel right about it the way she snuggled the photographer so affectionately (when he got to know her better he'd understand that she wouldn't have come anyway) and besides he was worried about the growing tenderness in his balls. He jerked off silently to Joy; it didn't hurt yet, just felt funny, so he could still pretend that it was nothing; as soon as he was done he wanted to get inside Joy as much as before, and then he had to piss again; that was a bad sign; as soon as he pissed he felt the need to piss again.

14

In his sleep he listened, and every time he heard the rustle of her in the sheets he woke up with his penis as hard as a rock, aching. It was a little before six. His desire seeped like the tropical light coming slowly in, first illuminating the white valleys in the curtains, next the white barred reflections of the curtains in the mirror, then the white sheets, his white sheets, her white sheets folded back down over her shoulders, the black oval of her head on the white pillow (could he see her fingers on the sheet?) Now the outline of the grating grew behind the window, now a white belly of light on the ceiling, the white upper walls, black wainscotting, the white closet shelf's black clothes. Her silhouette was sharpening; he began to see the shape of her hair, his socks and underpants hanging to dry on the curtains. He could see the outlines of leaves through the grating. Now the wall-blacks weren't quite black anymore. The frame of the TV had differentiated itself from the screen. The bathroom door detached itself from the wall-mass. Clothes and luggage were born on the tables. He could see her shoulder now separating from the sheet, the white bra-straps leaping out; her head was turned away, toward the photographer; he could see her neck, ear and cheek begin to exist as separate entities from her hair. He could see the border of paleness around the edge of her blanket. He could see her breathe.

15

The white hazy morning air was humid with the smell of fresh Brussels sprouts, not yet too thickened by exhaust. Little piebald dogs yapped on the sidewalk. Two policemen motorcycled by. The *tuk-tuks* were mainly empty, the buses only half full.

The sun was a red ball over the canal whose violet-grey fog had not begun to stink; a motorboat wended feebly down the middle of its brown water, which was thick like spit, and spotted with oil, trash, leaves; the boat vanished in the fog below the bridge long before its sound was lost, and birds uttered single notes from the vastly spread-out trees that resembled the heads of broccoli; aluminum-roofed shacks, siding and boards walled

the canal as it dwindled past piers and banana trees; beneath an awning a little brown boy squatted and shat while his mother dressed; a long tunnel of boards and siding ran along the canal, and in it people were going about their business; a brown dog and a white dog bit their fleas; a man in a checkered sarong dipped water from a barrel; a baby cried; a boy was washing his clothes. The dogs left wet prints on the sidewalk. The sun was whiter, higher and hotter now. The air began to smell more acrid. Another motorboat came, very quickly, leaving a wake; other boats started up. The man who'd been in the sarong came out of his shack, putting his wet shirt on. He walked barefooted. Other men got into their boats. This morning run of business reminded him of the evenings at Joy's bar when the girls gathered gradually.

16

At breakfast the photographer sat on pillows, a sweet brown arm sleeping around his waist. Eighty percent of the Pat Pong girls had tested positive for AIDS that fall. Probably she'd be dead in five years.

17

She watched the TV's cartoons as wide-eyed as before. Coffee was all she ordered from room service, giggling rapt with head on chin, while in the hotel's humid halls the maids in blue stood folding towels and talking, leaning elbows on the desk, and the *tuk-tuks* went by and the clothes dried from windows across the courtyard, barely moving, and rainwater dried on the tiles while one of the hotel's men in red livery went out to smoke and scratch his belly, and across the courtyard a brown man naked to the waist flickered past a window of shadow.

The journalist's balls glowed faintly. The soles of his feet stuck itchily to his rubber sandals.

Suddenly the sun came on like a dimmer knob turned rapidly up to maximum, and it began to get hot.

18

When Joy left, she was dressed conservatively, smiled blandly; she shook each of their hands. Did she become that way in the morning, after the photographer fucked her up the ass, and she saw that he was like the others? (The photographer told him she'd pointed to her vagina and said: Here OK condom OK and then to her anus and said: Here OK no condom OK.) Or was her affection just an act? Or was this public demeanor of hers an act? The journalist's heart sank. He'd never know.

19

And what's *this* injection? he asked.

The doctor's glasses glinted. – Pure caffeine, he said enthusiastically.

If I wear a rubber from now on so that I don't infect the other girls, can I keep having sex, starting today?

I think it would not be good for you, said the doctor. You see, the disease has already migrated far into the spermatic cord . . .

20

Receipt No. 03125 (two soda waters, 60 bhat) was already in the cup, and fever-sweat from the clap ran down his face. At the bar, the two girls watched King Kong, plump-cheeked, wide-eyed, almost unblinking. (Joy wasn't there yet; probably she was still sleeping in some other place of narrow alleys . . .) A girl in a blindingly white T-shirt came in, and then another. They leaned on the bar on that hot afternoon, talking, while the spots of disco-light began to move and the fan bulged round and round like a roving eye. No-see-ums bit the journalist's feet between the sandal straps, so he put some mosquito repellent on; business stopped as all the girls watched. The two plump-cheeked girls looked catty-corner at opposing TVs as King Kong roared; then, when it was only helicopters again, they went back to the click-click-click of red and yellow counters, thinking hard as the pattern built up, six by six, click by click; in their concentration they lowered their noses almost against the wall of that gameboard, hair long, cheeks smoother than golden nectarines, so young, so perfect; perhaps it was just to a coarse-pored Caucasian that they appeared perfect. Click, click. Soon the meaningless game would be finished (meaningless since they weren't betting ten bhat against each other as they did when they played the journalist; he always lost), and then one woman would pull the release and the plastic counters would clatter into the tray below with a sound like gumballs. Then they'd start again, smoothing back their hair, reaching, showing hand-flesh through the holes.

The journalist was working, and the girls sometimes gathered around to watch him write. Lifting his head from the bar, the photographer explained to them: My friend likes to write long letters to his balls.

In Oy's bar the Western video was repeating and dinner had closed because it was six o'clock now, Oy's hour to come to work as the photographer had kindly ascertained; and paunchy white guys grinned. The staff was getting ready for dancetime. Someone was chopping ice, and a girl in a beige miniskirt sat spread-legged by the register where the glasses were, scratching a mosquito bite on her thigh, and the great green ceiling grid was activated; then the blue fluorescents came on, then the yellow and green spotlights at angles, then the multifaceted ball, and a girl with a lovely face like all the others (who seemed increasingly ghostly) smiled encouragingly at the journalist and drew her arm grandly down as if to yank the ripcord of a parachute and went into the Ladies.

The journalist's teeth chattered with fever. – Man, I hope you make it, said the photographer.

I'm all right, the journalist said. Do you see Oy anywhere?

You wait here. I'll ask around.

Well, he said after a moment, they say she'll be in at seven or seven-thirty. You want to wait?

Sure.

At seven, Toy came in. She said hi, smiling; she said no Oy today. She smelled like perfumed excrement. There was something so sincere about her that the journalist almost said to hell with it and asked her, but she would only have said no. He wrote her a note for Oy, showing her each of the note's words in the English–Thai dictionary: *Oy – I worry you blood that night. Are you OK?*

Will Oy come today? he asked her again, just to be sure.

Toy patted his arm. – Not today.

You come hotel me, Toy?

No, sir.

You my friend?

OK friend OK.

Oy is sick?

Oy no today.

Then Oy came, smiling. Toy went off to dance.

He bought out Oy, saying: I just take you back. Just sleep watch TV no fucking just sleep you know OK?

OK, laughed Oy.

She seemed in perfect health. That annoyed him after all his anxiety. Oy? he said. Oy? I'm *sick* from you. From your pussy.

Oy hung her head smiling . . .

The photographer went back to the other bar to buy Joy, and the four of them walked down the hot narrow alley, the two

61

boys in faded clothes a little dirty, the two girls in fancy evening wear; what a treat! – Oy went to a store to buy condoms; he said no need and she was happy. They got a taxi to the hotel. Joy rode in front with the driver. Oy pressed against him. He held her hand, gave her leg a feel; her dress was drenched with sweat. – You hot? he said. – She nodded; she'd always nod no matter what he said.

How long have you worked in Pat Pong? he said.

Six month.

How long has Toy worked there?

Ten month.

(Toy had told him that she'd worked there for six months.)

The photographer grinned. – So, how do you know she worked there for ten months if you only worked there for six months?

Oy blushed and ducked her guilty head.

He led Oy into the hotel while the photographer paid off the driver.

The journalist went grandly up to the desk. – Two-ten, please.

All the Thais in the lobby watched silently. Oy hung back, ashamed. They began talking about her. She raised her head then and followed her owner up the stairs, into the humid heat and mildew smell . . . At the first landing, when she could no longer be seen, she took his hand and snuggled passionately against him . . .

He told her again that she'd gotten him sick, but that it was OK.

I go doctor; doctor me in here! she giggled, pointing to her butt. Later, when he'd gotten her naked, he saw the giant bandage where she'd had some intramuscular injection. It did not give him confidence that while her disease must be the same as his her treatment had been different. – Best not to think about it.

The photographer came in. – Same room? said Joy on his arm.

It's OK, the journalist told her. No sex. Don't worry.

That was truly his plan – just to lie there in the darkness with Oy, snuggling and watching Thai TV while the photographer and Joy did the same. Needless to say, once the photographer took a shower and came out wearing only a towel and cracking jokes about his dick, the journalist could see how it would actually be. He took his shower . . .

The photographer laughed. – You should really get back in the shower, he said. You finished, man?

The journalist just nodded. He was feeling dizzy. He wandered out with his shirt around his waist; the girls laughed; Joy shook her head saying *you baah* which means you crazy and he hopped into bed sopping wet. Obedient Oy snuggled up to him in her fancy clothes . . .

You take shower, he said to her.

Finally she did, wearing the other towel. The light was still on. Every time anyone flushed the toilet the floor always flooded; he could see the comforting sparkle of that water on the bathroom tiles . . . She crawled in, snuggling him, and he slid a hand between her legs and was happy to feel her narrow little bush.

I go ten o'clock, she said. Toy birthday party. Toy my sister.

Whatever you say.

He lay sucking her tits while she held him. She let him kiss her a little but she didn't like it. Her body was slender, her nips just right. Her face looked rounder and older tonight; her voice was hoarser. She kept coughing. After awhile she started playing with his penis, probably to get it over with. He had an erection, but no desire to use it; his grapefruit-swollen balls seemed to be cut off from the rest of his body. He still didn't plan to do it, but when he got up to go to the bathroom with just the shirt around him, the two whores sitting eating room service (the bellboy had carefully looked away when he brought it into the half-darkened room, the photographer and the journalist lounging like lords with their half-naked girls beside them), the head of his dick hung down below the shirt and they started laughing and then he started getting wild like the class clown. First he began tickling Oy. Then he started lifting her around, and pulling the covers down to show her off naked; she laughed (probably thinks you're a real pest! said the photographer, shaking his head); she kept rubbing against him to make him do something, and then she'd look at the clock . . .

Eventually, she rubbed against him in just the right way, and then he knew he'd have to do it. What a chore! But life isn't always a bed of guacamole. He squeezed K-Y into her cunt, handed her the rubber, and then she said she didn't know how to put it on . . . Wasn't that SOMETHING? She tried sincerely, but she just didn't understand it. He did it and then thrust into her. She pretended to come and he pretended to come; he didn't care. In the carpet of light from the half-open bathroom door the other two were doing it in the far bed; Oy lay watching the photographer pedaling slowly like a cyclo driver high between three wheels, and she clapped her hand to her mouth and snickered softly; meanwhile Joy suddenly noticed that Oy was on top of the journalist and rolled off her trick and went into the bathroom and turned the shower on loud for a long time.

He really enjoyed playing with her body, lying there relaxed and feverish, doing whatever he wanted while the TV went ai-ai − if he felt like sticking a finger up her he'd just grease it and pop it in! − *I have the clap!* he announced to himself, and he felt that he'd won some major award. Light-headed and distant, he enjoyed snuggling up to her and smelling her, sucking her shaved armpits, pursuing with kisses her face which sought to evade him; every now and then he'd catch her and kiss her lips and she'd laugh. Whenever he'd touch her between the legs she'd start going um um and begin swinging her hips as if in ecstasy, but her cunt stayed dry and her face didn't change and her heart didn't pulse at all faster beneath his other hand . . . He lounged, played, stroked in a delightful fog of disease like the foggy sprawl of Bangkok he'd be leaving in four hours, soaring east over big grey squares of water going into greyness, riding the hot orange sky. At the moment it was still dark. She tried to get him off again and he let her play with his useless and meaningless erection; later he lifted her onto his neck and ran around the room in his underpants with her on his shoulders clinging and laughing in fun or terror while the photographer and his whore laughed themselves sick.

He kept saying: Oy, you want go Kambuja?

No want! No want! Kambuja people is bad people! Thai people like this   (she prayed); Kambuja people like *this!* (she saluted fiercely). The journalist saluted her in return, and she cowered back . . .

21

Oy was feeling fine from her injection. – But what if she wasn't? What if she'd been in terrible pain that first time and then the other time; what if she'd just done it for the money to pay the doctor or for rent?

22

Joy stayed with the photographer until the last minute, of course. Joy had class. The photographer had class. The whole time he was in Thailand, the journalist (poor slob) could never get any but short time girls . . .

23

Grey-green and beige squares like a flaking dartboard showing its cork beneath; these and the other squares of grey water absorbed the plane's shadow as it sped through the morning-cooled patches of trees and rectangles of various greens and greys all shining wet . . .

Cambodia seemed a no-nonsense country. There was a line of soldiers on the runway, each soldier directing the photographer and the journalist on to the next.

24

He went into the hotel lobby and took a few stacks of riels out of the paper bag. – Help yourself to some money, he said to the concierge . . . and shot past the big traffic island with the monument to independence from the French. He was hot, weak and dizzy. Thanks to the caffeine injection, he hadn't slept for two nights. In the wide listless courtyard and porticoes of the Ministry of Foreign Affairs, which seemed almost empty like the rest of Phnom Penh (how many people had been killed off?), he and the photographer sat playing with their press passes, waiting for their fate to be decided. – *In our country, at the moment, the militia plays more of a role than the army,* an official explained, and the journalist wrote it down carefully while the photographer yawned. – A tiled roof was flaking off in squares of pink like weird rust or lichens. The afternoon smelled like sandalwood. An official led them into one of the rambling yellow buildings and told them to come back tomorrow. They took a cyclo back to the hotel, and the photographer went outside to snap some landmine beggars while the journalist lay down on the bed to rest. As soon as he rolled over on his stomach, something seemed to move in his balls, weighing them down with a painless but extremely unpleasant tenderness, as if they were rotting and liquefying inside and slowly oozing down to the bottom of his scrotum. Thinking this, he had to laugh.

It was evening now, just before curfew. The boys were shooting cap guns and everyone was cheering. A boy in sandals, a dark blue shirt and a dark blue Chinese cap pedaled a cyclo slowly down the street. The photographer brought some takeout from the French restaurant across the street – steak and fries. The journalist appreciated it very much.

25

The morning sky was a delicate grey, cats stalking along the terraces, ladies puttering among potted plants, the rows of cool doors all open in the four- and five-storey apartment blocks, rows of x-shaped vents atop each square of territory, gratings on the windows. The journalist lay in bed, clutching his distended balls. It was warming up nicely. His underpants steamed against his ass. The hotel maid came in and cleaned. She made seven thousand riels a month. The Khmer Rouge had killed her father, grandfather, sister, and two brothers. She'd worked hard for the Khmer Rouge in the fields . . .

26

A cloud blew over the street. Papers started to swirl. The vendors ran to cover their stands. Suddenly came a hiss of rain. A militiaman dashed. The almost naked children danced laughing. Potted plants shook on the terraces. Now as the rain slanted down in earnest, people braced themselves between the almost shut gratings, watching. A cyclo driver pedaled on; his two lady passengers held red umbrellas over themselves. Power wires trembled; the rain shivered in heavy white rivers. A boy prayed barefoot to Buddha in the street, then clasped his hands and danced, water roaring from his soaked shirt. A clap of thunder, then rain fell like smoke; rain spewed from the roof-gutters . . .

27

The English teacher wrote *sixteen* in standard and phonetic orthography on the blackboard while the children wrote *sixteen* in their notebooks, and the English teacher got ready to write

seventeen but then the power went out and they sat in the darkness.

Your English is very good,   said the journalist.

Yes,   the teacher said.

Where did you learn it?

Yes.

What is your name?

Yes. No. Twenty-two.

Well, that's *real* good,   said the photographer brightly. That's *real* nice. Do you know what the word pussy means?

28

Steamy-fresh, the sandalwood night neared curfew while water trickled down from the balconies and orphans sat down on bedframes on the sidewalk, huddled over rice. The grilles were drawn almost closed now. Only one was open. A lady stood with her child in yellow light, guarding rows of blue bicycles whose wheel-skins caught a glow of gold. On the sidewalk, boys were carving a deer. Its head hung from a hook. The rest, now flensed to a snakelike strip of steak, red and white ribs, danced as their knives stripped it down. The journalist went to watch, and everyone crowded to watch him, crying: *Number one!* – He hadn't picked up any whores yet; they still liked him. – Another long strip peeled off – scarcely anything but bone now. A boy with muscled brown arms held the swaying backbone like a sweetheart; another fanged the cleaver blade down. Skinny-necked like a bird, the carcass tried to flail against a grating, but the strong boy wouldn't let it.

29

How happy he was when on the third day of the antibiotics something popped like popcorn in his balls and he started feeling better! The tenderness was now in his lymph nodes, but it would surely go away from there, too.

To celebrate, he showed all the hotel maids his press pass. – You very handsome, they said.

30

They had an engagement with the English teacher who couldn't speak English. The small children were silhouetted in the dark, singing A, B, C, D, E, F, G . . . On the blackboard it said *THE ENGLISH ALPHABET*. The teacher pointed at this, and the children said: *Da iii-eee aa-phabet.*

Why does the alphabet only go up to S? asked the journalist.

Yes, the teacher replied.

The journalist pointed to a photograph that concentrated darkness like an icon. – My father is die by Pol Pot regime, said the teacher simply. He go to Angkor Wat to hide Buddha. They die him by slow pain . . .

For a moment the journalist wanted to embrace him. Instead he stared down at the floor, and the sweat dripped from his nose and forehead. As soon as he wiped his face it was wet again.

The English teacher and his friend took the journalist and the photographer to someone's house. The room was dark. Someone lit a candle and connected a gasoline generator outside. Then the lights flickered on. The wall-gratings looked out on darkness. The journalist sat in a corner consuming cool tea and cakes; the photographer sweated wearily. It was very hot. After a few minutes they thanked their hosts and went to dinner.

They sat at an outside table on the rainy street, while everyone watched them from underneath lighted canopies or leaning against trees; the rain gleamed on bike lights. There was a pot of cold tea on the table. One-legged beggars kept approaching, some in soldier's uniform; the journalist gave each of them a hundred riels because he and the photographer still had plenty of money. The English teacher ordered Chinese noodle soup with organ meats and peppers. Then they went for a walk. The English teacher's friend suggested a movie, which proved not to be a Chinese story about angry ghosts as the poster had suggested but a dubbed American thing; lizards crawled up and down the cement walls, and it was sweltering. After five minutes the journalist was ready to go. After ten minutes he slid out of his seat and walked down the dark stairs, knowing that the English teacher and his friend would be hurt, feeling guilty, but only a little; after all, he'd bought them dinner. At least the photographer wouldn't care.

The night was lovely at curfew time, the rain just barely

condensing out of the hot black sky like drops of sweat, motorbikes purring down the street. A woman pedaled slowly in the rain. It was very nice to see how her wet blue skirt stuck to her thighs. He passed the new market and saw a disco's dark doorway evilly serendipitous; I'll have to tell the photographer about that, he thought. (He didn't go in. The gaggle of taxi girls and motorbike drivers sitting hands on thighs, or looking sweetly, palely, over their shoulders, daunted him like pack-ice black and grey and all in a blue of mystery.) Every little chessboard-floored restaurant had become a movie theater of chairs packed with mothers and children raptly watching a TV screen placed high in the corner; two naked children, brother and sister, sat on the sidewalk staring in through a grating; every cell in the honeycomb was a cutaway world made expressly for the journalist to stare into and long to be taken into, just as the TV screens were for everyone else. Crossing a pitch-dark street he dodged cyclos and bicycles (all headlightless, almost silent). No one paid much attention to the curfew anymore; even so, as the hour shrank, more and more steel accordion-diamonds stretched taut to meet and lock everything into darkness. Girls leaned out of their terraces; doors opened to show darkness or brightly turning fans. The girls put both hands on the railings and leaned, their watch-dials white like fire; they gossiped across at each other, enjoyed the hot night's raindrops, watched the street where a boy crossed with long slow steps, the scrape of his sandals a continuous sound, his blue shirt glowing like a night aquarium. Lizards waited head down on hotel walls. The girls looked at the journalist and waved; he waved back. A black dog scuttered across the street like a moving hole.

31

In the hotel there were paintings of bare-breasted girls in butterfly-winged skirts standing waist-deep in the mist before science fiction palaces. The night was so hot that his face felt as if it had peered into a steaming kettle. He went into the room, turned the air conditioning on (he and the photographer, being boys of high morals, always traveled first class), and took a shower. He was standing naked in the cool water when the photographer came in with two whores.

32

They were from that same disco he'd passed, as he soon learned (the photographer's soul always gushed when he'd made a novel score). – I was gonna take the tall one because I kept thinking how it would be, you know, with her legs around me, but as soon as we got into the street the short one took my hand, so that's that. – I guess it is, replied the journalist, toweling himself off while the girls screamed and looked away. – They went through all his pills and medicines first, sniffing the packets, going *nnnihh!*, giggling at the condoms, whispering and pointing like schoolgirls. The photographer's girl was already in the shower and out, halfway demure in her towel. The journalist's girl stayed dressed. She did not seem to like him very much, but then that didn't seem unusual to him because girls never liked him; was it his fat legs or his flabby soul? Fortunately this was an issue he'd never be called on to write a newsicle about. – Look at 'em! shouted the photographer. They're as curious as fucking *monkeys*, man! – With great effort they mouthed the Khmer words in the dictionary section of his guidebook; they opened the box of sugar cubes, which were swarming with ants, and ate one apiece. The journalist's girl had a beauty spot over one eye. When she opened and closed everything, her eyebrows slanted in elegant surprise. She wore a striped dark dress. There was something very ladylike about her: she intimidated him slightly. He lay sweatily on the bed watching them; when they'd completed their inspection they neatened everything up like good housewives, so that it took

the journalist and the photographer days to find their pos-
sessions. Such *well-meaning* young women, though . . . They
stared with satisfaction into the mirror, the photographer's girl
tilting the purple tube of lipstick and drawing it along her lower
lip like a gentle loving penis while her earrings and necklace
shone gold, her hair spilling black and pure black like squid's
ink. Suddenly she turned toward the photographer, her nose's
beauty spot spying on him, something shiny and watchful in her
eyes and tea-colored face in the darkness as she made her hair
into braids for him, smoothing the electric blue dress down over
her tits; but the journalist's girl never looked away from the
mirror; she smiled into it or she leaned her nose against it so as
not to have to look at anything else; only the gold glitter around
her dark breasts like drops of light in the humid darkness of the
hotel room, her face level or low, maybe satisfied after all; or
maybe the smile was only some resigned grimace.

33

The photographer's girl got ready right away. But after half an
hour the journalist's girl was still silent in the bathroom with
the door closed. She stood staring at the back of her little
mirror, which had a decal of a man and woman together . . .

34

He communicated with her mainly by signs. She liked to smell
his cheeks and forehead in little snorts of breath, but not to kiss
him; whenever he tried, she'd whirl her head away into the
pillow, so he started Buddha-ing her in just the same way that
Oy had steepled her hands very quickly together for good luck
when he'd bought her out, she probably hoping he wouldn't see,

probably praying that he'd give her a lot of money; so he did this to the Cambodian girl; he'd seen the beggars do it; he'd do it to say please, then he'd touch his forefinger from his lips to hers – and she'd Buddha him back to say please no. Sometimes he did it anyway, and she'd jerk her head away, or let him do it only on her closed lips. Then sometimes he'd steeple his hands please and point from his lips to her cunt, and she'd wave her hand no, so he wouldn't do that; he'd pray to kiss her again, and she'd pray him no; so he'd pray and point from his crotch to hers and she'd nod yes.

35

He smiled at her as affectionately as he could. He wanted her to like him. It just made things easier when the whore you were on top of liked you. – The truth was, he really did like her. He traced a heart on her breast with his finger and smiled, but she looked back at him very seriously. Then suddenly she ran her fingernail lightly round his wrist and pointed to herself. – What did she mean? So many prostitutes seemed to wear religious strings for bracelets; was that what she meant? Somehow he didn't think so . . .

36

Give 'em more Benadryl; come on, give 'em more Benadryl, the journalist whined as the photographer's girl turned on the light giggling for the fourth or fifth time that night; he didn't know exactly what the hour was, since his watch had been stolen in Thailand, possibly by Oy . . . The photographer's girl loved to watch the journalist making love. Even when the photographer was screwing her she'd always be looking avidly at the other bed, hoping to see the journalist's buttocks pumping under the sheet; whenever she could she'd sneak up and pull the sheet away to see the journalist naked with a naked girl; then she'd shriek with glee. It was very funny but it got a little less funny each time. – Fortunately they obediently swallowed whatever pills the journalist gave them; the photographer told them that the journalist was a doctor and the journalist neither confirmed nor denied this report, which most likely they didn't understand anyway. So he gave them Benadryl; one for his girl, three for the other, who was hyperkinetic. Even so they both kept turning the lights on to see what time it was; they wanted to leave by the end of curfew. – The journalist's girl lay against him, her cool weightless fingers resting on his chest. Her face smelled sweetish like hair-grease. In the morning she pulled a towel about herself and slid into her gold and purple dress. Then she sat in a chair, far from the bed, making up her lips, using her eyebrow pencil, occasionally uttering brief replies to the other girl's babble. The other girl had a voice like a lisping child. The girl in the chair ran the lipstick very slowly over the outside of her lower lip. She saw the journalist looking at her and smiled guardedly, then raised the pocket mirror again. She smoothed her hair away from her cheeks and began to apply more of the sickly-sweet cream.

37

Once they'd left, he told the photographer he didn't want to see her again. Why, she hadn't wanted to do *anything!* – and she'd seemed so sorrowful he'd felt like a rapist. What did she expect anyway? – But as soon as he'd conveyed these well-reasoned sentiments, his heart started to ache. He didn't tell the photographer, of course. They rarely talked about those things. But he remembered how she'd hung his trousers neatly over the chair, how she'd ordered his money in neat piles without stealing any, how before leaving she'd taken each of his fingers and pulled it until it made a cracking noise, then bent it back; this was her way of pleasing him, taking care of him.

38

At the disco that night he didn't see her. He sat and waited while the crowd stridulated. Finally her friend, the photographer's girl, came to the table. She was slick with sweat; she must have been dancing. He asked the English teacher who didn't speak English to ask her where his girl was. The man said: She don't come here today. – Already they were bringing him another girl. He said not right now, thank you. He tried to find out more, and then there was another girl sitting down by him and he figured he had to buy her a drink so she wouldn't be hurt, and the photographer's girl was biting her lip and stamping her foot, and then his girl came and stood looking on at him and the other girl silently.

39

He pointed to his girl and traced the usual imaginary bracelet around his wrist. (He didn't even know his girl's name. He'd asked the photographer's girl and she said something that sounded like *Pala*. He'd tried calling her Pala and she looked at him without recognition.) Finally the other girl got up, carrying her drink, and began to trudge away. He patted her shoulder to let her know that he was sorry, but that seemed to be the wrong thing to do, too. His girl sat down in her place, and he could feel her anger, steady and flame-white in the darkness, almost impersonal.

40

But that night when he put his closed lips gently on her closed lips, not trying to do anything more because he knew how much Thai and Cambodian women hated kissing, her mouth slowly opened and the tip of her tongue came out.

41

You got her to french you? laughed the photographer, as the two chauvinists lay at ease, discussing their conquests. – Oh, *good!* She must have been *really* repulsed.

42

Sliding piles of fish empyred the dock, bleeding mouths where heads used to be, heads white and goggle-eyed and wheel-gilled at their new red termini like the undersides of menstruating mushrooms. The heads went into a big aluminum bowl; then the squatting girl with bloody hands and feet started picking through yellow tripe-piles, getting the yellow snakes inside; the dock was red with blood. – Another pile (smooth skinny silver fish) still flapped; the flies were crawling on them before they were even dead.

The rickety boards, which bent underfoot, were laid over a framework of wet knobby peeled sticks. Big fish and small fish flashed in the water-spaces. They were from Siem Reap. The fishers had been feeding them corn for four months. If all went well, they'd make more than a hundred million riels' profit. A big basket of live fish gaped up as sweetly as angels, winged with gills, their lips mumbling a last few water-breaths as their eyes dulled. They stopped shining. The flies were thick on them like clusters of black grapes.

A man tied two live fishes together through the gills with withes. Then he lifted them away.

Boys in dirty white shirts and pants scuttled on the planks. Then they leaped into the water. They began to draw in their nets. A gorgeous leopard-butterfly crowned them. – Why do butterflies love blood? the journalist wondered. The beauty of the butterfly seemed a sort of revenge that left him uncomprehendingly incredulous.

The glistening brown boys came up from the brown water, squatting on the frames. Fish splashed in the nets. The boys raised the nets a little more. The splashing was loud and furious now. The fish were fighting for their lives. The boys began their work. They grabbed each fish by the tail. If it was still too small they threw it back. That didn't happen often. Usually they whacked it on top of the skull with a fat stick. Then they beat its head against a beam until it was still, and blood came out of its mouth.

The butterfly had settled in a drop of blood, and was drinking.

A man with a notebook wrote numbers. He had a stack of money in his shirt pocket. Another man stood by pressing buttons on his calculator. It was like the Stock Exchange.

The dead fish were in a big basket. Two men slid a pole through, and lifted the pole onto their shoulders, carrying it away down the long wagging double planks onto the land, past the photographer who stood scowling like an evil dream, past the sweating journalist, past the people scraping earth into broad half-shell baskets which they dumped up onto the levée so that the pickman could tamp it down. (Everyone was worried about flooding.) The two men walked on and finally set the basket down in the back of a truck.

In the square wood-walled cells of water, the boys raised their nets until fins broke water. The squatting girl was already chopping off the heads of the other fish with a big cleaver. Her toes were scarlet with blood.

43

The disco was stifling hot, and everybody mopped their faces with the chemical towelettes that the hostess brought. Waves of stupid light rusted across the walls.

You happy?   he asked the English teacher who couldn't speak English.

Good!   the other replied.   I'm berry excited . . .

It was long and low in there with occasional light bulbs. Girls said   aaah   and   ooh   and   aiee   while the crowd swarmed slowly and sweatily. Semen-colored light flickered on men's blue-white shirts and women's baggy silk pajama-pants or dresses; the accustomed smell of a cheap barbershop choked him like the weary Christmas lights. The barmaid brought a tall can of Tiger beer. Hands clutched all around, as if in some drunken dream –

44

She almost never smiled. Once again that night she traced an invisible bracelet around her wrist, then his. He watched her sleeping. In the middle of the night he pulled her on top of him just to hug her more tightly, and she seemed no heavier than the blanket.

45

She lay hardly breathing. He could barely hear her heartbeat. Her hands lay folded between her breasts. Her nipples were very long, brown and thin.

46

In the morning she cracked his finger-joints and toe-joints for him; she stretched and twisted his arms and legs; she slapped him gently all over. Then she made her rendezvous with the mirror, where she stood painting her eyebrows in slow silence. When she was finished he sat her down with his guidebook, which contained a few dictionary pages. He pointed to all the different words for food, pointed to her and then to him. She just sat there. He made motions to indicate the two of them going off together. She followed soundlessly. He locked the door. She came downstairs with him, into the lobby's world of eyes which shot the weak smirk off his face, and the eyes watched in silence. She was behind him on the stairs, creeping slowly down. He dropped the key onto the front desk and she was far behind him. He let her catch up to him a little, not too much because she might not want that, and went out into the street that was filled with even more spies, spectators, jeerers and hostile enviers, and she was farther behind than before. It must be difficult for her to be seen beside him. He concluded that the best thing to do was to walk without looking, which he did for half a block, then sat down at an outdoor restaurant where they brought him tea and bread. She had not come. He drank a few sips of his tea, paid, and walked wearily back. He said to the cigarette vendeuse: You see my friend?

Market. That way,   she said.

You tell her, please, if she go to hotel, she come in.

No, no. You go market. She that way.

He did, but of course he never found her.

47

He felt miserable all day. He didn't want to fuck her anymore, only to straighten things out. He'd find someone to speak English to her . . .

Again and again he circled the market's yellow-tiered cement dome. The traffic was slow enough to let jaywalkers stand in the street. He loitered among the umbrellas and striped awnings, under each a vendor's booth or table; and sometimes they tried to sell him things: moneychangers studied him behind their jagged walls of cigarette cartons; but there was only one vendeuse he wanted, and what she had, it seemed, he couldn't ever buy.

The photographer's girl, on the other hand, had stayed. The photographer was getting sick of her. He told her that he and the journalist would have to go to work soon; he pointed to her and then to the door, but the girl tried desperately not to understand. In the middle of the morning she was still there. She wanted him to buy her a gold bracelet. They were out on the street, the three of them, and the photographer said to the journalist: All right. We'll each grab a cyclo and split.

Where to?

Where *to?*   cried the photographer in amazement.   *Anywhere!* Just as long as we get rid of this bitch . . . Oh, shit, she's getting a cyclo, too!

Finally they went home with her. She took them down a very dark narrow dirt lane, then right into an alley, then up a steep plank ladder two inches wide to a dormitory that smelled like wood-smoke and was rowed with tiny square windows for light and air. Puddles on the floor darkly reflected the ceiling's patchy plaster. Mosquitoes and fleas bit the journalist's feet. The room was filled with beds, enclosed by patterned sheets hung from strings like laundry; sturdy beds, neatly made up. People lay one or two to a bed, very quiet, some sleeping, some not. The photographer's girl said that she paid ten thousand riels a year to stay there. She lived with her aunt, in a bed against the wall.

She pulled the photographer down on top of her, tried to get him to marry her – with a gold chain –

How many times has she been married?   asked the journalist.

The aunt smiled and fanned him.   – Five times.

He heard the sound of a thudding mallet, saw the shadow of a woman's bare legs darkening the nearest puddle on the dirty-grey cement. The photographer lay listless and disgusted on the bed, his girl on top of him whining, working him slowly but determinedly like a cyclo driver polishing his wheels. The journalist felt sorry for her.

Now they brought another girl for the journalist to marry in the dimness; she'd gone through it three or four times at least from the look of *her* gold chains; she took over the task of fanning him, smiling so wide-eyed that the journalist began to feel sorry for her, too; he already had a girl. – Pala, Pala! he said. – The photographer's girl knew what he meant, and she gnashed her teeth. This rejected matrimonial prospect turned away and put on a new bra, kneeling on her pallet two feet away. The disks of her gold necklace gleamed consecutively when she turned her head, like the bulbs of a neon sign. While she was away the aunt resumed fanning him. Her teeth were perfectly white except for one of gold. She wore a ruby ring from Pailin (where he had promised his editor he'd go; he had no intention of going because the Khmer Rouge were still in control of the town).

I can't stand this anymore, the photographer said. Let's get out of here.

They'll want us to take them out to lunch.

So we'll take 'em out to lunch. Then we'll dump 'em.

The aunt didn't come. So it was only the photographer and his girl and the journalist with two new ladies, each hoping and vying, who went to the nearest sidewalk restaurant. He was a little afraid of one of them, a very pale girl with a Chinese-porcelain face (was she albino, or sick, or just heavily powdered? The longer he looked at her, the more corpselike she seemed . . .); she, noticing how he studied her most frequently, said something in a smug undertone to her rival, who then withdrew her solicitudes. The Chinese-porcelain girl kept lowering her head and smiling, fingering her strings of gold, while the other girl, still hopeful to a small degree, gazed lovingly from time to time into the journalist's eyes. Crowds lined up behind their chairs, staring unhappily. By and large, they did not seem to

admire whores or foreigners who whored. But of course there wasn't a damned thing they could do about it, thought the journalist as the Chinese-porcelain girl peeled him the local equivalent of a grape, which had a green rind, an inner sweet grey substance the texture and shape of an eyeball, and then a round seed – did it taste more like a grape or a cantaloupe? Being a journalist, he really ought to decide the issue once and for all – oh, GOOD, he'd have another chance (she'd hardly touched her soup; she looked very very sick; quite suddenly he was sure that she was going to drop dead any minute) . . . She called the fruit *mayen*.

48

So after lunch they dropped the girls, and the girls were very disappointed.

49

The photographer had to go back to the hotel to get more ointment for his rash, which had spread from one arm to the other and itched practically as bad as scabies or crabs (which the well-traveled photographer had already experienced; of course he'd never had *** **GONORRHEA** *** so the journalist was one up on him there). The journalist sat waiting for him in an open square of grass riddled with wide walkways and rectangular puddles between which children ran. On the far side (this park was quite large), two-storey houses whose roofs were truncated pyramids strutted stained balconies. Between the roots of a tree, a boy was digging with a stick.

The journalist thought about the gold chain that his prostitute wore about her naked waist. He wondered who'd given it to her, and whether the man had loved her in his heart or whether he'd just paid her. Did he still see her?

There were red lines running down her skin in slanted parallels from her shoulders to her breasts, three lines on her left side, three on her right, the two triads arrowing symmetrically inward; they reminded him of aboriginal tattoos. Most likely they'd been made with a coin's edge. Someone had told him that Cambodians did that to ease the blood when they were ill. Suddenly he recalled the nightmare pallor of the Chinese-porcelain girl, and he almost shuddered.

50

Night having smothered the wasted day at last, he set out for the disco while his dear friend the photographer lurked in the rat-infested shadows of the garbage heap, not wishing to show himself to *his* girl, the five-time bride, whom he'd dismissed definitively, and who was in corresponding agonies. The journalist knew very well that by returning to the disco he'd be disturbing her, and the photographer as well, but this was the time to actualize his own reproductive strategies. So he passed through the hot outer crowds alone. Every time he came here they seemed more menacing. It was all in his head, but that was his problem; as the saying goes, he was thinking with the wrong head. As soon as he'd been sucked into the sweaty inner darkness, the photographer's girl came running up, seizing him by the hand, weeping, pleading in a rush of alien singsong. He shook his head, patted her shoulder (this was becoming his stereotyped Pontius Pilate act), and she stamped in a rage. Just as nightshade grows tall and poisonous in American forests, its spider-legged veins hung with red balls, black balls, and milky white putrescences, so grew her fury in that long narrow cavern whose walls dripped with lust-breath. She ran away into the cigarette fumes between the crowded tables and though he'd lost sight of her, her terrible howling made his ears ache. She was back again, snarling and groveling monstrously (did she need to eat so badly as that? what didn't he understand?) and he wondered whether she only wanted him to buy her out so that she could rush to the hotel in pursuit of the photographer, or whether she wanted *him* now, whether he was her fallback; anyhow it was clear that she wasn't Pala's friend (that night she finally took the trouble to tell him that the woman he was falling in love with was not named Pala, but Vanna) because that afternoon she'd tried to get him to go with the girl in the bra, the Chinese-porcelain girl, or failing that the other one (did she get a commission?); she wasn't loyal to Vanna! – Thinking this helped him harden his heart. (In truth, what could he have done? His loyalty lay with Vanna and with the photographer, not with her.) – I want Vanna, he said. – Excuse me, sir, said a low-level pimp or waiter or enforcer, presenting him with two other girls, each of whom slid pleading hands up his kneee. – I want Vanna, he said. – The photographer's girl said something, and the others laughed scornfully. Then they all left. (Later the photographer said that he saw his girl come running out, and he hid behind the garbage pile so she wouldn't discover him; she got on a motorbike and went to the hotel to sniff him out; not finding him, she came back weeping.) – Vanna must be dancing, probably. There was no possibility of finding her if she didn't want to be found. She was a taxi girl; it was her profession to find him. If she wanted him she'd come . . . He sat back down, and a waiter said something in Khmer that to him sounded very eloquent. Evidently it was a question. Tall, white, conspicuous, the journalist sat at his table facing the stares from other darknesses. – Seven-Up,   he said. The waiter trotted off, and returned with a long face.   – Sprite,   said the journalist. The waiter brought him three cans of ice cream soda.   – Perfect, he said wearily. The photographer's girl was sitting down beside him again; he slid one can toward her. His own girl came from the dance floor at last, eyeing him with what he interpreted to be an aloof and hangdog look. A man said to him: YES, my friend! . . .   and began to explain something to him at great length, possibly the causes and cures of hyperthyroidism, while the journalist nodded solemnly and Vanna stared straight through everything. The journalist offered him a can of ice cream soda as a prize for the speech. The waiter remained anxious at his elbow; the two staring girls needed so badly to be taken out . . . – At last the man pointed to Vanna and then to himself, joined two fingers together . . . Then he said something involving many vowels, concluding with the words *twenty dollah*. Buying a girl out was only ten. The journalist reached into his money-pouch and handed the man a twenty-dollar bill. The man rose formally and went behind the bar, speaking to a gaggle of other smooth operators as the journalist took Vanna's hand and tried to get her to rise but she made a motion for him to wait. The man came back and announced: *Twenty-five dollah.* The journalist shook his head and popped up from his seat again like a jack-in-the-box. He was required to stand and sit several more times before the man finally faded. Then he took Vanna's hand. She walked behind him without enthusiasm. Every eye was on them. The photographer's girl made one more attempt,

53

He'd made up his mind, as I've said, not to fuck her anymore. He just wanted to be with her. When they lay in bed that night he kept his arm around her and she drew him close, drumming playfully on his belly, pinching his nipples; but then she was very still on her back beside him and he could see that she was waiting for him to do what he usually did (as meanwhile in the street the photographer met his former girl, who'd come hunting for him again alongside the girl with the Chinese-porcelain face, who still entertained hopes of majoring in journalism on her back; the photographer's girl was sobbing and screaming in the street . . .) He didn't even kiss her or touch her breasts. He just held her very close, and the two of them fell asleep. All night they held each other. He wanted to respect her. In the morning he could see that she was waiting for it again, so he got up and took a shower and started getting dressed. He couldn't tell if she was surprised. She got up, too, and pulled her bra on, while in the other bed the photographer lay grinning.

You mind if I hop her while you're in the shower? he said.

I don't think she'd like that,   the journalist said evenly.

That's a good one,   the photographer jeered.

54

He made eating motions and she nodded faintly.

He took her downstairs, this time holding her hand and introducing her to everyone as his girlfriend, but she didn't look anyone in the eye.

At the restaurant they pretended she wasn't there and asked him what he wanted.

Ask her,   he said.

They looked at him incredulously.

He said it again, and she said something.

Uh, they said, she want, uh, only soup, sir.

Two soups, please, he said.

When the soups came she put pepper on his and smiled a little. She picked the meat and noodles out of hers, leaving the broth as people always seemed to do in Cambodia, and then she just sat there. He suddenly wanted to cry.

He drew an imaginary gold circlet on her wrist, and she nodded.

They went out, and he was about to take her by the hand to go to the market where he'd seen some gold things for sale, but she took *him* by the hand and led him to a motorbike and they got on. They traveled far across the city, down shady lanes of coconut palms, past clean white two-storey houses already shuttered against the heat, then a sudden crowded marketplace, then a sidewalk lined with the checker-clothed tables of the cigarette vendeuses, ahead more palm trees receding infinitely . . . He gripped her shoulders. Everyone was looking at him as usual. He kept expecting to get used to it; instead, every day it got harder to bear. There was a young soldier in fresh glowing green who lounged in sandals, smoking and talking with a friend sitting on a Honda; the soldier looked up suddenly and locked his eyes on the journalist's face; when the journalist looked back, the soldier was still watching. Two old brown faces leaning close together, smoking Liberation cigarettes over a bicycle, peered round and caught him. They stood up slowly, never looking away. A cyclo driver with veined brown pipestem legs saw him, and there was almost an accident. The journalist never tightened his grip on Vanna's shoulders; he did not want to add to her shame. They vibrated past shady chessboard-floored chambers open to the street, their corrugated doors and grilles retracted to let the last of the morning coolness in, glass-fronted shelves not quite glinting in the dimness, people resting inside with their bare feet up on chairs, schools of child-fish watching TV; and the journalist drank them in almost vindictively because so many had drunk him in; everywhere soldiers and gorgeous-greened police rode slowly on motorbikes, looking both ways.

At last they reached a video arcade which was also a jewelry store without any jewelry, without anything in the glass case except for a tiny set of scales on top of a cigar box. The Chinese-looking man in the straw hat opened the cigar box and took out three gold bracelets. Vanna gestured to the journalist to choose. He smiled and signed that it was up to her. She smiled a little at him. Already a new crowd was secreting itself, like the swarm of black bees eating the sugar and flour in the market's open bowls . . . – Two of the bracelets were slender and lacy. The third was quite heavy and had three blocks that said A B C. That one would obviously be the most expensive. She took that one. He took a hundred-dollar bill from his pocket and gave it to her. She looked at it as if she'd never seen one before, which she probably hadn't. The man in the straw hat said something to her; the motorbike driver joined in, and they all began to discuss the alphabet bracelet with its every ramification. There was one chair, and she gestured to him to sit down; he gestured to her to do it, but she shook her head. The man in the straw hat gestured to him to sit down; he gave in. The man in the straw hat got a calculator from somewhere and clicked out the figure 30 and said *dollah*. The journalist nodded. I guess I can give Vanna a lot of change, he thought. They all talked some more. The man in the straw hat clicked out 137. They were all watching him to see what he'd do. When he got out two twenties, everybody but Vanna started to laugh. Were they happy, polite, scornful, or sorry for him? What did it matter? The man in the straw hat brought out his miniature scales and weighed the alphabet bracelet against a weight. Then he switched the pans and did the same thing again. The journalist nodded. Vanna took the bracelet and draped it over her left wrist. He realized that everyone was waiting for him to fasten it for her. He bent down and did it, taking awhile because the catch was very delicate and he was clumsy and nervous with his fat sweaty fingers. The man in the straw hat came to help him, but he waved him away. When he'd finished, he looked up. An old lady was standing at the edge of the crowd. He smiled at her tentatively, and she stared back stonily.

Then he looked at Vanna. The smile that she gave him was worth everything. And she took his hand in front of them all.

They got back on the motorbike and went to a bazaar. She paid the driver off with two of the one hundred-riel notes he'd given her last night, and led him into the awninged tunnels. People stared at them and snickered. A woman with her three young children was sitting on a bedframe on the sidewalk, eating rice. When they spied Vanna and the journalist, they forgot their rice. Someone called out: *Does you loves her?*   – She stared ahead proudly; he hoped that their cruelty did not touch her.

55

She went to a bluejean stand and held a pair of black ones against herself and then put them back. (Did she want him to buy her something?) She looked at a white blouse and a yellow blouse. She put them back.

She kept looking at her watch. Had he already used up his hundred thirty-seven dollars' worth of her time? She caught them another motorbike and brought him to a place that looked like a prison. Soldiers were sitting at a table behind a grating, with their pistols lying pointed out. There was a ragged hole in the grating. She put some money in, and a hand reached out and gave her two slips of waste paper with hand-written numbers on them.

Then he realized that they were going to the movies.

Taking him by the hand, she guided him upstairs through the molten crowds and bought them fruit. Then they went into the auditorium. It was almost unbearably hot, and the shrill screaming crackling echoing movie was interminable. But he was very happy because she held his hand and snuggled against him, and he could watch her smiling in the dark.

There was a newsreel about the latest floods. She pointed, held the edge of her hand to her throat like rising water.

Then she brought him back to the hotel. People lined up on the sidewalks to watch them pass; he longed for one of those Chinese rockets-on-a-string, to clear the landmined path . . .

Well, what have you been up to?   said the photographer, on the bed, nursing his skin rash.

Got married.

Oh. Well, I guess that means I'd better clear out. Is an hour enough?

He still didn't really want to fuck her. He just wanted to be naked next to her, holding her for the last ten minutes or two hours or whatever it would be until she went to work. He stripped and took a shower. While she did the same, he looked for his gonorrhea pills. When she came out he got into bed with her. She pointed to her watch. She had to go soon. She snuggled him for a minute, then pointed to the tube of K-Y jelly. He didn't want to confuse or disappoint her anymore. If that was what she expected, then he'd better do it. She touched his penis, and he squirted the K-Y jelly into her and rolled the rubber on and got ready to mount her, and then something in her face made him start to cry and he went soft inside her and rolled off. – She was not pleased, no two ways about it. After all, it was their honeymoon. She was rubbing him; she wanted him to try again. He put more K-Y jelly inside her and took the rubber off and threw it on the floor. The doctor had said he wouldn't be contagious anymore; sex was only hurting him, not anyone else. As soon as he was inside her, he went soft again. He was crying, and she smiled, looking into his face, trying to cheer him up; he was behaving like a baby. He traced a heart on his chest, pointed from himself to her, and drew a heart between her breasts. She nodded very seriously. He made a motion of two hands joining and she nodded. He said: You, me go America together . . .   and she shook her head. She drew a square on his chest, not a heart, then pointed to a heart-shaped chain of gold that some other man must have given her . . .

She got up and took a shower. He started to get dressed, too, but she gently motioned him back into bed. She dressed very quickly. She came and sat with him for a moment on the bed, and he pointed to the number eight on his watch and signed to her to come to the hotel then and she nodded and he said: *Ah khun.* * – Then she stood up to go. She clasped her hands together goodbye and he was crying and she was waving and kissing her hands to him and she never came back again.

THE END

* Thank you.

56

But the end of the story is not the end of *the* story; that doesn't happen until THE END when they lower you into your pitch-dark grave. The punchline of the closed episode recedes as experience continues, which must be why it's so difficult to learn anything.

57

I wonder if she's waiting for me at the disco,   the journalist said.   Maybe she misunderstood –
    I'm sure she is,   drawled the photographer.   Yep, she's just sitting around waiting for her knight in shining armor.

58

That night he had a dream that he was getting married and everyone was so happy for him; all the street orphans were there drumming and dancing; reformed Stalinists made him fish soup; the cyclo drivers donated their vehicles to serve as chairs . . .

59

When he told the photographer a little more about it, the photographer said: She must have thought you were a real pain in the ass.

60

They were on the way to the battlefields, although not much was going on there; truth to tell, that was how they liked it. Their official driver (the interpreter assured them that he was not in the secret police) sped importantly down the road in the government car whose insignia meant secret police; every fifteen seconds the driver honked. A woman rode side-saddle on the back of a motor scooter, holding a basket of green fruit in her lap. The driver honked and the motor scooter skidded aside; the woman almost went flying. The driver gunned it and pulled ahead, drowning her in dust. Down the hot white road where cyclists bore bushy loads of grass, the pale car rocked and bumped. The driver honked, and pedestrians leaped for their lives, scrambling up the dyke of yellow dirt. They passed angle-roofed tin-walled houses on stilts. A naked brown child was fishing in tea-colored water. A water-buffalo sucked its mother. – There are two kinds of land mine, the interpreter was saying. One explodes if you touch it anywhere. The other kind explodes only if you step on it. – The journalist was barely listening. He could not stop remembering the way she'd been looking at him when he started crying and she was trying to cheer him up by smiling and teasing him with her finger though her eyes were sad and distant like always, so he tried to smile back like a good sport even with the tears running out of his eyes and he could not miss her looking at him so searchingly and then she rose to pray her hands *ah khun* and goodbye, gently going out the door.

You see,   an English student had told him (another of his
myriad helpful interpreters),   sometimes I too like to play with
taxi girl. But, you see, I have girlfriend.

61

And I think you have already had a taste of Cambodian girls?
the interpreter said suddenly.

Uh huh,   said the journalist, thinking: Which spies and
busybodies in the lobby *didn't* report us?

A poster of a worker, hammer in one hand, gun in the other.
Jungle to the left (to the far left); that was where the Khmer
Rouge were. More empty orange rivers; a kid barfing out the
window of the Red Cross van . . . The journalist rubbed his
balls.

62

The Chief of Protocol received them on a high porch. He was
pleased with the journalist's French. He read their dossiers and
clapped a hand to his mouth in mirth.

Ah, a beautiful girl there – did you remark her?   he said in
the car.

No, Monsieur,   said the journalist.

But I believe you do regard them.

Yes, I do regard them,   replied the journalist in the most
pompous French that he could muster.   For me, every girl in
Cambodia is beautiful.

The Chief of Protocol laughed so hard that he had a coughing
fit.

Clearly it was his job to amuse the Chief of Protocol.   – In
Phnom Penh, every girl is a delicious banquet,   he said.

Delighted, the Chief of Protocol embraced him.

What did you tell him?   asked the interpreter.

I said that it is very hot today,   said the journalist.

The Chief of Protocol said something to the interpreter, who giggled.

Yes, yes,   said the interpreter,   and Battambang is famed for its lovely roadside flowers.

Sounds like we'll be gettin' some pussy tonight,   said the photographer.

Well,   said the journalist cautiously,   that's up to them. But at least we know it's in our file.

63

At the expensive restaurant where they had to take the driver, the interpreter and the Chief of Protocol, two hostesses came to sit with the white boys. The journalist tried to give his girl to the Chief of Protocol, who sat constantly at his right hand talking until his ears ached, but no matter how many circum-flexes the journalist piled on, the Chief of Protocol said: I am married!

So am I,   said the journalist, kissing the hole on another can of Tiger beer.   You see, Monsieur, I married a flower in Phnom Penh.

A flower – in Phnom Penh! Hee, hee, hee!

The journalist did not want a Battambang flower. He wanted Vanna. But he did not want to disappoint or humiliate the hostess. And he did not want to make the Cambodian officials think less of him. It seemed so important to them . . .

The woman smiled at him shyly. He smiled back. He could think of nothing to say to her. He was exhausted.

Tell her I'm in the KGB,   he said.   Tell her I want to take her to Russia with me. My name is Communist Number One.

She says, she don't want to go with Russian. She afraid. She go your friend.

So the photographer got two girls that night. The journalist was relieved. He yawned and blew his nose. The Chief of Protocol was very sorry for him. It all worked out well: the journalist with a good night's sleep, the driver and interpreter well amused, the photographer with his girls grinning vanilla-teethed, nodding on his shoulder, the Chief of Protocol grinning hilariously in the dark doorway behind . . .

64

Riding atop the jolting Soviet tank in the rain, he saluted the staring or laughing girls, kissing his hand to them, waving to the kids, the old men and ladies, tossing ten-riel notes down into the road like bonbons (the photographer and the driver did the same; the driver was dressed in a black uniform today, and wore his Russian pistol especially for the occasion); and the interpreter and the Chief of Protocol and the soldiers with their upraised machine guns watched the journalist, grinning, and the journalist saluted for hours as they rolled back in from the tame battlefield. He was utterly and completely happy. In Cambodia he could never disappear; now at least when people gawked at him they saw someone comic and grand, a man with a private army who gave them money; he felt like God – a loving God, moreover; he loved everyone he saluted; he wanted to love the whole world, which (it now seemed to him) was all he'd ever wanted when he had whores; his balls still felt funny; all he wanted to do with people was hug them and kiss them and give them money. His forehead glowing with sunburn and three beers, he sat against the spare tire, blessing everyone like the Pope, nodding to his elders, wishing that his lordliness would never end. Most of the time they waved back. Girls on bicycles giggled to each other. Children saluted back with slow smiles. Skinny white-grinning men waved back. These gratifying demonstrations almost balanced those other stares they'd given him and Vanna . . . He ached to hold her. Since he was drunk and only a flightless butterfly, he squeezed the spare tire instead.

65

The Hotel Victoire, which just after the liberation they used to call the Hotel Lavatoire, was a very good hotel, possibly the world's best. It had running water, electricity, air conditioning, a toilet and screen windows. No matter that none of these worked. Sleeping there was like sleeping in a sweltering locker room. It cost two thousand a night for the photographer's and the journalist's room, and five hundred for the driver's and the interpreter's room. This infuriated the photographer, but the journalist said: Look on the bright side. We're paying for everything. At least we don't have to pay twenty bucks a night for their room, too. – He went up to the room, and the interpreter told him that it was his turn to get a girl that night.

I only want to salute her, he said.

Excuse me? said the interpreter.

OK, I'll make her happy, he sighed.

His fever was getting worse. Even his lips felt sunburned. He picked a cunt-hair out of the K-Y jelly and slathered some on his forehead . . .

He went for a walk in the rain to cool down; everyone laughed at him. After awhile he came back drenched, and a dirty gentle little boy came into the lobby (which was otherwise utterly empty) to slap palms with him and smile. The journalist had a nasty cough from Vanna. – Every time you get a new whore, you get a new disease! growled the photographer, shaking his head. – The boy stood very sincerely wiggling the sheets of glass that lay evenly spaced upon the long white-clothed table that no one used, and the boy hummed to himself and said unknown words, yawning and smiling and stretching his neck; he sat down in an adjoining chair, and when the journalist winked at him the boy winked back, singing and holding his knees. Outside the big fancy windows it was grey and dripping and peaceful. The palm-trees seemed to stretch, drinking in cool mist. – He went out again and saluted a line of white cows running in the rain, necks down, halters dragging, ears flapping; somehow it wasn't the same . . .

66

So are you going to do one or not?   the photographer wanted to know.

Not me. No whores for me. I'm going to wait for Vanna.

Oh, *Jesus,*   said the photographer, covering his face in disgust.

Besides, my balls ache.

All right, all right.

So,   said the journalist,   the long and the short of it is: maybe. After all, I'll never see Vanna again . . .

At these cheerful tidings the photographer brightened markedly. He came out from under the sheet, killed two mosquitoes, played with his flash, and initiated a fabulous conversation on a subject which they had never before discussed: namely, whores. For hours the two of them discussed whose cunts had been tightest, what the differences were between Thai and Cambodian women, how many times the photographer or the journalist had been so low, cowardly, perverted and immoral as to use a rubber, and so they whiled away the suffocating hours until it was time to pick up the Chief of Protocol and head for the Blue River restaurant . . .

67

Ask this sixteen-year-old if she wants to marry me, said the photographer, with a mirthful glance at the journalist.

She says, she will bear you children, cook for you, do dishes, but she cannot marry you because she is too far beneath you.

The photographer shrugged. – Tell her she is prettier than a flower.

She says, a flower that is smelled too many times begins to wilt.

68

Interesting that the photographer, who wanted to break as many hearts as possible, and the journalist, who wanted to make as many happy as possible, accomplished the same results . . .! Does that prove that the journalist was lying to himself?

69

A sweet fat girl in yellow silk pajamas was already sitting next to him, cutting up his food. Her flesh had the odor which fat girls sometimes have; he'd always found it pleasant. If it weren't that such tidings would further complicate this already intricate tale of betrayed commitments, I'd tell you that he once almost married a fat girl . . .!

I don't want her to get sick from me, he said. That would be too cruel.

But no, it is nothing! cried the interpreter. It is her duty, her occupation!

Tell her I'll be blowing my nose all night. Tell her I have so much nasal mucus I hope she knows how to swim.

The interpreter only laughed. The Chief of Protocol winked –

Tell her it's up to her. Tell her I'll pay her regardless, but she doesn't have to come with me. It won't hurt my feelings . . .

She says she don't mind about that. She says please don't worry. She *want* to come with you.

70

Please believe me when I say that he did not want to be unfaithful to Vanna this time, that he took her to the Hotel Victory for the same reason that he bought other girls drinks: when anyone asked him for something, he hated to cause disappointment. I honestly think that the journalist was fundamentally good. I believe that the photographer was fundamentally good. Even Pol Pot must have meant well.

71

The photographer was already doing his sixteen-year-old while Marina washed up with buckets of water in the bathroom, and the journalist lay feverish and blowing his nose and coughing in the double bed by the window. The night was as thick as Stilton cheese. She came back in and let down the mosquito netting around the two of them so that they were in their own nest of darkness; the air became even thicker and mosquitoes still found their way in, but who knows, maybe the mosquitoes that had malaria were excluded; why not look at the bright side, which is to say why not look at Marina in the darkness, a yellow-silver shimmer of pajamas with a pattern like flaking gold; most of all, a dark kind face . . .? – He coughed, burped, sneezed, farted, and blew his nose. No, she was nothing like the hypersexually

103

sophisticated Thai ladies sequined in green science fiction light, the Thai transvestites' faces like skull-bubbles in the lightning-jagged darkness . . .

All night her hand checked his forehead and throat. She never slept; she was worried about him. She hugged him tight, held his hand; her hands were big, rough and callused; she was a farm girl. What had the Khmer Rouge done to *her*? He couldn't bear to ask the interpreter . . . She didn't like him to touch her body, and he tried to respect that; but whenever he wanted she'd open her legs and put him inside her, and she was always wet; she threw the rubber down in disgust, never did let him do that . . . In the middle of the night she woke him, moaning to have him make love to her again; her cunt was fiery, dripping wet like his feverish face; she went   oh oh   and squeezed him very tight . . .

In the morning she and the other girl left early. They didn't want anyone to see them.

72

Just for variety's sake they went to the Blue River for breakfast, the river lower and browner by the table, everyone eating chicken noodle soup, ants in the sugar jar (which had previously served as a bottle of Ovaltine), and the Chief of Protocol, grey-haired and bespectacled, kept laughing shrilly and slapping the journalist's shoulder.

My dear friend, how is your health today?   said the Chief of Protocol.

Much better, thank you, Monsieur. I was cured by Dr. Marina.

Hee, hee, hee!

The girls sat at the table by the TV, looking over at them from time to time. So Marina was his girl now. Well, he seemed to have a lot of room in his heart; he was as accommodating as any other whore . . . She was wearing her yellow chemise again. Sleepily she put her head down on her soft arms. On his way out she looked up and smiled at him . . .

And did you enjoy your lily?   asked the interpreter.

Always,   replied the journalist calmly.

How many times?

Three. Since I was sick, you know. Ordinarily it's four. And you, what's your rule?

Two!   laughed the interpreter nervously.   Or one!

Surprisingly enough, it was going to be a very hot day. The journalist was sticky with sweat already; the Chief of Protocol had a big fly on his forehead . . .

73

Sliding the press pass across a wide table to a lieutenant who sat making notations far away in an immense notebook, the journalist surreptitiously cradled his aching balls. Displaying duly sycophantic attention to the irritable-mouthed Deputy Commander of the Provincial Army, who glared in dark green, the journalist thought of his various love-secrets. They don't know who I really am, he thought smugly; but then he thought: But of course they do. They put everything in my dossier. In a way that pleases me, because sometimes *I* don't know who I am, either. – He had to give every official something: a carton of cigarettes, or twenty US dollars, or a bottle of Johnny Walker Black; on the whole (so to speak) he liked the whores better. These people wouldn't translate the battle program on the blackboard; they wouldn't explain the pushpins on the Vietnamese-made topo maps, whereas Marina . . . On the way out he saw a pair of Soviet-made PPM guns squatting on wide low spade-footed tripods. They wouldn't let the photographer take a picture of that. – What are we doing here when we could be fucking whores? said the photographer loudly. The interpreter turned and frowned; the Chief of Protocol looked very sad . . .

They went to see waist-high green .107 shells, captured exploded Khmer Rouge trucks with bullet holes in the Chinese-starred windshields, golden narrow AK-47 bullets; they squelched through the mud between sheds.

Take care, the interpreter said. That grenade may explode.

It's all a crock, said the journalist.

The journalist had to bite his lip not to laugh. Oh, he was happy; he kept thinking of whores! Why couldn't he be as conscious and watchful as the driver steadily guiding their car of state over bumpy roads, his big shoulders moving easily, his big hands gripping the wheel, the brim of his black cap absolutely level, his black hair going straight down the back of his neck, the dark green Thai army uniform rendering him a living shadow and concentration of the light green rice paddies that he flashed his passengers through; why couldn't the journalist be *professional* like him?

Another hospital to visit (a little too close to the jungle, maybe; that must be why the interpreter was anxious). The kid's long skinny leg ended abruptly in a bandage; he'd stepped on a Khmer Rouge mine. The baby girl lay with her mouth open; a mine had found her, too. – And the journalist thought: I do feel for them, but what about Vanna dancing and fucking for almost nothing; what about Marina so hopeful and trying so hard to love me when I love only Vanna?

(It cost two hundred and fifty riels to dance with Vanna. The English teacher who didn't speak English had said that she got paid a hundred and twenty-five, but the journalist wasn't sure whether that meant per dance or all night, which was from seven to midnight . . .)

The director of the hospital was talking to him in French. He didn't understand a word. He was tired; he wanted to lie down in Vanna's arms and sleep forever.

I suppose the photographer and I are going to get canned when we get back to the States,   he said to himself.   We're not really doing our job. It's really more sad for him than for me; I know he'd like to see the whores of Rangoon someday . . .

Now it is the wet season,   a doctor was saying.   So we have many children with diseases like malaria and dengue. What is very fantastique in Kampuchea, is that they are so alone, so isolated. And so we feel it is getting worse and worse. And this lack of sanitation is another grave problem –

What about AIDS?   the photographer cut in.

AIDS? Ah, SIDA. There are no cases reported so far in Kampuchea.

Is that right? Is *that* right? You see, doc, I fucked this GREAT sixteen-year-old whore without a rubber; I practically had to rape her. That pussy was *nice*. Come to think of it, I didn't use a rubber on the other one, either . . .

74

The photographer and the journalist became security risks after that. When the journalist was waiting to interview the Commander of the Provincial Army, he shifted in his seat there at

HQ Battambang, and as suddenly as he moved he found the driver standing an inch behind him with his hand on the holster, watching him with ferocious care . . .

75

At dinner he got Marina again, and she was so happy and sweet. He took her in just the same way the driver would hurtle along on the good stretches, honking his horn to make other vehicles in both directions pull over so that the mud-spattered government car could forge ahead; and sometimes the journalist would see a child or an old lady leap out of the road into the mud as the driver barreled forward, honking maniacally. He groaned and grunted on Marina until the photographer doubled up laughing. In the middle of the night she woke him up again; she wanted him to fuck her again. He couldn't do it; his balls ached. She touched his biceps to show that he was strong enough to do it; then she wept. He wanted to do it, but remembering what had happened with Vanna, he only embraced her and rubbed her back (he wanted to stroke her hair, but it's bad manners to touch anyone's head in Cambodia); then he went back to sleep . . .

76

On their last morning in Battambang they breakfasted at the Blue River, of course. There was a thatch-roofed canoe in the water; a man poled a skiff past the empty tables; the blue river was brown and the floorboards creaked. No one had turned the fan on yet, but the music was already blaring; it was six-thirty. The interpreter sat blinking. The girls were nowhere in sight. The Chief of Protocol had already been paid off. The driver stared down at his coffee, the heavy Russian pistol strapped to his belt, his uniform fresh and green; he was calm, alert. His steel watch caught the light. His eyes flickered around.

Marina was at the table far away, and when he turned and smiled at her she smiled back.

How many times? asked the interpreter. The driver leaned forward, too, extremely interested.

Only seven, said the journalist.

Seven! You are not joking?

I never joke about such things.

When it was time for them to go to the car, Marina came with him, in full view of all the customers. He was face to face now with a Buddha as huge as a whore's face about to kiss him, the eyes half closed, the mouth smiling like a ripe pea-pod, lips parted, skin mottled black and gold . . . He embraced her.

She says she want to come to the jungle with you,   said the interpreter.   She don't care how dangerous . . .

The journalist was stunned. Was she the one who really loved him, then?

Should I take her?   he stammered.   Maybe I should take her –

We are not bus drivers,   said the interpreter contemptuously.

THE END

77

The night that the photographer and the journalist got back to Phnom Penh, they dropped by the English teacher's house. The English teacher was not back yet, and they could not communicate with the English teacher's mother except by signs. The English teacher's little sister was there, and she did her best, crooning to him: One is for *man*, two is for *voman*, three is for *boiee*, four is for *guhl*, five is for *motahcah* . . . and he gave her a ride to the ceiling and was happy to be with her although she stank and had lice, and he dressed her up in his raincoat so that she laughed, and when the English teacher and his friend came home he invited the little girl out with them, and her mother hastened to dress her in her best, there in a dark corner where the candle did not reach, and then they all set out for a Vietnamese restaurant whose waitress the photographer had had his eye on for a week. The journalist put the girl on his shoulders. She was very small and light. At first she was happy to be carried, but then when everyone kept staring she became uncomfortable; the journalist put her down. He walked along beside the English teacher, holding her hand, and they kept staring . . . In the blue glow of the Vietnamese restaurant's TV they sat laughing around the table and drinking beer with their friends and the waitress, who kept dropping ice in everyone's drinks (the little girl had Seven-Up; everyone else had Tiger beer) and she lifted more ice with the tongs, robbing the treasure of coldness from the blue plastic bowl, and her fat brown face gleamed with exciting TV shadows while a TV monster roared around and the beers shone and got more and more watery with melting ice until they became one with the

111

sweat that ran down everyone's cheeks, and the little girl looked up at the journalist with her gaptooth glistening, slowly stroking her glass, only wanting to add from the bottle to her pleasure little by little, like the sweat that crawled down the journalist's neck; and the ice in the blue bowl glistened more and more while the waitress laughed slit-eyed at the little girl and the checkerboard floor was like TV static. – Ask that waitress if she likes Ho Chi Minh, said the journalist, who was getting drunk. – Yes, the English teacher replied. – The photographer was making good progress with the waitress. – She want to come to your room tomorrow at twelve o'clock, said the English teacher's friend. – The waitress had a friend who asked the journalist's age and he thought that she was gorgeous but he didn't need any more complications; she thought or pretended to think that he was sleeping with the eight-year-old girl. – Well, it *is* true that the photographer had said: I bet you'd like to get into that! and it *is* true that the photographer had said: You know what the difference between us is? There's no difference. We're both assholes.

78

He went to the disco. The photographer did not come because he did not want his girl to know that he was back in town. The journalist knew that he was starting trouble for the photographer by going in there but he missed Vanna too much; maybe he loved her; maybe he really did. As always in that hot darkness, he felt that he was doing something stupid and dangerous by being there. He could see nothing. The air was brownish-black like the tree they'd shown him at Choeung Ek, the tree whose bark was ingrown with hardened blood where the Khmer Rouge used to smash babies' skulls. He fumbled his way to a table sticky with spilled beer.

Is Vanna here?

You want one beer?

Vanna. Girl. I want Vanna. Tall girl.

You want Tiger beer?

No – no – Vanna – she here?

No no you miss *mistake,* my friend.

Vanna –

My friend –

I want to take home Vanna. Only Vanna. Vanna and me like this.

No no no!

I want to marry Vanna. I buy her gold ring.

No no no my friend no no!

Gripping the journalist's upper arm firmly enough to bruise, the pimp or waiter or bouncer or whatever he was led the journalist outside. He looked back at all the faces watching him in darkness, the fat yellow cat-faces –

79

Well,   said the photographer,   why *should* she come to work? You got her a fucking gold *bracelet* for Chrissakes. She probably sold it ten minutes after she got rid of you. *That* money should last her a few weeks.

80

I used to not have enough money to spend on whores,   the photographer said.   Now I don't know what else I'd ever spend my money on.

The photographer had fallen in love with the money-changer just outside the hotel, and asked her to marry him. All day she sat smiling at the world. So they were engaged. After that, practically every time the journalist went in or out, he'd see the photographer leaning on her glass-topped table grinning down at her as she sat there among her rubber-banded bundles of money sideways stacked; when customers came she'd look up with her calculator already in hand; she'd be ready to sell anyone her pink packs of Ruby Queens, her silver-topped red packs of Marlboros, her red-topped Bentleys, gold Dunhills, green Wrigley's spearmint gum; and then she'd go back to giggling with her fiancé, making him write down everything he said so that she could have the other English students translate for her, and the photographer said: I will come for you in one year . . .   and the photographer asked again: Do you love me?   and she nodded radiantly and sold the customers cartons of cigarettes from her secret glass shelves.   – Well, I guess I'll have to divorce my wife,   the photographer said glumly.

So they went to the market to get flowers for their girls. It was the journalist's idea. He wanted to give Vanna something. He wanted to get down on his knees before her, in the disco with everyone watching; maybe then she'd know he meant it even though what did he mean?

The Vietnamese waitress, henceforth known as the plump girl, was coming to meet the photographer at the hotel at seven although she was scared because she wasn't a taxi girl so she asked the English teacher who couldn't speak English to take her there. That rendezvous had to be taken into consideration, explained the photographer as he led the journalist into the market where a woman passed by with a wide plate of fruit on her head.   – I'm pretty sure I know where the flowers are,   the photographer said. – Down the long aisle crowded with combs and light bulbs and locks and cords of string, a series of counterbays enclosed the people who worked beside the orange flames bending out from sooty ash cans to stroke the undersides of gigantic frying pans mountained with sprouts and noodles; underneath the ash cans, tables were stacked with cordwood to feed them; there was a sound of sizzling; steam came out just like the vapor from the journalist's ice-crammed soda glass; and the girls who shooed the flames away from their bowls of rice and occasionally added pinches of flour to things and stirred thick sauces and spooned purple slush into plastic bags for whoever paid, topping the treat with crushed ice, laying the banknotes down on top of a tray of dried yellow fruit for a minute while they went to retrieve their soup bowls, these girls stared at him and the photographer just as everyone always stared at him in Cambodia, maybe considering him a tall fat-buttocked white idiot or maybe just considering him a novelty; the answer was surely as complicated as the bewildering central polygon with its glass counters of watches, gold bracelets and lenses, where he was always certain to get lost, and they did get lost but since the journalist had learned the Khmer word for flower and kept saying it they got where they were going finally and they each bought bouquets which immediately began to wilt in the heat.

When they got back to the money-changer's stand she was busy piling bundles of banknotes into other men's paper bags, so she had the photographer sit down in her chair. The street kid called the Playboy came up to see the photographer's bouquet. Usually the photographer bought the kid cigarettes. This time he yelled: These flowers aren't for you! Can't you see that? Get lost, fuck off, *screw!* For two cents I'd knock your block off! — The photographer's fiancée giggled nervously.

82

Raise the curtain on the next act, the plump girl on the bed laughing, the English teacher who couldn't speak English and his best friend laughing at their ease, basking in the reflected glow of their masters, the plump girl glittering the place up with her white teeth and black eyes, sweeping and gesturing until the photographer dug her in the ribs. The photographer was talking with the money-changer, his fiancée, when the plump girl came to the hotel, so the journalist had had to bring her in himself, to keep the photographer's fiancée ignorant of this minor unfaithfulness; as a matter of fact the photographer had already made up his mind not to screw the plump girl so her very presence was pointless but she didn't know that yet; the journalist led her into the lobby and all the bellhops, maids, concierges and Ministry of Foreign Affairs underlings who just happened to be there watching him go in and out did not exactly stare him down in any unfriendly way but somehow conveyed that the world disapproved of this his latest action; he took the plump girl upstairs and made her comfortable and then the power went off so he found his headlamp. Just then the photographer came in, glum because his fiancée had not been fooled (probably because the plump girl had gone right up to the

photographer as he stood at the money-changing stand and she'd squeezed his shoulder); then the English teacher and his friend knocked, and the party began which I have just described. The plump girl was starving. The photographer had promised to take her out to dinner. He'd already eaten. – Well, I really think you should do it, the journalist said. I feel kind of bad for her. – Tell her I'll take her out to any restaurant she wants, the photographer yawned to the English teacher who couldn't speak English. But tell her I'm very sick; tell her that after that I must rest. – The plump girl was giggling and the journalist played with her feet to make her laugh because the photographer was ignoring her and the photographer groaned: God, I'm tired. How did I ever get myself into this?

The English teacher (who did not always speak English) said: She is not a taxi girl.

She isn't? said the journalist in amazement.

Yes.

You're trying to tell me that she isn't a taxi girl?

Yes.

So why's she here?

Yes.

She comes to sleep with my friend?

Yes, sir, she sleep here, in hotel, with your friend.

And she wants him to give her money?

Maybe yes, she want money your friend.

Then if she sleeps with him for money, isn't she a taxi girl?

Yes. Yes, she is taxi girl.

That point having been cleared up and epistemologically grounded, the taxi girl who was not a taxi girl led everyone to the Hotel Pacific. She knew exactly where she wanted to go. She took them past the dancing girls going slowly *aieeeeeyoo* in the grid of flickering spots and before he knew it she'd brought them into a private room in the back where the waitress came at once, bearing menus in French with no prices – always a bad sign. The journalist sat thinking the same things he'd thought at noon, while the photographer slept and he lay staring up at

117

the ceiling's fan and blue decaying paint, wondering whether Vanna had been there last night and he hadn't seen her or whether she'd been out fucking, whether she'd sold the gold bracelet yet, whether she wanted to see him again; she always seemed so sad and distant. – Meanwhile the plump girl ordered lobster and rice while everyone else got Tiger beer or Coke, and it was already five of eight, which meant that in five minutes the journalist's new English learner was due at the Hotel Asie to go with him to the disco to interpret for him with his now possibly never to be seen again Vanna; this same slender boy in the high-collared white shirt was the one who'd written out at the journalist's dictation that letter suitably transposed into Khmer which described the journalist's truest feelings. – Well, it felt quite jolly to be racing back for this new appointment even though his balls ached. The plump girl, pouting, said she'd see him tomorrow –

83

No, sir (the boy interpreted),   I'm sorry; she's not here today.

Then she came like a ghost in the darkness, smelling like her sickly-sweet face powder, giving him for awhile her triangular face, and he had to concentrate too hard on everything to be happy but he knew that later on when he had time to remember he'd be happy, and she sat beside him and he slipped her ten thousand riels under the table, a middling stack of money which she made vanish; then the photographer showed up with the English teacher and the English teacher's friend, saying that he'd given the plump girl the slip but she'd be back tomorrow, and here came the photographer's girl, the same one that he'd dropped before Battambang, and the photographer was saying: Now, do you think my fiancée's gone home yet? I can't bring this one back to the hotel until she does . . .

Can I buy you a beer before I go?   said the journalist to the new interpreter.

But, sir, I have not had any supper! the boy whined.

The journalist started to despise the boy then. He'd showed up uninvited at lunch time; the photographer had yelled: *Fuck off! Screw!* – but the journalist had said: All right, if you want to come to lunch you can come to lunch, but you have to pay for yourself . . . and then the photographer said: Aw, you can't make him pay for his own meal; the kid's probably got no money . . . – and so they'd taken him out, handing the waiter rubber-banded blocks of hundred-riel notes that smelled like mildew; it was after lunch that the journalist had gotten him to write the love letter, a commission he'd fulfilled in beautiful script, even folding the sheet of paper as delicately as if he'd studied origami, so the journalist had been grateful, but this request to be bought dinner at a rip-off place was too much, especially with Vanna waiting to be taken home; he told the boy he'd buy him a beer and a dance but that was that. He was already on his feet following Vanna out. She never wanted to take his hand in public. She walked the way that many a lady walked with her tray of wares balanced between right shoulder and upturned palm, the conical hat hanging from the crook of the other elbow; those vendeuses walked in an effortless-seeming way because there was only one thing for them to do and so they had to do it; without any tray or cone-hat Vanna walked the same way, specialized and powerless. Now he was behind her on the motorbike, telling the driver: Hotel Asie . . . and they were speeding toward that lobby of spies where everyone waited to frown upon his latest activities, and Vanna paid the driver two hundred from the money he'd given her . . .

As soon as he'd closed the door of the room behind them he gave her the love letter, and she sat down to read it. (I have one sure rule for you, one of his friends said to him much later, when he told the friend about her. The rule is this: Whatever you think she's thinking, you're going to be wrong.) It took her half an hour to read the letter. He saw her lips moving three times or more over each word. Then he saw that instead of explaining himself to her and making the situation easier, he'd

119

only set her another ordeal. But he had to know. He had to
know! He gave her pen and paper and waited, drinking her in
like the kids did clutching the grating of the Muslim restaurant,
peering in at the video wide-eyed like beggars while the bicycles
crossed silently behind them in the empty sunlight and they
stretched their necks to see better and nosed the grating and
held the grating tighter . . . She smiled anxiously. She strained
over her writing, sounding out every letter in her whisper-sweet
passionless voice. Then she crossed out what she'd written –
only a single word – and turned the page. She tried again and
again. Finally she had three or four lines for him. It had taken
her twenty minutes. The next day he got his government
interpreter to translate, and the man laughed and said: But it
is all together like nothing, all these words! She does not know
how to write! I cannot, I . . . uh, she say, uh, that she watch
you very carefully the first time, and she is very happy with your
letter, her happiness, uh, beyond compare.

84

The English teacher translated: *Thank you when I wrote letter to
sent to you I'm please so much. It hasn't find to as.*

85

The English teacher's friend translated: *Thank you when I write
letter to you I'm very glad. It nothing to say.*

86

She was so slender, like a thin hymen of flesh stretched over bones; he could feel her every rib under his palm. Her long brown nipples did not excite him, but enriched his tenderness. She held his hand all night. In the morning she turned away from him with a sour face; she didn't want him to walk her out . . .

87

That same morning the photographer had said as before: I'd sure like to hop on her. Why don't you send her over here for a minute?

I don't think she'd like that, the journalist said levelly.

When she left, she sounded out the syllables of farewell one by one, and as always it seemed the first time that he had ever heard her speak: – Bai-bai.

88

He had lain beside her thinking she was already asleep and touched her hand but at once her fingers closed around his very tightly. He began to play with her but she was still. He touched her cunt but she kept her legs closed. So he patted her and rolled over to sleep. Suddenly she was smiling and slapping his butt. Pretty soon he was pointing to his dick and her cunt and she was nodding and he got out the K-Y jelly –

89

That afternoon the Vietnamese girl came back for one more try; since the photographer was paying no attention to her and the journalist felt sorry for her she started smiling at him and his heart ached because he couldn't help her but by now those feelings were nothing personal. After awhile she got into a cyclo and went away. The English teacher said proudly: I tell her you no want her, because she Vietnamese! Rob you, steal you, Vietnamese no good! I no like!

The English teacher was so happy, knowing he'd done the right thing like a pet cat that brings you a bloody screaming bird in his jaws . . .

90

Back to the disco, with the photographer and the English teacher. He had a sinking feeling of what's the use. He always dreaded going there. – So! he said.   You have a good day today? – The English teacher looked at him. – Everything good for you today? – Yes, the English teacher said. – They sat in the loud hot darkness, waiting for her to see him and find him. Drunken monsters grinned at them like the green sun-frogfaces in temples that waited to swallow the moon at eclipses; would the moon come out on the left side or the right side? – that would determine the harvest. Maybe something in the way those faces drank blackness would determine whether she'd come or not, but the photographer would say that that was all bullshit, and it was; the photographer was always right. The photographer's girl had come right away with loud cries of delight. For some reason he thought of the rubber-band game that the children played on street corners, shooting elastics from a distance to try to strike other elastics and win them. What did his game mean? Across the table, the photographer and his girl were drinking something canned, probably carbonated water or cream soda; in the disco you always had to order something. The journalist had a Tiger beer; he bought the English teacher who didn't speak English a Tiger beer . . .

She came like a ghost, looking at him.

She say she's busy with another guest,   the boy said.   Do you want her to come to your bedroom, sir?

Oh, I dunno,   said the journalist despondently.   Let me think about it.

He sat there and the waiter came back and he said: Tiger beer.

He took one sip that he didn't want and said: Tell her it's OK. Tell her she doesn't have to come. Tell her I'll say goodbye.

Eyes bulging, the English teacher repeated this information in a voice of machine-gun command. Or maybe he said something entirely different. That was the beauty of it.

She said something to the English teacher, who said: She is very happy to have meeting you.

Well,   the journalist thought or tried to think,   that's it. Really it's just as well . . .

. . . as Vanna came to him and gave him something wrapped up neatly in a square of paper, and again he had a sinking feeling, believing that she was returning his letter, and it seemed right and fair but also very sad, and then because she was still standing there he opened it to learn that it was something very different, lines of Khmer written very neatly (possibly professionally) with loops, wide hooks, spirals, heart-shaped squiggles, everything rounded and complicated, flowing on indecipherably.

The English teacher said: She go to get free from customer.

OK,   he said –

He was happy and amazed. He sat there and the English teacher sat with him.

She came back and said something to the English teacher, who said: She will go home now to dress. Please wait for her. She return in twenty minutes. She come for you.

123

She comes for me at the hotel?

Yes,   said the English teacher.

He took the English teacher outside and sat him down in the light outside an apartment building. He asked him to translate. The English teacher looked at the letter for a long time. Then he said: I will tell you only the highlights . . .

Please tell me everything. Can you write for me everything? Then I go to the hotel to wait for her.

The English teacher wrote: *Dear my friend.*

She comes for me at the hotel?

Yes.

The English teacher wrote: *It's for a long time wich you went to Bat dom Bang provinc by keep me alone. I miss you very much and I worry to you.*

She comes for me at the hotel?

The hotel?   said the English teacher in surprise.   No. She – she arrive for you at disco . . .

He rushed back across the street while the English teacher sat translating. The doorway to the disco was very crowded. As he tried to enter, a man stuck out a leg, and he clambered over it. Another man pressed a glowing cigarette against the thigh of his pants. He pushed the hand and cigarette away, and brushed off the sparks, which were already half quelled by sweat. The photographer and his girl were still there, drinking Tiger beers at the same hot sticky table, while the music pounded indistinctly through the dripping air that stank of ghosts and sweat and lust and fear and unhappiness.

Has she come back?   he said.

No,   said the photographer. The photographer's girl looked at him owlishly from under the photographer's arm.

Tell her I'll be waiting right across the street,   he said.

The English teacher had translated: *I think that maybe you was abandoned from Kambodia & not told me.*

Why can you write so much better than you can speak?

Yes,   the English teacher said.

91

She wouldn't ride in front of him on the motorbike anymore. She made them ride separately and pay both drivers. Had people been torturing her too much, or was she just lazy? His driver paralleled hers, so that all the way back to the hotel he could watch her sit side-saddle on the bike, gripping some handle between her legs, her clown-pale face almost a toy, smiling like a happy mask.

He was desperate to know what her letter said. It was so hard not to be able to talk with her. He wondered if she'd had to pay someone to write the letter for her, or whether they'd done it for nothing.

He held her, and when the photographer came in and turned on the light, he saw that she'd fallen asleep smiling at him.

92

The letter said:

> *Dear my friend.*
> *It's for a long times wich you went to Bat dom Bang provinc by keep me alone. I miss you very much and I worry to you. I think that maybe you was abandoned from Kambodia & not told me.*
>
> *Since you were promiss to meet you at hotel I couldn't went because I can't listen your language. So you forgive me please. In fact I was still to love you and honestly with you for ever.*
>
> *After day which I promissed with you I had hard sickness, and I solt braslet wich you was bought for me. So you forgive me.*
>
> *When will you go your country. Will you come*

*here again? And you must come Cambodia don't
forget I was still loves you for ever.*

*In final I wish you to meet the happiness and loves
me for ever. I wish you every happiness and loves me
for good.*

Signature

love VANNA xxx

93

He sat rereading the letter under the rainy awning where the
cyclo drivers sat drinking their tea from brown ceramic teapots
with bird-shapes on them; they recounted their skinny stacks of
riels as lovingly as he retold her words to himself; they rubbed
their veined skinny brown legs; and he thought: Am I so far
beyond them in soul and fortune that I can spend my time
worrying about love, or am I just so far gone?

After a quarter-hour the rain stopped, and the cyclo drivers
took the sheets of plastic off their cabs and dumped masses of
water out of them. The proprietor of the café brought them
their bills. The Khmer Rouge had put his family to work near
Battambang. They'd beaten his wife and three children to death
with steel bars because they couldn't work quickly enough. He
had seen and heard their skulls crunch. They did it to them one
by one, to make the terror and agony stretch out a little longer.
They'd smashed in the baby's head first; then they deflowered
his four-year-old daughter; then it was his seven-year-old son's
turn to scream and smash like a pumpkin and spatter his parents
with blood and bone. They saved the mother for last so that she
could see her children die. The proprietor was a good worker;
they had nothing against him. He knew that if he wept, though,
they'd consider him a traitor. He had never wept after that. His
owl-eyes were wide and crazy as he fluttered around the café

126

exchanging bread and tea for money. He was like a mayfly in November. And the journalist thought: Given that any suffering I might have experienced is as nothing compared to his, does that mean I'm nothing compared to him? Is he greater than I in some very important way? – Yes. – So is there anything I can do for him or give him to demonstrate my recognition of the terrible greatness he's earned?

But the only thing that he could think of to help the man or make him happy was death, and the man had refused that.

Then he thought about giving the man money, and then he thought: Yes, but Vanna is as important as he is. And because she loves me and I love her, she is more important.

As for tragedies (which were a riel a dozen in Cambodia), what about the circular white scars on her brown back, put there forever by the Khmer Rouge when as a child she couldn't carry earth to the rice field dykes fast enough? If he could have gotten into his hands the people who'd done that to her, he would have killed them.

94

Another boy who longed to learn English lured the journalist up lightless stairs to a lightless apartment which was empty except for a table, two chairs, and a wooden sleeping platform: six thousand riels a month. He took the journalist out to the terrace where they could look down on the yellow dome of the central market, bugeyed with terraces, bikes and motorbikes lined up in rows; and all the journalist could think was: The disco is on the other side; I wonder if Vanna is there . . . – But I have no good teacher, the boy whined; I have no money for good teacher . . . – and the journalist thought: Your obsession is no better or worse than mine. – When the boy's begging began to get under his skin, he went out into a new rainstorm, all the people laughing at him sweetly; a woman came running up with

an umbrella to hold over him and he smiled and thanked her
and then stuck his arms out wide into the rain and flew away,
laughing so happily while she laughed; he splashed drenched
through the street puddles, and, giving everyone his best
thumbs-up, yelled: *Number one!*

95

At the base of the great bridge which the Khmer Rouge had
destroyed almost twenty years ago now, during the Lon Nol
time, were barber stands, which is to say greyish card tables and
old chairs in which soldiers, police, cyclo drivers and others sat
to have their hair snipped; the street was black with hair. A
barber stropped his razor at a desk. There were little mirrors on
the tables, and a styling poster . . . On either side of barber's
row was a cement well whose stairs were pancaked with excrement; there was no way to avoid stepping on it. The journalist
ascended this stinking way and came out onto the bridge, which
seemed very far above the wrinkled brown water with its thatch-
roofed junks. The Khmer Rouge had done a good clean job,
shearing through steel, concrete and asphalt to leave a squared-
off edge of sunny air. Remembering this much later, he thought:
Three steps, and I would have been with Vanna forever, even
if she stayed alive . . .   – But at the time he entertained no
such designs because Vanna was present and urgent; he'd see her
as soon as darkness came . . .

96

Her hand and face were amazed at the ice cube tray in the
freezer; he knocked a cube out for her and she crunched it
happily between her teeth. She was finally laughing and smiling

and going   *psssst!* . . .   – she finally trusted him;   yes, she loves you,   the interpreter said;   she trusts you; you can see it in her eyes . . .   – She lay in bed with him singing Khmer songs in a soft voice until the photographer, who was very ill, sat up in bed and started mimicking her in the ugliest way that he possibly could, and Vanna became silent.

97

The photographer had made a mess of things. He'd bought everyone a dictionary, but then he was too sick to be there when they made a banquet to thank him. He'd caught a fever from the journalist, who'd caught it from Vanna . . . Then the money-changer saw him with two different women and cried her eyes out and hated him . . . He'd made up with his girl at the disco, probably for the journalist's sake since the journalist was going to go there for Vanna no matter what; now the photographer's girl was weeping because the journalist was asking Vanna EVERYTHING (by means of the English teacher), while the photographer only lay there not caring whether she stayed or went – preferring, in fact, that she'd go, because the photographer knew it was only a matter of time before he had to puke, and anyway Cambodia wasn't exactly his country the way Thailand was; the girls here didn't attract him as much, and everyone seemed so docile and lazy to him whereas he only respected people like his next door neighbor in San Francisco whom he'd caught pissing in the hall and the photographer started yelling at him but the neighbor only swung round his bleary terrible face and shouted: Next time I'll shit on your head!   and then the photographer had to forgive and admire him; his girl in Cambodia didn't do that, not quite; and when the time came to send her away forever because they were leaving for Thailand early next morning, the girl began to weep and grovel again, soaking his knees with tears, clinging to him; it was horrible to see her; as affectionately as he could, the journalist kissed her hand goodbye . . .

THE END

98

B ut that wasn't the end, either, because in the morning,
very early, there was a tapping at the door, and when
he got up sick and fat and groggy in his underwear to see who it
was he still didn't know; he opened the door and shouted
VANNA! with glee and thankfulness and she was glowing at
him; she'd brought loaves of bread for his journey; he shared one
with her; the photographer, who'd passed out puking on the
floor, lay feverish in bed; and the journalist opened the refriger-
ator door where the photographer had left his fruit to be
abandoned and gave it to her, a gift for a gift, and she smiled
and took it so that it became something special; lying in bed
beside him she peeled a fruit somewhat like a giant grapefruit,
each sector of it walled off by a bitter cuticle as thick as a flower
petal, the reward inside being a mass of rubbery pale yellow
teardrop-shaped fibers with bittersweet juice; and she put the
segments into his mouth, and she said: *I wuff you* –

THE END

99

When they got back to Bangkok, the journalist said to the photographer: Well, that was it. No more whores for me. – And he'd start talking about how he was going to marry Vanna, until the photographer said: Aw, you're driving me crazy! – The photographer went and got laid. He really wanted the journalist to do it, too. He looked out for him. When the journalist's balls had been at their worst, the photographer always got him meals in bed. But the journalist wanted to be good now; he said no. – Can I at least bring you back something? – Red-boiled by the sun until he resembled a vulture, staring blearily, grimly ahead, the harsh light of Bangkok illuminating the insides of his ears, the photographer had had a hard time getting through the daylight hours. But now all his grace was back. As ever, the journalist envied him and wanted to be like him. – Oh, that's all right, he said. You go spread one for me. – He stayed in and washed his underwear in the sink. The room was bright, cool and quiet, with hardly any cockroaches – this being the world-famous Hotel 38, you see, which they'd never heard of before; the two lower floors were all whores; and their room number was special also, for the Pakistanis down the hall had said: Room 302? Very unlucky. Whenever someone in Pakistan gets murdered in a hotel room, it's always 302! – Looking around and smiling, the journalist had said to the photographer: I think I'm going to LIKE this place! and the photographer laughed so hard he had to hold onto the wall. – I wonder, said the journalist to the air conditioner, do they call it the Hotel 38 because it has thirty-eight stars? I'll give it that many in my book . . . – but the air

133

conditioner didn't answer. When he'd scrubbed his underwear from brown to grey, he squeezed them out and left them hanging and dripping on the bathroom doorknob. (The photographer sometimes rearranged his laundry for him neatly. The photographer, pitying his incompetence in almost every sphere of life, did what he could to help him. – Don't ever leave your wife, the photographer always said to him. Without her you'd *really* have problems!) The journalist stood in the empty room. His mouth was very dry. Too tired to pump the filter anymore, he decided to go down to the alley to buy bottled water. The miniature pagoda was illuminated in the courtyard; the neon sign darted on its pole like a string of lizards, a spill of water on the concrete below twisting rhythmic orange in sympathy . . . His guts churned a little, and so did his balls. Time for dysentery. The second-floor girls were coming down the corridor arm in arm, linked by pink lights, laughing harshly. One had already snagged some geek in a white shirt . . . The girls poked the journalist in the belly and he poked them back. He stood on the landing between the second and third floors looking across interstellar darkness into the window of a garment factory where girls in pale uniforms sat sewing; it seemed to him very strange and bleak; the prostitutes probably had a better life, in spite of the shame . . . Just after he'd turned the light out and gotten into bed, the light came on, and he opened his eyes to see the photographer with someone else in the hot glowing doorway. A moment later, Joy, the photographer's old Bangkok girl, was on the journalist's bed, holding his hand and hugging him so naturally like he was her brother while the photographer laughed. – Only one boyfriend me! she said, pointing to the photographer. I love *him!* – You are so sweet, said the journalist in wonder, meaning every word of it, wondering how many times he'd meant it . . .

Joy went into the bathroom. Then she and the photographer went to bed. The journalist told them both goodnight. Soon he heard Joy's soft rhythmic moans, faked or unfaked, while in the hall a cat in heat went *aaoow, aaoow* . . .

100

At six-thirty in the morning, when the maid was sweeping the courtyard and hooking up various-colored lengths of hose to water the plants, he stood on the fire escape watching an old lady across the street turn slowly on her heels while a dog ran in circles around her, and two schoolgirls in uniform marched down the alley; a boy balanced a huge book on his head; the maid swept water across the concrete, toward the wicker baskets loaded with papers and trash; the photographer slept on with his whore in the cold dark room.

He'd given away most of the bread that Vanna had given him, because he couldn't eat it all before it went stale. Last night he'd shared the last loaf with the photographer as they'd stood together in this very place. The photographer had taken one bite and then thrown the rest down onto the roof-ledge. The journalist had felt a weird heartache when he saw that. He ate his half without saying anything. This morning the bread was still there, brownish-black with dirt, rocking under the surges of voracious ants.

101

What is she to you?   a cyclo driver had shouted from among the crowd that encircled him as he walked her across the street on that last morning, his fingertips gentle and careful against her back.

She's my friend,   he said.

102

And what *was* she to him? She said she loved him, and he did believe that if he asked her to marry him she would do it, come with him, bring her child (her other husband had kicked her in the face and abandoned her), and he thought that she must love him as she understood love, and he loved her as he understood love; was that enough? When he drew sketches of the Hotel 38 maids they kissed him on the lips and asked him to take them out dancing; later that day one said to him very tentatively: I *love* you?

103

The next night the photographer brought some pussy back for each of them, a sort of midnight snack; he'd asked again before he went and this time the journalist had said: Go ahead; twist my arm.   – The photographer's pussy was Joy again. The journalist's was a greedy thief smooth-shaven between her legs and he kissed her but her breath tasted horrible and he ate her out but as soon as he'd stuck his tongue in her he knew that it was a mistake. He got up and rinsed his mouth out. Then he put a rubber on. The next day his tongue was coated with white fungus and his throat was so swollen that he could hardly breathe. Over and over a fierce fever grabbed him by the scruff of the neck and lifted him out of his dreams, then let him fall back to sleep exhausted. Afterward, the crusts of something on the sheets pricking him like needles, he remembered Vanna's face. Well, doubtless Vanna wasn't celibate, either. Was it then that he began to get the unbounded confidence and ease that permitted him to cut any pretty girl who caught his fancy right out of the Pat Pong herd and take her straight back to the hotel, so that later, when he awoke in the middle of the night, jet-lagged, and saw a woman sleeping beside him, at once, not knowing who she was, he pulled her underpants briskly down to her ankles and rubbed her fuzz and spread her until she stirred and muttered: *What . . . ?* and he suddenly remembered that this was his wife? The next day he walked back and forth very quickly and his wife said: Why are you pacing? – I guess I need the exercise. – His wife said: There was a look on your face just now as if you'd done something naughty. – There was? he said in amazement. He inspected his reflection in the window of darkness, but learned nothing; his reflection decomposed in just the same way that the white dogs scuttling in front of the TV in the beauty parlor and the whirling checkered sign became part of the same blur after a giant Singha beer on an empty stomach. He wanted to say to his wife: Who am I? – only to see her expression when he said it, of course. – I'm thinking of leaving my wife and marrying an illiterate prostitute from Cambodia whose language I can't speak a word of, he said to one of his friends. – That's very interesting, his friend said. Maybe you should sleep on it. I wouldn't do anything drastic. – How much do you think I'd need to support her and her baby? he said. – We can run through the numbers together, his friend said. A thousand a month for a two-bedroom place. You'd need that; you'd need a room to work, a room for the kid. That's twelve thousand. Then there's food and health insurance. Transportation. She'd be learning English the first year; there'd be a bill for that. Maybe day care. Figure twenty-five grand. That's after taxes. So you'd need thirty-five, forty grand. – So much? whispered the journalist in dismay . . . Turning left, he found himself by the Snake Farm. He went into the ice cream parlor and ordered. – Okay, sir, said the waitress, whom he'd seen before. Won mickshake waniwwa. – I love you, he said, and she giggled and said: I you my heart . . . Now he became in truth a crazed and greedy butterfly, no longer pretending to know who he was or what he was looking for, dreading the weary moment when he must stick it in, dreading the moment when the lady must leave, but avid to have and have had, his tips becoming smaller as the money went, the girls giving him colds, coughs, sore throats, weird new aches in his balls . . . What he was doing was systematically dismantling his own reality, blurring faces and names (sometimes he couldn't remember the name of the woman he was on top of; of course she couldn't remember his, either), forming mutually exclusive attachments that left him a liar and a cheat attached to no one, passing his own reckoning by. When he wanted to eat out a whore, he'd say: I want to *kin kao* you, which means, I want to eat rice you, and then he'd point to her pussy –

104

Butterfly! Joy crooned drunkenly. Go work, go dance, go dingalow, go fuck a lot! I say hello how are you where you come from, what city? I say buy me drink. I go work six o'clock thirty. I no show; you give me money too much OK I show.

When the gunfire drumming of rain disturbed the metal roof, Joy jumped up to bring her laundry in, sat back lotus-legged on the green plastic, folding her bluejeans neatly shipshape while Pukki came back bare-shouldered in her Pat Pong dress, having just showered (remember Pukki? The journalist didn't. But she remembered him. She'd tried to get him to buy her that night in Joy's bar when he told her he loved Oy. He'd never seen Oy since coming back to Thailand. He'd been faithful to Oy; so if he saw her again that wouldn't be faithful to Vanna . . .) Joy's lingerie became square white bales. In her bra and white-striped black skirt, Joy sat folding and smoothing; then she made the bed and lay beside the photographer and stretched –

The journalist sat staring at her long smooth brown legs. He didn't love her the way he loved Vanna; but he LIKED her, of course.

Faces peered in the door-crack.

Joy yawned into the photographer's ear. – I want to take shower and uh –

Pukki came back from another shower, wet, wrapped in a towel, and borrowed a tampon. – Pussy accident, said Joy. You know?

She straddled the photographer and lovingly drummed his shoulders. – No butterfly, you? she whispered anxiously.

105

They'd checked out of the 38 to sleep at Joy's just for a day; that might be cheaper. On the way out, one of the maids called the journalist into the room once more and said: You come back? – I don't know, he said. – She kissed him full on the lips while the other maid watched. Then she said: Ten bhat. – He reached into his pocket and gave her a hundred to divide with the other maid. Her eyes glowed like Christmas bulbs. As he went out, he heard them both laughing at him hoarsely, no doubt believing that he must have made a mistake with the banknote . . .

106

The transvestites skull-grinning with black cobwebs made up over their sparkling eyes didn't tempt him, not even the ones with black bridles and nostril-slits and double eyebrow-slits cut into their sweating glistening faces leering sheer and sweet out of darkness, but by now he'd begun to understand De Sade's prison scribblings when the sex object no longer mattered; an old man was as good as a young girl; there was always a hole somewhere; but unlike De Sade he didn't want to hurt anyone, really didn't; didn't even want to fuck anyone anymore particu-

139

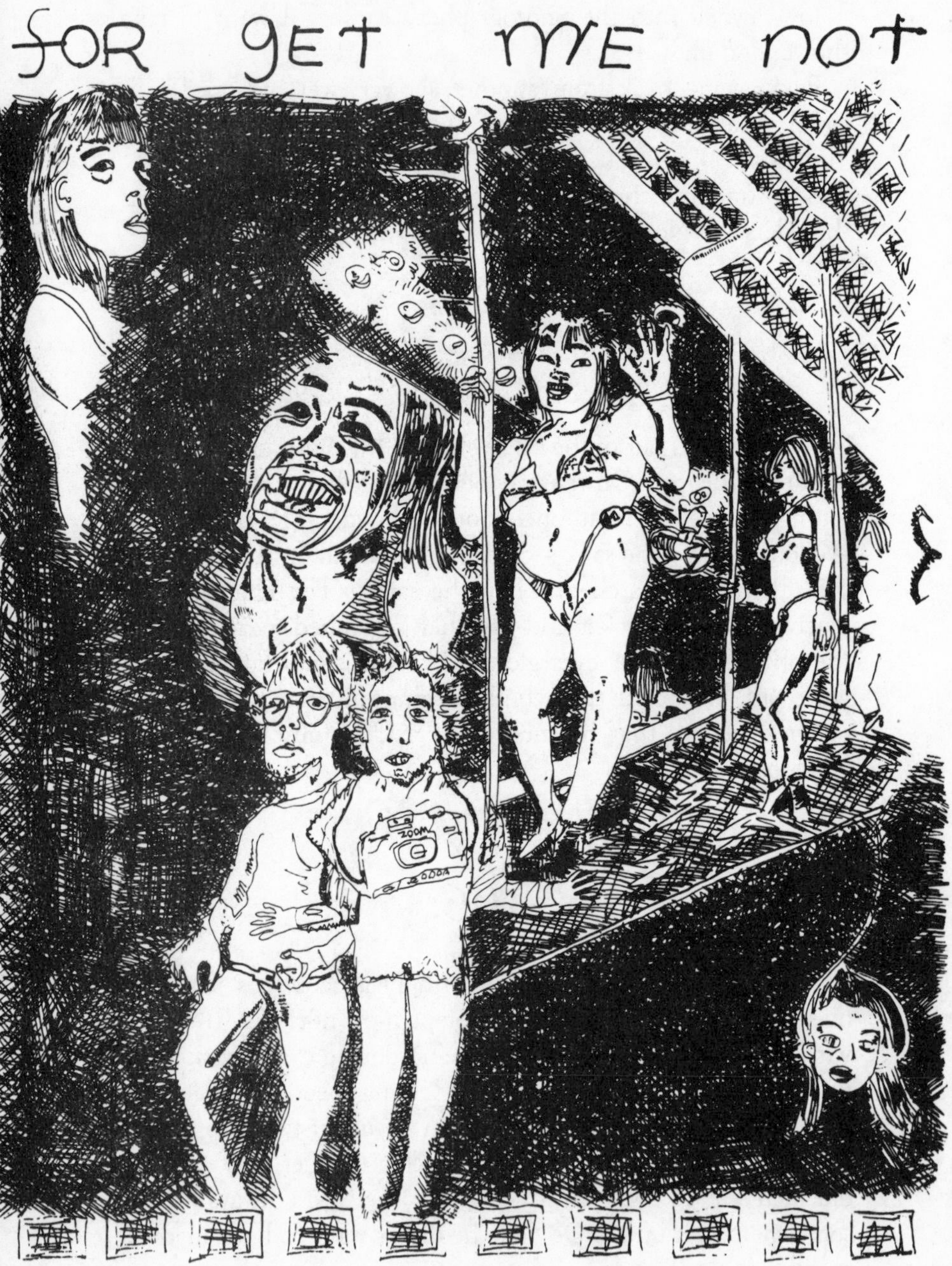
for get me not
ZOOM

larly; it was just that he was so lost like a drifting spaceman among the pocked and speckled and gilded and lip-pinked grinning heads that floated in flashing darkness, cratered with deer-eyes, holding Japanese-style umbrellas like darkness-gilled mushrooms; he was so lonely among them that he wanted to love any and all of them even though loving any of them would only make him more lonely because loving them wasn't really loving them –

107

He was feeling sick again; his balls were aching again. He certainly didn't know what he'd done to deserve *that*. At the Pink Panther, lights reflected through his mixed drink; high heels clickclacked on the bar-enclosed platform; black bathing-suited ladies danced slow and sure while overhead the balloons aped red traffic lights. The first one that came to him was very fat and desperate. She kept sticking her tongue in his mouth. – I'm sick, he said, but she started jouncing on his lap. – Pussy accident, he said, and she laughed. – I have VD, he said, and she laughed. She kept asking him to buy her out tonight, tonight, and he said maybe tomorrow and she started screaming no no no and cramming her tongue into him, becoming more horrible every second until he almost wanted her to catch the white fungus on his tongue.

Finally she gave up. – You sick OK no problem you come bar tomorrow darling buy me out tomorrow?

OK, he said.

Promise? You promise? I say you promise me now?

Sure, he lied. I promise.

On a cocktail napkin she wrote NAME and then her name, first and last; she wrote NO. and then her bar number; then she wrote:

for get me not

and seeing that, how much she needed him, how deeply she longed for even one night's worth of his money, how much she was counting on him to come tomorrow when if he could help it he'd never come to this bar again, he was so sorry for her that he looked down at the floor; she, misinterpreting this or perhaps understanding all too well but still hoping to make something of it, spread her legs and jiggled her crotch into his line of sight; when he gazed into her sweaty face she hissed: You sick OK! You go other Thai lady I see you I . . . – and she leaned forward, panting her desperate wet breath into his nostrils, and slid her hand's knife-edge across his throat –

108

I can't take you anywhere! the photographer cried in anguish. Whenever a girl asks you to buy her a drink, you buy her a goddamned drink! I can stay in a bar for hours and tell 'em all to go screw, but you're such a pushover it just blows my mind. You'd better never leave your wife. You need someone to take *care* of you, man!

I agree a hundred percent, said the journalist, who like the photographer agreed with everyone on everything; it was so much easier.

Then he felt contrite and said: In the next bar I'll do better. I'll watch my money better.

So in the next bar, just barely out of sight of the Pink Panther, a woman said to him: You buy me drink? and he said no and she said: You buy me drink? and he said: Sure, honey. If it'll make you happy I'll buy you two drinks.

109

In that bar, which he was to think of as Noi's bar, Noi being the name of the woman he was buying all those drinks for, he kept handing out Cambodian money like party favors and they swarmed around him; Noi on his lap pleaded with him to give her another even though he kept telling everyone that the money was worthless in Thailand; the boy-girl on his left kept wriggling a nightmarishly long tongue at him like some corkscrew parasite that penetrated into his all too fresh memories of the Pink Panther whore's tongue whose sour-sweet uncleanness he could still taste, and suddenly he wondered how often these girls thought of penises as he was now thinking of tongues, these slimy snaky things that were determined to enter him whether he wanted them to or not; glumly and with aching balls he sat at that bar (a weird open-air place in the middle of the alley, hot crowds passing on either side) while the boy-girl bartender wiped the journalist's nose for him and cleaned his glasses: — you buy me drink? prayed Noi, already sloshed (such a tiny girl! such big drinks! it seemed so cruel that the girls couldn't drink colored water; that would be the journalist's first reform if they ever made him King of Thailand); the boy-girl on his left held his hand captive on a squishy bazoomba; Noi (45 kilos) now more firmly in his lap had his other arm cuddled around her most tenaciously; with that hand he sluggishly unzipped her fly and stuck a finger in to see if she were hairy or shaved — so many things to learn about Thailand! — and she was hairy. After that she had him buy her another drink, and since in his situation he couldn't clink glasses with her she clinked hers against his and even raised his to his mouth for him while the moon-faced bartender rubbed his nose once more; he felt like a king surrounded by ass-wipers . . . — Buy me drink? said the boy-girl on his left. — One more, he said. But just one. — Why not me? wept the bartender.

143

110

When at last he took all the slips from the wide teak cup and added them up, he saw that he was short by almost 500 bhat. He had to call to the photographer for money.

I don't fucking *believe* it, said the photographer in the most genuine amazement that the journalist had seen in a long time.

111

The two of them went back to Joy and Pukki's to sleep. They couldn't afford the Hotel 38 anymore except on special occasions; it was 300 bhat. (They'd given Joy twenty dollars apiece, each without knowing what the other had done; but all the same, Joy told them that they owed the landlord 200 bhat per night . . .) Her room was an oven at night, bright and bleak and reeking of insecticide. Splashing sounds came from the hall where ladies took turns doing the laundry. In the corner crack, a foot or two below the ceiling, a hairy curled wire protruded. The wire began to vibrate. After awhile the photographer got up and pulled it; something squeaked; it was a rat's tail . . .

112

While we are waiting for Joy and possibly Pukki to come back from work, while the two sexist exploiters sleep (at rest, the photographer's face still looked almost sweet sometimes the way his eyelashes curved and his lower lip swelled; his cheek rested against his bent-back fingers), I may as well describe Joy's place, which one gained by going down a dark corridor deep in toilet-smelling water; then, just at the foot of the stairs where another girl stood scratching her shoulder-bites, one turned right down a hall whose left wall was a barred partition behind which a family lived with big slow rats (one as big as a piglet); on the right were tiny padlocked doors like entrances to storage lockers. Joy unlocked one of these. The room, whose walls were part concrete and part wooden slats, was maybe ten by twelve feet. The floor's grey cement was partly covered by a sheet of green plastic patterned like bathroom tiles. On the wall hung a broom; Joy and Pukki kept their room very clean. In the corner was a one-piece unit of open wire shelving, then a beaten-up card table on which the two women kept their purses, some lotions, a photo of Pukki with her English boyfriend; then there was a wastebasket where they kept their dirty laundry, and a narrow vinyl "wardrobe" for all the clothes. These items were all ranged along one wall, on the bare concrete. On the green plastic, which covered most of the cell, there was nothing but a fan, an ashtray, a box of matches, and in the corner a folded length of ticking too skinny to be called a futon. Joy kept her stuffed animals there. – This baby for me, she said, squeaking her soft pink teddy bear. I love. – That was everything. There were no pictures on the walls. (On the ceiling was a mobile of shells, it's true, hung from the same beam the bare incandescent bulb was mounted on. I'd forgotten that.) The rent was 900 bhat per month.

My place no good, said Joy softly. You no angry me?

113

She came in at four in the morning, staggering, falling, laughing, stretching her long legs over the pillow, her brown toes soaking up light, saying: I drinking too much! I'm sorry I drink two beer, three whiskey, one champagne, two vodka –

It's OK, said the journalist. You're a good girl –

Thank you, she whispered.

114

Early in the morning a rat squeaked upstairs, and the monsoon rains came steadily down, eating all light except for a dreary brown or khaki luminescence that showed the clothes hanging outside the window-bars and then the stairs, underneath which was the toilet on its raised platform. Pukki had never come home. She'd had to go to Pattaya for an Australian boy's holiday. (The girls seemed to dread those "holidays" more than anything else, probably because they could never get away from their assignment then and always saw the same things, just beaches or hotel ceilings . . .) Joy and the photographer were lying very still. The journalist waited as long as he could, the sweat gushing from every inch of his body, and still they slept; he got up and put his sandals on. Outside, the alley was now a gutter calf-deep in brown water through which sandaled people slowly splashed; radios were playing beside the families on the open platforms brushing their teeth and spitting into that canal; scraps of newspaper floated by; there was the usual crush of flies, as eager as boys (or girls) at Pat Pong; men sat on their wooden porches which had become docks; ladies splashed steadily from stand to stand, buying food; awnings stretched across the narrow sky, almost meeting each other, and beneath them ran the unreal canal city. By ten in the morning it was hot and sunny, the street bone-dry.

He went back inside, down the hall, past the toilet and right to the tiny door with the padlock; when he pulled the door open he caught a gleam of thrusting buttocks and said: I'm sorry but Joy said his name and said no problem.

115

Back to the National Museum he went alone, to enjoy an hour of beauty without love, but he was just like the photographer who'd shouted on the bus: *I can smell a pussy a mile away!*

because after a diversionary visit to some bird's head swords he found himself sniffing out Khmer art (there was more here than in Phnom Penh! – the Khmer Rouge hadn't forgotten much); raining his fever-sweat down on the courtyard grass, he stood lusting for the Bayon-style Dvarapalas of the early thirteenth century.

The stone head leaned forward and down, not quite smiling, not quite grimacing, the balls of its eyes bulging out like tears. Too familiar, that face; he wished now that the photographer were here, to take a picture of it. – Marina? – Maybe. Yes, Marina, plump, blurred and round. Her mouth was definitely grimacing. He stepped back, stood a little to the left so that her eyes could see him. She looked upon him sadly, without interest or malice; this Marina was long dead. Her nose was eaten away as if by syphilis, her breasts almost imperceptible swellings on the rock, her navel round and deep, her vulva a tiny slit that may have been vandalism from the same axe that cut off her right hand and left arm . . . She stood square-toed and weary in the heat.

Beside her was another Dvarapala in the same style, stunningly beautiful, the contours too soft to be human; her face, neither a Buddha nor an Egyptian deathmask, merged eerily into her sweep of hair and bust; she could barely see him; her thick lips smiled; to make her smile at *him* he stood slightly to the right to meet her gaze; she smiled the way a whore smiles when you didn't pay her enough –

116

She looked into the photographer's face very earnestly. – You boyfriend me, or you butterfly? If you butterfly, we finit.

I love only you, the photographer grinned. Me no butterfly. Me suck only your flower. You my sweet rice girl.

117

That night while the photographer went to turn his cruel hawkeyes on other bargirls until Joy should arrive, the journalist sat drinking and preparing the final draft of his article, which would surely appear on the front page of the *New York Times*: **Thailand's 3 main cash crops: rice, fish and women**... and he started to feel something crazy lurching up inside him just like that time in Phnom Penh when Vanna wasn't there and he hopped on the back of the cyclo driver's vehicle and started pedaling the driver crazily down the street, the driver covering his eyes and smiling in dismay, everyone else laughing and pointing and staring, and the journalist had been full of spurious mirth that made him pedal desperately until he crashed the cyclo; now, knowing that something similar was about to happen, he left his friend, made his speedy escape from the square white, red and yellow lights of Pat Pong glowing down the alleys like soft drink signs. He didn't take Noi because she'd gone home early. The bartender said that a man had bought her too many beers and she'd gotten drunk and puked. For every 55 bhat per beer that the man had paid, Noi received 20 bhat, and she was required to drink it down to make the man happy; otherwise how could she wheedle another one out of him? – The journalist was sorry. He'd been thinking all day about what a tight pussy she must have. (But he loved only Vanna, of course . . .) Sitting in the *tuk-tuk*, he smelled the blue smoke of the stalled traffic; he watched a lady with shoebutton eyes sitting side-saddle and miniskirted on the back of a motorbike, carefully gazing at nothing; then his *tuk-tuk* driver switched the motor on; the golden bulb lit up the naked green 𝕷𝕬𝕯𝖄 𝕺𝕱 𝕳𝕴𝕲𝕳𝖂𝕬𝖄 decal guarding the driver's back and the bloodspatter decals on the window; now they were moving so fast that the breeze was actually cold. Stop again. More blue smoke. Another side-saddle girl beside him, this one staring wide-eyed through her crash helmet. He saw other faces suspended behind the dark windows of taxis. Then the *tuk-tuk* growled off again. They turned by the lighted garden of the World Trade Center, bound once again for the Hotel 38.

118

Short time mean I fuck you two time, one hour,   said the Hotel 38 girl.   All night mean until twel' o'clock. Then I go home Papa-san.

He tried to tell her that he was a journalist, just to tell her something, just to reach her, and then he asked if she understood and she said yes and then he wondered how many men asked her if she understood and how often she said yes.

He showed her the rubber.   – You want to use this? Up to you.

Yes,   she said.   Good for you, good for me.

Well,   he thought (a little dashed),   now my perfect record's spoiled. Now I've actually used a rubber from the beginning with one of my girls.

That's how the cookie crumbles,   he said to himself.

Well, there was that one I caught the white fungus from, but I started by eating her out so that didn't really count.

This girl cost three hundred bhat. He'd told the night manager to pick one out for him, whoever wanted to come.   – Be good to her!   the night manager had said. He tipped her two hundred. When he saw the expression on her face, he thought:

149

Well, at least once in my life I've made another human being completely happy.

He tried to get her to stay a little longer, but she wouldn't. Later, though, she came back because she worried that he might not have had a clean towel . . .

119

You butterfly too much,   Joy said to him when she and the photographer came in that night.   Too much Thai lady! No good for you, no good for her. She no good, no good heart! She have boyfriend! Not me. I no boyfriend. I love you, I go with you; I no love you, I no go. Before, I have boyfriend. He butterfly too much. He fucking too much!   (Joy was shouting.) One day he fucking one, two, three, four. I say to him: OK, you no come here again, we finit.   I say: You want marry me, see Mama me, Papa me – why?   He crying. He say: I don't know.   I say: You don't know? You finit! Finit me!

What did you think of *that?*   laughed the photographer. Boy, you looked *scared* for a minute!

He pointed solemnly to the journalist and said to Joy: He butterfly too much!

120

Lying in that absurd round bed at half-past four in the morning, he blew his nose, cleared his throat, coughed, and spat on the floor, listening to the rain outside while the air conditioners droned and the blue curtains hung dirty, fat and listless like diseased cunt-lips. It was not very dark because the rooms with round beds had windows at the tops of the doors to let hall-light in, probably so that the whores wouldn't lose money for the hotel by falling asleep. He coughed. Finally he got up, turned on the light, and sat alone in the middle of the round bed, weary and calm. The shrill shouts of the whores had ceased; he could hear nothing but the rain and the air conditioner. A big bug scuttered across the floor. (In Pat Pong he'd seen the whores eating bugs roasted on a stick.) The late night feeling went on and on, and he cleared his throat and spat white fungus.

121

There weren't any other rooms in the hotel, and though he'd invited the photographer and Joy to take the round bed (he didn't mind sleeping on the floor), they went home to Joy's to sleep.

When he went into Joy's box, there was nothing but small-ness, heat and darkness humid with sleeping breath; the photographer and the two women didn't make any sound as they slept.

122

You go Pattaya? said the journalist to Pukki.

She looked guilty, and he was sorry he'd said anything. – How you know?

I know everything, he said with a wink. My name King Pat Pong. Your boyfriend good?

So-so. Not good, not bad.

When the photographer had gone out to the toilet, Joy said to him right in front of Pukki: Do you love me?

The journalist didn't want to hurt her feelings. He didn't know who he loved anymore. He was fond of her . . . – Yes, I love you, he said lightly.

She didn't say anything.

After awhile he said: Do you love me?

No. I like you. I don't love you. I love only him.

Then he felt a little ashamed, as usual; why did he have to either hurt people or lie?

But maybe he did love her. Like a brother, of course . . .

Joy seemed so sweet and patient and all-seeing with the towel around her, cigarette in hand, other hand between her legs, casting her black shadow against the day, her eyes and mouth and nostrils perfect slits, the towel-folds fanning down like sandbars from her left breast, a dark fingertip of shadow between her right breast and her arm, her expression maybe not quite so sweet after all, maybe only neutral.

123

Well, 200 bhat for a stifling sleepless night at Joy's place *versus* 300 bhat at the air-conditioned Hotel 38; perhaps (thought the weary white boys) Joy's place was a false economy. – Back to the 38.

While the journalist squatted at his ease in the puddled bathroom, having diarrhea and cleverly vomiting between his legs at the same time, the photographer caught a *tuk-tuk* to Pat Pong to buy Joy and Pukki (whom the photographer, though he no longer hated her, still enjoyed calling Porky). The journalist was not that interested in Pukki, but he wanted to do Joy a favor, and it seemed important to her to set him up with Pukki: fine, he'd stick it in. (I want to *kin kao* her, he said to Joy, right in front of her. – No problem, she said tonelessly.) So many times now he'd seen Pukki dancing on top of the bar beside Joy, grasping the cool shining pole whose reflected light rocketed invitingly up her half-cocked thighs, and Joy would be looking away, moving her knee up and down while Pukki in the silverlime bathing suit smiled open-mouthed *hi!* like some comedian bringing thumb and forefinger together in a circle which summed up all holes, poor Pukki dancing on, never getting as much attention as Joy . . . So all right, let's be Mr. Nice Guy. Oh, the problems you can have with women when you're popular . . . They came in already half loaded, and Joy had bought a giant-sized Singha beer for each of them. Pukki sat

on the journalist's bed scarcely paying any attention to him; her face was full of Joy, who lay hugging the photographer and glancing over her shoulder every ten minutes or so at Pukki, who would giggle again; the photographer had said he thought they were lesbians, which the journalist hadn't believed, but now he wondered and said quietly to Pukki: You go with ladies sometimes?   and Pukki blushed and said: Sometimes   and he said: You go with Joy sometimes?   and she nodded. – He said to her: You no want stay with me. It's OK, honey. I pay you same you stay, same you no stay; up to you . . .   – and Pukki whirled on him in a flash, scared now, and started snuggling him, and he felt very sad.   – I stay I stay!   she whispered.   I

stay short-time you want short-time; I stay all night you want all
night! and this got his hopes up a little bit; so maybe he'd
finally found a Thai lady who'd stay all night with him (all the
photographer's had been all-nights), so he said: OK, you stay
all night, please, Pukki and she smiled. – Joy said something
to her very sharply and she opened her fingers to show him a
condom and said: You use this please. – That's only fair, he
said. I've been telling you I'm a butterfly. – Butterfly no
problem me, she said. – Kap kum kap,* Pukki. Why don't
you go and take your shower? – So, not too long afterward,
she'd fumbled the condom onto him and for variety's sake he
put K-Y jelly on the condom instead of inside her and after a
few half-hearted caresses he slid it in good and deep, semi-erect
like a banana leaf, wanting only to sleep, and he pulled it out
and stuck it in and pulled it out and stuck it in and could feel
himself starting to go soft just like with Vanna, from whom he
was sinking farther with every thrust, and he got softer which
he didn't like one bit because it would only make Pukki feel
worse about herself (as it was, she couldn't be exactly enjoying
herself, but the similarity between whores and wives is that you
don't have to consider their pleasure when you fuck them,
unlike sweethearts such as Vanna who probably don't enjoy it,
either), so he did his best to feel in the mood and the bed
creaked cheerfully and he stopped noticing the other two in the
other bed and her face was gentle and kind; she was trying to
make him happy; and after awhile he started thinking he'd
finally mastered the art of enjoying himself with a rubber; it felt
better than it ever had before; he could feel the heat of her cunt
right through the rubber, and the harder and faster he did it to
her the hotter and wetter and more slippery she got and he was
sailing and flying thinking to himself this is great! and her
cunt was so good, almost too good, and then just as he came he
saw the same thing in her face that he'd seen in rush hour
people at the beginning of a sudden rain, the lady running with

* Thank you.

154

her shopping bag, the man in the soaked white shirt, the man on the moving truck quickly throwing pieces of plastic over a cargo of cardboard, raindrops spilling off the *tuk-tuk* awnings, the air no cooler, a sudden hot wind coming, the pavement now a river, and she said urgently: Let me see condom please!

and he pulled out of her with a slurp and the condom had dissolved.

Now I have bay-bee!   she wailed.

124

He helped her wash.   – I go now!   she said.   Go talk friend stop baby, sleep home, not with man, OK?

Whatever you want, Pukki.

You not angry?

You butterfly me, I butterfly you, no problem, I not angry, Pukki . . .

125

All morning and all afternoon the photographer lay in bed, helpless without his fix of pussy. The journalist wandered in and out with his heart racing for Vanna. At the park gate two men were playing checkers with bottlecaps on a piece of cardboard, and the journalist went in and sat beside the mud-brown lake as rainclouds guttered like greasy candles in the sky.

He reread her letter, as he'd done every day . . .

126

Joy had told the photographer that she had to see someone before she came that night, so she'd be late. – Probably got to make some money, said the photographer. It's not like I've been giving her much . . .

She came at four or five in the morning, smiling and swaying. – I drink too much! she giggled.

Are you happy? asked the journalist quietly.

Yes, me very happy, 'cause I drink too much! I bring something for you. Here your clothes; I wash them for you; your shirt not yet; I no iron –

The photographer lay on the bed, his eyes closed.

You angry me?

No, not angry, Joy, just tired.

Look! I got toy monkey! You see? From lady! She like me too much! You go America Friday, I go her Saturday for holiday. No make love! No make love! Only go with her . . . You not angry?

Nope, yawned the photographer.

He looked at the monkey on the bed for awhile. Then he flung it to her, or at her; what he was doing was never entirely clear. But surely he was only playing with her . . .

She froze in just the same way that Thais jogging in the park freeze into rigid attention when the national anthem comes on the loudspeaker. Then she whirled on him. – Why you do that? You angry me?

No. Just tired.

You no like me?

I like you fine, Joy.

Why you angry me?

After that, the photographer's face hardened. The journalist knew that something bad would happen.

Joy stood by the mirror. She had been about to undress. She fingered the topmost button of her Pat Pong uniform, undoing it and then doing it up again. Then she began to speak in a rapid monotone:

You no like me? You no like me OK I go home sleep. You no like me? You no like me?

The photographer said nothing. He didn't even open his eyes.

OK you no like me I go. I go now. You no like me. OK.

She began to pack very rapidly. She slipped her sandals back on. She stood waiting for the photographer to say something, and the journalist wanted to call out to her and take her in his arms, only to take her pain away – as if *his* embrace could do anything; he had to PAY to embrace . . . and he wanted the photographer to say to her once more that he loved her (although that probably wasn't true) but he knew that the photographer was not going to say anything, and even if it had, that wouldn't have helped her, and even if the journalist or the photographer or anyone could have smashed the collar of anguish that was strangling her, she'd be choking again tomorrow night; so he lay watching her in silence, saddened to the bottom of his heart, knowing that there was nothing he could or should do, nothing to do, in that long long time when she stood by the doorway waiting, and then she said: OK. I go. – And she waited a little longer. Then she turned out the light, opened the door, and shut it behind her. Now she would be walking toward the stairs; the photographer could still have leaped up and caught her; now she was downstairs; now she'd be walking very very quickly in the rain to find a *tuk-tuk*. Lying in the darkness, he heard the photographer groan.

127

In the morning he decided to set out for Joy's to tell her that he was worried about her, and possibly to give her flowers or money. The photographer had her address, written in Thai for the *tuk-tuk*. He didn't want to tell the photographer where he was going;

the photographer might feel (and rightly) that it was none of his business. He decided to walk. He didn't know exactly where it was but he thought he knew the direction that the *tuk-tuks* went. It was near a large park, which he was confident he'd find. Soon he was in places he'd never been before.

The fungus between his fingers itched. Thais immaculate in pressed and sweatless shirts eyed him as he trudged and dripped. – Where are you going, butterfly?   a man called. – He came to a translation service, and remembered that he had a letter for Vanna with him.   – Can you translate from English to Khmer? he said.   – No,   they laughed. – They always laughed. It was the tenth place he'd tried. He came to an international calling service and asked them if he could call Cambodia. Yes, but he must wait one to two hours to get through. – Anyhow, he didn't know whom to call, how to reach her . . . He came to a department store and then a vast spacious park with fountains and playing fields; a grand white structure rose in the distance, multiple-roofed like a *wat*. Probably it was a girls' school. Everywhere he saw girls in white blouses and navy blue skirts. They sat in ones and twos on the edge of a brown pool, their homework on their knees. No, evidently there were boys, too; here came a procession of them in white shirts, navy blue trousers, marching along the outer perimeter of the pool. – Too bad there had to be boys. Now the place was polluted. – He sat for a long time and watched the water.

128

He arrived at Joy's with his heart in his throat, and knocked, seeing light under the door. At least they weren't sleeping.

Joy?   he said.   *Sawadee-kap.* *

Yes,   she finally said listlessly.

* Thai greeting.

He went in and said: My friend no angry you. I worried you.
You drink too much. No problem. OK?

Pukki's face had lit up when he came in, but now it dimmed.
– You no come for me?

I have something for you, Pukki,   he said, giving her his last
twenty dollars.

For me? Why?

I sorry maybe you have baby.

OK. No problem.

The girls were not their bar selves. They sat sweating and
trying to rub away beer headaches. Two Thai boys (whom they
vehemently assured him were not their boyfriends, and he
thought: Why does it have to be my business? Why can't they

159

be your boyfriends? We have no claim on you; we're only sick butterflies) were lying on the futon. Soon Pukki began to pay the journalist his due attentions. She sent one of the boys out to get lunch. When he came back she spooned the journalist's food onto the plate for him, just right. She peeled the skin off his chicken. She poured his water while the boys ironed his shirt and bluejeans. She had him lie down, and she sat fanning him. – Time to work. He wrote: *Article about a whore who kisses a locket with her (dead?) boyfriend's photo before every sex act.* – You good wife, he teased, and she laughed in delight.

You marry me?

Maybe next time.

When you come back?

I don't know, Pukki. I no lie you. Maybe never. I no good. I butterfly. I butterfly you forever.

But later, when she snuggled against him and the boys massaged his legs, calling him Papa-san and bumming ten bhat off him (he gave them twenty), he thought: Well, I could do worse than marry Pukki; Pukki is really a dear, dear girl . . .

129

The photographer came and made up with Joy. The journalist stayed and stayed. – I really should cable something to the newspaper, he thought. Well, maybe I shouldn't; if they know how to get hold of me they may tell me I'm fired. Shit. Maybe I'll write something. What I need's an idea . . . an idea – by God, I have an *idea!* That means LIGHT BULBS!

Proper selection of Thai whores vital to good marriage

By You-Know-Who
New York Times

BANGKOK – In and out or in-out? That's the fundamental decision and a real dilemma for the matrimonially inclined. But Pat Pong girls really do hope for marriage if they're lucky. That is why they're loving and affectionate; that is why they hate the "butterfly men." Here are some helpful hints from one who knows:

1.   If she goes with you only short-time, not all night, then she's no good; she'll butterfly you.

2.   If she pays for the *tuk-tuk* herself or bargains the driver down, that's a good sign.

3.   If she . . .

Finally Pukki said to him: OK you go hotel now.

You come with me?

No. I go see friend. You come bar nine o'clock, say goodbye me. I buy you beer from money you give me.

OK.

But at nine o'clock, rolling into Pat Pong on a *tuk-tuk* with the photographer, who should he see but Noi, the short girl he'd bought all those drinks for and hadn't seen since, and Noi ran up and grabbed his hand, crying: I wait you, I wait you – every day I wait you!

130

Noi, I don't have any money left.

No matter me. Marlee say you save your money come looking me; you have good heart –

I can't even buy you out of the bar. How much is it, three hundred bhat?

How much you have?

The journalist turned his pockets inside out. He gave her everything he had: a hundred fifty.

OK,   she said.   No problem. I love you . . .

131

She paid fifty bhat for the drink he'd bought her. She paid another fifty for the *tuk-tuk*.

It was raining again. She was very little and frail; she barely came up to his waist. He took off his raincoat and gave it to her. She squeezed his hand. She draped the raincoat around her like a cloak. He put the hood over her.

You have raincoat at home?   he said.

No. I am poor.

I give you.

Thank you. It rain Bangkok every day; sometimes I sick . . .

They reached the Hotel 38, and Joy was standing on the balcony looking down. She called his name.

Pukki little angry you,   she said.   She see you. She say she love you. She cry little bit.

I don't think she really does love me, Joy. She hardly knows me.

Oh? OK.

Yep,   said the photographer, his hand on Joy's ass,   I get the feeling old Porky's used to disappointment.

132

Joy kept showing skin for the journalist, looking at him over the photographer's shoulder, making sure to herself that she could still cast her spell on him even when he had a new girl. She was only twenty-one (she said), but looked older, though she was still gorgeous. The smoking and drinking were working against her. – You like my girl, Joy? he said. – She shrugged. – You like her I like her OK no problem, she said. (Later she told the photographer that Noi was no good.) – Lying in bed with Noi, the light still on, the butterfly fluttered excitedly knowing that Noi's vulva was going to open up for him like one of those Ayutthaya-style gilded lacquer book cabinets: – gold leaves and birds and leaf-flames on black, every line in black; it was almost as tall and wide as a tomb; and like a tomb the doors could not be opened to just anyone; that was why it was so neutral and pretty like Joy's face, its birds bright and open-beaked, a tense-antennaed butterfly questing below, more leaf-flames, like swirling golden kelp, enclosing a lion, an elephant, dragons, horses dancing, their manes scaled like leaves and butterflies' wings; monkeys clutching at branches, a bird gobbling berries, a bird feeding her little ones; all gold on black, gold on black . . . but on one side the gold had been worn half away, as if a black night-fog were streaming down poisonously; it was the same black that had been so beautiful elsewhere. That was her wizened old face, her wrinkled belly. He saw himself, though, as some old white palace with gilded lacquer doorways and windows, the courtyard still and green, his bamboo hearts curving up from a common hillock, his stonewalled pool rippling green. Inside him there was definitely room for Noi. Inside Noi there was room for him.

It was the best yet. Noi let him eat her out to his heart's content and didn't make him use a rubber. It felt so good inside her that he almost went crazy. When she left he was very sorry. – When Joy left, saying goodbye to him forever, she kissed him on the lips. (He'd told her to tell Pukki that he was sorry.) He said to the photographer: Joy really has class. I hope you do marry her. – Aw, yawned the photographer, I doubt I'll see her again. I never cared about her one way or the other.

THE END

133

The photographer had gone out with Joy, to buy her some shoes with bells on them that she craved; the madam could give the photographer a good price. Probably she was leaning up against his belly on the bar stool right now (supposed the journalist), his hand on her ass which was bathing-suited, hence multicolored like a baboon's, and there'd be a gleam on the shot glasses and the liquidlike ceiling, a shimmer on her silver bracelet and gold earrings; he knew; he'd seen a bar or two by now . . . He came to the Hotel 38 at the beginning of a rainstorm. The men at the first-floor landing gazed at him with contemptuous hate-filled faces. When he got the key from the office he said *kap kum kap,* and one of the men sneered *kap kum kap* falsetto. – Thank you, the journalist said to him wearily. Thank you very much. He climbed the two flights of stairs. When it was cool and damp like this, the sweat still dripped down the back of his neck; the only difference was that he didn't mind it because it wasn't hot sweat. Sometimes a breeze blew so softly that he could not feel any motion from the air, only a faint coolness where the sweat was. In the halls of the Hotel 38 there was never any breeze, of course. He let himself in, turned on the light, closed the door, and sat down on a chair. Giant red ants swarmed on him. He got up. The rain was coming down harder now. He turned off the air conditioner, unhooked the screen window over his bed, and pushed the shutter open. Then he stood there watching the rain spear down, rattling on tin roofs, splashing on streets, waxing and waning with gravel sounds beneath the thunder, making new unsteady vertical bars between the bars of windows, solid bars of rain nailing themselves down to concrete ledges and lower roofs from which they instantly ricocheted and then puddled like softnosed bullets, falling faster and faster now so that the air darkened; a flicker, then it thundered directly overhead . . .

The rain continued long after dark. He closed the shutters finally and sat on the unmade bed. One of the photographer's used rubbers was on the floor. A fresh one waited on the bureau, like a fresh battery pack ready to be plugged in. The rain trickled on outside.

The bathroom door, a little ajar, was gripped by claws of humid darkness. The dirty walls, splattered with the blood of squashed bugs, seemed his own walls, his soul's skin and prison. How could he set his butterfly free?

Then he remembered the Benadryl, and smiled.

His balls ached.

Pukki had bought him another Singha beer, the 630 ml size. There was about an inch still left in the brown bottle. It would be warm and flat and thick with spit, but it would do to get the pills down. He lifted the bottle idly, and a cockroach crawled away.

He got up and began to search listlessly through the first aid kit. He felt neither happy nor sad. For a long time he could not even find the Benadryl, but in the end he saw that he was holding the jar in his hand.

After awhile he unscrewed the top and swallowed a capsule dry. It went down fairly easily, and so did the next, but the third one didn't, so he took his first swallow of beer, which was no better than he had expected, but if he could eat whore-pussy this was a cinch. The pills were sticking on the way down, but eventually the bottle was as empty as his heart. In the next room, someone coughed. He lay down on the bed feeling a little sick and stared at the ceiling for awhile; then he got up and turned the light out. It was very dark. He undressed down to his underwear and got under the covers.

Later, when the dark figures bent over him and he didn't know whether he was in hell or whether he'd simply flubbed it, he strained with all his force to utter the magic words: More Benadryl, muttered the journalist.

THE END

134

Ahem! – Benadryl, you know, is only an antihistam-
ine – not one of those *profound* and *omnipotent*
benzodiazapines that can stop a man's heart even better than a
pretty whore –

No, he didn't really know his drugs, just as he didn't know
why all the Cambodian whores had taken Russian trick-names;
but when he walked down Haight Street one foggy afternoon
after he got back it was all   *buds? buds? indica buds? get you
anything?*   wide-eyed faces wanting to help him get high; he'd
never been offered drugs so many times at once his entire life! –
and he thought: Has something about my face changed over
there? Since I said yes to so many women, is my face somehow
more open or positive or special or weak?

Blackish birds circled in minions over the power and streetcar
wires; drunks were spinning in the trees; the people he'd thought
were panhandlers were sellers, and even when he said no they
took his shoulder and tried to turn him around; they were so
certain he'd made a mistake! – No one had ever done that to
him before. (The photographer would have punched them.)   –
A cigarette!   a man in a skullcap was screaming. It was so
different, but not really; it was only as strange as the American
flag above the McDonald's.

135

Back at the city clinic again because his balls still ached, he listened to the other victims of sexual viruses and bacteria explicating their woes: — That's what happens when you get BORED. — Well I tole that bitch I wanna become a personal trend. — . . . and I said please touch my mouth I'm a competitive bodybuilder and she says I wanna hug and I says ya want anything more and I DIPPED her like THIS! and then I tole her if a man touch *my* doll like that I'd kill 'im! — He gimme five dollahs an' then he stick it in me an' now I be gettin' these night sweats; well sistah if I was serious I be scared so I can't be serious.

You should really take the AIDS test, the doctor said. How many sexual partners did you say you've had in the last month?

Seven, the journalist said. No, eight. No, nine.

Well, now, said the doctor. I think that puts you in our highest risk group, right in this red area at the top of our AIDS thermometer. Did you know the sexual histories of all your partners?

Oh, I know their histories all right.

Well, that's very good, Mr. Doe. Because, you see, if you didn't know their histories you might not be aware if they'd engaged in any *high-risk* behaviors such as unprotected sex, anal intercourse, IV drug use, prostitution . . . They wouldn't have engaged in any of those behaviors, now, would they, Mr. Doe?

I don't *think* they were IV drug users.

Mmm *hhm*. Now, Mr. Doe, do you always use condoms?

I couldn't go so far as to say that, doctor.

Well, (the doctor was still struggling to keep a positive attitude), would you say that you use condoms more than half the time, at least?

I did use a rubber with *one* of 'em once, the journalist grinned. But it was kind of an accident.

Mr. Doe, said the doctor, I really believe you should take the AIDS test.

I'd rather not know. How about if you just wrote me a prescription for some Benadryl? I'm fresh out.

THE END

136

With all due respect, his wife was saying, maybe even because you're so smart, I don't know – they say there's a fine line – you've definitely got problems. (The journalist had just told her that maybe, just maybe, they should consider a divorce.) You need analysis, his wife said. You've got something to work out. You always say my family's screwed up – *well!* I'm telling you, *your* family's screwed up. Really screwed up. Actually the rest of them aren't so bad. It's you. Everyone thinks you're a freak. All the neighbors think you're a freak, even if they're too nice to say it directly to me. I'm normal; I'm tired of being married to a freak.

I see that, he said.

All your friends are freaks. Either society's rejected them or else they've rejected society. They're the lowest of the low. You've spent years building up a crew of freaks.

I wouldn't necessarily call them freaks, he said.

Tears were snailing their accustomed way down the furrows in her cheeks which all the other tears had made, so many others, and so many from him – why not be conscientious and say that those creek-bed wrinkles were entirely his fault? They shone now with recognition of his guilt; they overflowed until her whole face, sodden with snot and tears, reminded him of a beach where something flickers pitifully alive in every wet sandbubble when the waves retreat.

And that photographer you hang out with, she said, it doesn't do your character any good to be with someone so irreverent –

Hearing that, no matter how sorry for her he was, he could

171

not prevent a happy brutal smile from worming to his lips, twisting his whole face; he could hardly wait to tell the photographer what she'd said and listen to him laughing . . .

137

He kept waking up in the middle of the night not knowing who this person beside him was. After she started sleeping in the other bedroom they got along much better. Sometimes he'd see her in the back yard gardening, the puppy frisking between her legs, and she'd seem so adorable there behind window-glass that he ached, but as soon as she came in, whether she stormed at him or tried desperately to please him, he could not feel. *He could not feel!* For years he and his wife had had arguments about the air conditioner. He'd turn it on and then she'd turn it off and he'd wake up stifling and turn it on again and then she'd start screaming. These days, he did nothing when she turned it off. He could hear her bare feet on the hardwood floor of the other bedroom; then her door opened and he heard her in the hall; then the air conditioner stopped. Sometimes he couldn't sleep. Other times he dreamed of struggling in blue-green jungle the consistency of moldy velvet; the jungle got hotter and deeper and then he'd find himself in the disco again, no Vanna there anymore, only the clay-eyed skulls from the killing fields, white and brown, a tooth here and there; from the Christmas lights hung twisted double loops of electrical wire (the Khmer Rouge, ever thrifty, had used those to handcuff their victims); no girls, no beer; they kept bringing him skulls . . .

He was not inhibited by mechanical rules or
by metaphysical thinking . . . To follow rules
would have been to court sure disaster.

> N. SANMUGATHASAN, General
> Secretary, Ceylon Communist
> Party, *Enver Hoxha Refuted*
> (1981)

1

O ne night his wife did come into bed with him, in the
middle of night, when the attentions of his dreams
had already been fixed on pink flowers at the tips of outspread
fronds, like some Pat Pong beauty's painted fingertips; waking,
rolling away from her even as he woke, he found his eyes flying
open in the darkness as fast as someone falling, and his chest
already ached with dread of this woman whom he considered his
old wife. Not yet having the courage to tell her that he was
leaving her (well, perhaps that's unfair; let's say he just didn't
want to be hasty), but meanwhile knowing that he probably
would leave her, he hesitated to transmit any signals of intimacy;
he couldn't! – but he couldn't stand to be cruel, either, so he
found himself adopting a position of polite distance; when she
came into bed the next night he gave her a pillow without
saying anything; when she thrashed sleeplessly he said: If you
wake me up one more time I'm going to ask you to leave.   –

Thank God there was no mirror to terrify him with his own harsh mask. – For a long time he lay beside her, listening to what he construed to be her bitter breathing. She breathed rapidly and shallowly, as if she were trying to suppress a tremendous anger. Had he been less eager to establish his own doctrine, he might have admitted that she could equally well have been terrified. He lay rigid with his own heart thumping hatefully. There was an unpleasant taste in his mouth. He closed his eyes, trying to get back among the fresh wet air, the unpreaching leafy stalks straining and drinking with all the greed of shortlived things. There had been jungle like that in Battambang, but only in patches. It thickened, he supposed, beyond the tame battlefield. When he got up to go to the bathroom she got up, too, thinking that she'd failed and he was moving to the other bedroom; his mouth was full of mouthwash so he couldn't explain it to her right away, so he put his hand on her shoulder and held her until he could spit the mouthwash out. She did not try to pull away. It felt very strange to be touching this woman. His emotion was not loathing, but something less familiar. – It's OK, he said to her at last. You can stay, if you want to. – He led her back to the bedroom and he deduced from her quick submissive steps that she was very happy and grateful not to be sent away, and he felt revolted at himself, that he couldn't be nicer; and it made him sad but also grimly triumphant that before their discussion she would hardly have been grateful; she needed him and had only now realized it after so many years; she'd never been so sweet to him before! Needless to say, if he gave in and decided to stay, she'd go back to being herself. She'd have to!

In the night she woke up and said: I had a nightmare.

He stroked her face. – What was it about? he said wearily.

They – they were trying to chase me in a car, when I was driving . . .

OK, he said. Go to sleep.

In her sleep she started whimpering, and he wanted to kill himself.

2

He called all the magazines and newspapers he knew. – I've got to get back to Cambodia *fast!* he said desperately. Things are changing there; now's the time to see it all happen . . .

In the last two years we've done three pieces on Cambodia, an editor said. Our foreign desk is overbooked. It won't go through; I can't even try. I'm afraid I'll have to steer you elsewhere.

I just don't think it'll wash, an editor said. So you were the first American journalist to interview Pol Pot's brother. Big deal. So I was the first American journalist to piss green.

3

He had a dream that his wife was in charge of a massive jumping-off-skyscrapers competition. Lofty as some saint of parthenogenesis, she bustled about smiling. Unlike many dreams, this one was entirely accurate in its characterization: his wife loved to tell others what to do. In the dream she didn't jump off buildings herself, but yelled and pushed the contestants until they did. She was an MC. The contest was being conducted on the roof of a broad tower level with many other towers. Representatives of each television station were there; and crowds watched from other highrises. The first two contestants were led by his wife to the edge and they leaped into the shaft of shade between buildings. Let it be said that they were PROFESSIONALS in brightly colored technical jumping gear; *they* didn't have to be forced! He stood beside his wife watching them dwindle speedily into darkness, and then they vanished forever. They'd won. Now his wife was digging her fingernails into his arm, screaming at him. He was on the edge, and then he saw a way to let himself down gently by his fingertips into a carpeted hallway between offices. Once he'd done that he felt guilty that he hadn't jumped. She couldn't see him. If she had, she would certainly have screeched. – Maybe I'll jump from the next floor down, he said to himself. – He took the elevator. At the next floor he still didn't feel ready, so he took the stairs. That was how he eased his way safely down. May I inform you that his wife caught up with him breathlessly? She approved of him now. All the ones who jumped had never been heard from again. So he was the winner after all, the men after him emulating his sane descent . . .

4

Now that the lust for a new wife had spread through him like viremia, we can't really call him the journalist anymore, so we'll call him the husband. As soon as he had the money he'd be back in Cambodia to claim his prostitute bride in some happy morning of green leaves all around the windows, although the English teacher who couldn't speak English had said to him, in a sudden amazing gush which had obviously cost him dictionary hours: Do you want to get marry? Or you want to be still single forever? I think you are old enough to get marry. Or you want to be taxi boy? Carefully, please! You know AID? It's a bad kind of sickness. You can die by it. I'm afraid it. Therefore I never sleep with a girl at all. So I only want to get marry with a pretty girl. But I'm poor and she's rich . . . – Too bad, thought the husband. Through all his assignments Cambodia lurked and waited, moistening in his memories like a fungus, like an obscene orange orchid-bowl rotting between compound leaves that tapered like paintbrushes; and thinking of Vanna (whose face he could no longer see quite as readily as if she'd been tattooed on the insides of his eyelids) his heart butterflied as it did when he waited to go on studio, the second hand of left clock and right clock clicking like synchronized eyelashes, the green nipple on the wooden breast not yet glowing so that the husband could ignore life's tests yet a little longer, afloat and irrelevant like his styrofoam cup on the blue felt. – *Do not consider what you may do* (thus Claudius Claudianus), *but what it will become you to have done, and let the sense of honor subdue your mind.* – But the grammar of his particular shoulds and oughts was beyond him. Not finding answers, he asked himself the same questions; no need to know whether he lived on the left clock or the right; being in either case a second hand, he clicked round fruitlessly. Life's dreary stretch and trickle was making him forget Vanna month by month; sometimes it seemed that he remembered far more vividly the Chinese porcelain-faced girl with her head down in the darkness offering her round maggot-pale cheek so dreamily to her glass, as if she were listening, while another pallid lady who wore an ice-blue butterfly bow elongated her silver braceleted arm out toward the Chinese porcelain-faced girl in the darkness; a lady with an ice-pink artificial flower in her hair got to the husband first, grinning cautiously downward with her lip lifted from her upper teeth. – Vanna, Vanna! he shouted.

5

He dreamed that he was cutting his wife up with a saw, and she never cried out, not when he cut her ankles off, not when he severed her knees; but when he began to saw her heart out she wept very very quietly.

6

Why should we send you to Cambodia? yawned the editor. You've already been, right? And you didn't get what you went for?

Well, it's just that it's such an exciting time there, the husband blabbered, they're just now getting reliable electricity again, and soon the import–export businesses will be going; history's being made and I want to be there when it happens . . .

You know what? said the editor. I really don't think I'm interested.

7

There was a famous writer named Ned who had been invited to read at what is called an "event" because nothing happens there; they permitted the husband to be the warmup act. The whole time he made his appeal, he thought he saw Prince Sihanouk smiling at him from the back row. Everyone else was yawning. He stopped in the middle of a sentence and two or three people clapped politely; Ned leaped up on the stage and began to crow and snort and fart while everyone shouted for laughter, and when he was through the audience was on its feet shouting madly: NED! NED! NED! NED! and Ned came back and gave them another raspberry.

No, I just don't see how we can send you to Cambodia, said the editor, a magnificent lady who was very vague. – If we made *money* off you it would be one thing, but you know that hardly a soul reads you. And then there are the budget cuts. That office is a *minefield* right now. It just wouldn't be safe to bring you up. If I did, you might lose everything . . .

Well, but what should I *do*? asked the husband with such pathos that she couldn't duck him with brightness.

There's always Ned, she replied. You might learn a little about writing from Ned. Ned's very generous with lesser writers.

The next time he was on stage with Ned, the husband watched his act very carefully. The husband was up next. His attention hovered like a butterfly over a pool. Doing what Ned did would be pulling down his pants in public. It would be giving head. It would be doing what Vanna did.

His turn came. Tentatively, into the horn of the audience's deepening embarrassed silence, the husband began to crow.

8

Hello, Sien?

Yes.

This is the journalist. Any news?

No news. Not yet.

That's not too good. You think anything is wrong?

I think maybe I wait one two more week, then I send another letter. Early next month. I have backup copy.

I can see you know how to do business,   the husband flattered him.

Sir, I do my best.

You think everything's OK with her?

I think maybe I send a letter soon.

9

He'd heard that every now and then, capriciously, the government cracked down, and the prostitutes were put in a place where there wasn't enough to eat.

His worry about her was no less than anguish; he loved her, his dear new wife as narrow-waisted as a fresh-tied bundle of light-green rice . . .

After two weeks he called Sien, who said: I learn nothing sir no news of her I try again maybe one week.

10

(Sien, like Ned, was only doing his job; the husband reminded himself of this. Sien was doing his job as the clerks did theirs in the post office on that street in Bangkok where gems and fossils and hill tribe silverwork were sold, the placid postal clerks stamping rows and rows of little papers, and on the walls white reliefs of unknown grand gentlemen, serration-bordered like stamps. They'd done their jobs, too.)

11

Finally he got some post-Hungarian magazine to send him to the Arctic for a couple of weeks – lots of work and morose nose-blowing and maybe eight hundred bucks at the end of it; well, her passport out of Cambodia alone would cost two grand so he'd better start somewhere. – It's the recession, you see, the editor said. We just don't have the advertising. All the magazines are skinnier these days.

The ice's bumpy snow massaged his feet through the kamik-soles with tiny tingles, the orange sun one sun's length above the blue. Dogs wagged tails over old polar bear tracks. The low cliff-sweep of Signal Hill was already waiting for the darkness to get darker, the hill-edge closer to night than the sky, everything going storm-blue or death-blue; and the lights of the village only increased the dreariness. Thinking about his new wife, he had the usual feeling of anxious despair; hour by hour the bond between them was dissolving. She was getting AIDS. She was moving to another disco. She was in the re-education camp. She was giving up prostitution. She would never give up prostitution. She was forgetting him. The way he should have felt was exultant, because the eight hundred dollars was the first step back to her. Instead, it seemed to him that everywhere he went just got him more lost.

There was a children's Halloween party. Probably the post-Hungarians would want him to cover it. But who knew what they wanted? Children were always good for a paragraph. Honking their noisemakers, faces corpsened with pale paint, wearing tinsel on their skeleton-heads, they dashed about, their parents lurking shy. Paper and plastic pumpkins hung orange and absurd from the ceiling; what the hell were pumpkins doing in the Arctic? Swirly white paper bones and skeletons kissed their hair. They danced and ate treats loaded on styrofoam plates. Ladies with faces painted pink and green and white flounced around in Arctic boots, sneakers, kamiks. The principal wore a black witch's gown and a pointed hat covered with orange stars. A lady trudged, her baby quietly eating a cupcake in the armauti. The husband thought: Nothing belongs anywhere anymore. All the cats have been let out of all the bags, and they've gotten mixed up.

12

The husband did not illuminate himself in the same harsh checkpoint light that other minds would have cast. Oh, he deprecated himself, all right, but only for the highest reasons. *He* wouldn't have graduated from the College of National Smiles! His somberness was sometimes misunderstood; they thought him harder on himself than he actually was. To his thinking, the sin (now fortunately no more present than an echo) had been the vacillation between two wives. It had reflected badly on his self-knowledge, impaired his efficiency, and, worst of all, made the opposed women into playthings (he remembered a hairdresser's sign in Phnom Penh: two curly permed ladies like in the movies) – not even his playthings, since he wasn't in command of himself, but the playthings of his impulses, which in turn were controlled by random happenings. When he made the decisive break with his old wife, he continued to feel guilty, of course; now he'd hurt her more than ever, probably for life. (If you believe you've done a kindness, you've probably done an injury. If you believe you've done an injury, you've probably done an injury.) Yes, the husband was quite sorry about that. On the other hand, if he'd stayed with her he would have been as unhappy as he'd made her (so he reasoned), and Vanna of course would have been waiting and wondering. It was true that he'd been married for eleven years, and had known Vanna for less than two weeks, but the patent truth which gleamed before him like a gold-painted gate with gold lions was that he'd been miserable for eleven years. He'd only been miserable with Vanna for two weeks – much more promising. As for all the whoring he'd done, before and after meeting Vanna, if someone had raised *that* as a character flaw he wouldn't have been surprised, since prostitution was so generally disapproved of that one could take it for granted that the questioner was probably infected with the usual prejudices, enough said! If, however, the interlocutor could have been skilful enough to thrust past the husband's guard, persuading him that in fact the issue was one of fidelity, then he might have faltered for a moment, but he had the answer there, too: Fidelity was another very relative and hence misunderstood term. (He scarcely thought about Oy, Noi, Nan, Marina and Pukki anymore.) There was nothing wrong with sleeping around if you loved everybody; you could be faithful to a hundred wives. – But how much can you really love them   (our interlocutor might have said)   if one is as good as another? More to the point, are you happy and are they happy?   – As it happened, there was an answer for that, too. The husband loved Vanna the best. He'd keep being promiscuous only until he had her forever. Then he wouldn't need anyone but her. And if it turned out then that he was still unfaithful after all, surely a whore would be used to it.

186

13

Those of you who frown on such a strategy will now be cruelly gratified by learning its results. The first challenge to his constancy (if once more we ignore Oy, Noi, Nan, Marina and Pukki) had occurred on his return from Cambodia, when he'd encountered his companion of eleven years. That test he'd passed honorably, as we know, by filing for divorce. The second challenge, far more formidable, put its claw upon his shoulder in the Arctic. It's customary for a new wife to be a phagocyte,

devouring all the foreign bodies that precede her in the husband's psyche, so that only she is left to shine. Poor Vanna's problem was that she was not the newest, for within the husband's cuckoo-dipping mind another presence now inserted itself, as he'd feared it would; that had been the real reason for his lack of enthusiasm about going back to the Arctic; there was somebody up there whom he'd once almost married. It was not that he wanted to marry her now; no, he was not like the pigeon that nods so quickly when eating crumbs; he was Vanna's husband now. But as soon as he came back in sight of the Thule ruins (skeleton of whale ribs over a snow-filled pit, the wind blowing . . .), he remembered again what the Inuit had always said, that to gain more wisdom than others one must do abnormal things. The Inuit had done it by going off into the ice alone until animal spirits came. The husband would do it through promiscuity.

14

Somehow, the knowledge that he sought was the same as being one with Vanna. He knew that, although he didn't know how he knew it. And while fucking the whores in Bangkok had taken him farther away from her, fucking from now on would bring him closer. What had changed? – Only this, that he sought her faithfully. Now every thrust of his penis would be like an Olympic swimmer's stroke, drawing him closer to the end of the humming blueness. – Was that really true? – He knew that it was not. But here he was so far away from Vanna that she faded from the inner walls of his eyelids faster than ever! How did it go in Dante? *In the forest journey of our life I lost my way.* Something like that. Whenever that came to him he remembered the jungle beyond the tame battlefield at Battambang, and although he had not particularly noticed the jungle at the time because the interpreter and the commune leader and the Chief of Protocol kept him so busy looking at shell-holes, it became ever more lushly menacing in his memories. Plant-phalli towered, so well leaf-scaled that nothing of their underlying structure or origin could be seen; they were studded with pale blue flowers. This was the jungle of his life where he had lost his way, and it was also Vanna's jungle, so he should have loved it, but it terrified him. Sometimes it seemed to him that in divorcing his other wife he'd thrown away his compass, and the Inuk woman whom he'd almost married was his last unlikely chance not to be lost —

15

At the Bay store when he went to give some acquaintances a present after not having seen them for years, they greeted him most cordially but only stopped for a dozen eyeblinks from their work of cross-checking the register tapes so that he soon felt dismissed even though they invited him down for dinner any time, "any time" being less the perfect generosity that it appeared than a courteous tautology whose complete form was: "you are invited any time we invite you" — of course that wasn't fair, because in the north people really don't mind if you drop in; nonetheless he knew that he was not going to drop in, knew it already as he zipped up his parka, burrowed his wrists into the big mitts, and worked his face mask back up from around his neck; then he turned to say goodbye and saw them so young and fine together, he a white man born and raised in Indian country, hardy in his ways, at ease with boats and guns and heavy loads, sunny and steady, she a full-blood Inuk of such striking loveliness that men meeting her for the first time couldn't look away because her traditional topknot of blueblack hair seemed to concentrate all the snow-shadows which spilled down to cool her elegant forehead; her long-lashed eyes were usually half-closed, but when she looked directly at anyone there came a stunning flash of liquid black purity; her nose was Egyptian like a sphinx's; as for her lips, to see them was to long to kiss them . . . and most beautiful of all about both of them was that they wanted no one but each other, he cherishing and protecting her with his strength while she loved and gladdened him; so they went on doing the accounts together, a self-sufficient couple, and barely acknowledged his goodbye; they had work to do. – He thought: Is this how my new wife and I will be together, so happily hiding under the sheets?   – And that seemed good to him. He decided not to talk to others about Vanna anymore, to pare away all the world except her . . .

16

Of course, he wouldn't be able to talk with *her*, either.

17

Inside the Narwhal, a man was laying down strips of a silver substance in the hallway, painting them with solvent which some teenager would probably want to sniff, and a man sat reading and smoking a cigar by the pool table and the hanging plants grew, but the wind kept blowing and the ceiling kept thumping and creaking. Outside, snow blew in thin puffs and streamers across the snow-packed road and parking lot that were the same blue as snow-shadows because it was only a bit past sunrise, the orange still a long narrow triangular intrusion in the sky (nested in it, a flag on one of the airport buildings, straining like a horse's thirsty head, the flagpole bending fantastically but always straightening), and now the sky had lightened to a calm cold blue but the moon hung on, half gone, thickly yellow-white around the edge, the rest so distinctly mottled that it almost seemed possible to make out individual mountains and craters, and because the moon was pretty and far away the husband couldn't believe that it would be a more difficult place than Resolute. Meanwhile the snow-dust continued its empty rushing, not just in stripes as before but also in discrete fog-clumps which rose as high as the power wires, skating across the blue snow with the frictionless insatiability of spotlight beams. The crisscrossed tracks and treads on the snow reminded him of the dance floor in the community hall at Pond Inlet, a scratched slab of dull gleam in the warm darkness whose loud scratchy music made his ears ache; little kids in boots and parkas ran across the floor while the high school students whose dance it supposedly was sat shyly on wall benches, girls with girls, boys with boys, waiting for midnight or some even more impressive hour when things would happen; he danced with a girl once and then she wouldn't dance with him again. Maybe at one o'clock something would happen. It was for that something that people were drinking home brew, potent but thin, at a house in Clyde River, telling the same old polar bear stories, making plans to get rich, talking about ladies and dogs and distances, eating black hunks of barbecued caribou, dipping into smoked char and roasted char with onions, getting louder and more insistent about their own greatness until one of the quietly smiling Inuk women, having drunk a glass, began screaming obscenities and smashing things and then everyone had to leave. The husband imagined marrying her and getting her drunk, knowing that she wouldn't remember what she did; she'd stab him and hit him; when she came out of it she'd be amazed and tenderly concerned, unable to believe she'd done it; so he'd offer her another drink and watch the complicity in her eyes as she swallowed eagerly, knowing she was going to be transformed . . . At the dance one woman was already leaving, a beautiful young mother in a white parka, the baby in the armauti, and she walked white and silent through the white silent streets, brightening and fading in accordance with the laws of streetlamps, and a little girl opened the orange square of light, leaned out and cried: *hello, hello!*

and a skidoo went by and the mother passed the last streetlight, turned snow-blue and vanished. Once she was gone, the husband began to ache with longing. He believed that if only he could have convinced her to love him, then he might have advanced a step away from his old errors. Now, although he might love other women, and although he had utter faith that soon he'd be with Vanna, he would never learn whatever it was that the woman in the white parka might have taught him.

18

He wondered about the girl he'd almost married. She'd worn a parka of blue duffel . . . Was she well and happy? If he'd married her, would he be closer to where he wanted to be as Vanna's husband? If he married her now, could he marry her and Vanna at the same time? Suppose they all lived together, the husband with all his wives (even the one he'd put off could come back then), all loving one another like the inmates of a monastery, walled off from sadness because none would ever have to go away . . .? This ideal city of wives might well be the answer, or at least part of the answer. Certainly it wouldn't be a shortcut to his ultimate union, but it might be a flowering from it. It was so simple! If he could keep them all with him, then he could make them all happy!

19

There was a Peruvian lady who was working with the flying court while her divorce pended (the notion of a flying court always made the husband think of red-buttocked gibbous judges leaping through rings of fire, landing perilously on legal tightropes which they clenched between their hairy toes to pivot their bodies three hundred and sixty degrees through the air, to the accompaniment of stormy cheers; from this conception it was an easy progression to imagining sexual trapeze acts with the court stenographers, which the Peruvian lady was), and just for amusement's sake he started calling her his wife. She was warm and plump; how good it would be to snuggle her while the wind slavered outside . . .

But I am married! she cried in indignation.

Exactly, he said. To me.

Everyone else laughed, and she pretended to pout. – Eh, what will you give me, if I am to be your wife?

He still had oodles of Cambodian money, which he carried around with him everywhere. He started swirling the almost worthless notes down around her by the handfuls, and everyone had a good time . . .

On the day he had to leave he went into her room to say goodbye and she said: Wait! I have no clothes! I am undressed for the shower!

Well, that's perfect, he said.

She laughed, but kept the door closed until she'd put her dress on.

Can I kiss you goodbye?

Kiss me where?

On the mouth.

Her roommate came in just then, and the Peruvian lady said: He wants to kiss me on the mouth!

Pig! laughed the other girl.

Okay, okay, just one time on the mouth. You sure you don't have herpes?

I'm sure.

They kissed a few times. The husband was really enjoying himself.

But you know I am really married, said the Peruvian girl. I am not yet divorced. And you?

The same.

Why is it no good with your wife? I think you are very
intelligent. Is that true?

I guess so.

And your wife, is she intelligent?

Very intelligent.

Ah, then that is why. You are intelligent, so you need a
stupid girl.

Maybe you're right,   said the husband thoughtfully.   Maybe
that's what I need.

I think so – husband,   she laughed.

Well, wife, you're always right.

And now I must get undressed again. No, you can't stay. But
here is my telephone number in Jeune-Lorette. Call me some-
time . . . when my husband isn't around.

20

At the co-op hotel in Grise Fiord he met a white man who was
almost bald; what hair he had left was bluish-white like the
snow outside. The man said little at dinner, but from what he
did say the husband began to understand that he was wise and
good. The husband believed in wise men because he had to. He
was desperate for someone to explain to him what he should do,
and why. Having advanced beyond any picayune hopes of those
paid mirrors, psychiatrists, he'd been torturing his friends with
questions for years every time any of them showed signs of
wisdom. (That was when he still allowed himself to mention
Vanna directly to others; now the most he could do would be to
mention the Inuk girl.) A year or two ago, he'd nerved himself
up to go to a priest, thinking that if he could only be made to
BELIEVE he'd gladly COMMIT or RENOUNCE; he was with his
other wife then and they were so unhappy together because he'd
done everything possible and she'd done the same and they'd
both given until they were exhausted and couldn't give anymore

and were screaming at each other hating each other so much; these arguments had always come out of the blue, so at first he'd been stunned by them, and then after awhile he was continually waiting for them – oh, how he needed wise men! – maybe the priest could help . . . but just as he walked into the church he saw a newsletter with photos of the priest's henchmen blockading abortion clinics, and he came to his senses. After that he'd given up on wise men for awhile. But as he spoke with the old man, he began to feel a thrilling sense that this had been meant to happen, that this person had been sent to him to help him, if he had the courage and intelligence to ask the right questions. Once he'd told a French-Canadian friend how he'd been lost and hallucinating in the snow and had seen angels and the woman said: Mon Dieu! and he said: But I think they were all one angel who was meant to help me; I think maybe I saw my guardian angel, because she told me what to do and I did it and I lived! – and she said in a low voice of utter belief: Yes, I think so. – This wise man, then, was his guardian angel. The husband knew it. And he knew that this time he'd not be tested cruelly beyond his faith; the answers he'd receive would make sense in and of themselves.

The wise man said that he had an Inuk wife who was twenty years younger than he. They were ecstatic together. She was the granddaughter of one of Baffin Island's last shamans. The shaman had never said anything against his enemies, and never seemed to do anything against them, but by some coincidence they all came to horrible ends. The wise man's wife had inherited some of his power. Whenever the wise man started thinking about how he was ready for a cigarette or a cup of coffee, before he'd even said anything or started to move, his dear wife would be handing it to him. One night he was dreaming beside her and he felt her somewhere very near and when he opened his eyes he was speaking Inuktitut to her even though he didn't know that language. Another time he was dreaming of sailing and his wife shook him awake quite angrily and said: Get out of my dreams! and he said: What was I dreaming of? and she said: Sailing . . . and he shivered because she was so very special and strange. Whenever he went anywhere on a trip, the phone would be ringing when he walked into the hotel; somehow she'd know that he had just arrived and would be calling to say she loved him.

I almost married an Inuk girl, too, the husband said. But she kept sniffing too much gasoline. It never would have worked.

The wise man smiled gently and said to him in the voice of truth: You made a mistake.

21

After that he was on assignment in Hall Beach – which is to say eight million frozen tussocks away from the wise man – and it was exactly as cold as Phnom Penh had been hot and his friend Jeremy started swearing because the pilot light had gone off; they felt the winter instantly even through the triple thick walls. They sat drinking Scotch. Jeremy said that the first time he'd been unfaithful to his Inuk wife he'd gone to a dance and picked up a Greenlandic girl, a friend of his wife's. He'd done it with her once and then she called him and so he did it with her again. Then she called him a second time, and he said he wasn't interested. Jeremy told the husband proudly that he'd never enjoyed it, had only done it for revenge against his wife; therefore he'd been extremely moral. The husband nodded and drank his Scotch.

Well, Jeremy, what *was* the reason you did it?

My wife, you see – I still don't like to talk about it. I'd moved in with her, aye? And we were getting married; everything looked good. Then I found this letter she'd been hiding. Something about it, just the way those hooks and symbols lay on the page, well, I didn't like the look of it. So I got it translated. And it was a love letter. It talked about all the things he did with her. And I'd been drinking with the bastard the same night! I went over to his house and he was asleep. I told him that I was going to kill him. I smashed a few things in there and whacked him a couple of times, and then he apologized, aye? But I never could quite make up with the wife. She's such a witch sometimes! That was around the time she'd started getting cold to me, you know what I mean? At night she always brought one of the kids into bed between us so she wouldn't have to do anything. That was when I started screwing around. And I've done it with ten or twenty girls now – some real young ones, too, I'll tell you! – and I am proud to tell you that I've never enjoyed it once! I'm a man of principle! But I don't know what to do about this new AIDS business . . .

And how are you getting on with your wife now?

Pour you another shot?

Sure.

Well, just recently she started coming on to me again, but she's getting older and doesn't attract me quite so much, aye? And now she's having some kind of *mid-life* crisis. Suddenly she wants to be Inuk more than ever. She insists on eating walrus meat, which she always hated before and which I hate because it's a putrid jelly. It really stinks up the house. But that doesn't matter; she has to do it. And then there's the matter of striking the kids. That's what burns me up. I think it's a good idea to discipline the kids a little. Hell, the rest of the world does it. Maybe those Inuks should realize that if everybody else does it, maybe there's a reason. Maybe they could learn something, aye? Look how fucked up all the kids are up here! But no, the wife won't have it. One time she wanted some caribou from the freezer to boil for dinner, so I said to our eldest, Cecily, I says, go and get your mother some caribou. And she had the cheek to refuse! Well, I said, if you don't do as your mother wants you'll have nothing to eat tonight. – I was defending my wife! – And my wife *turned* on me and said: Don't you dare threaten your children!

So you think you made a mistake to marry her?

Damned right I did! Just last night she struck me again with the hairbrush; tell me if you don't see the mark!

What about Stuart and his wife? They don't have problems, do they?

Oh, yes, Stu has problems.

Well, what about Roger and Annie?   the husband said in triumph.   Roger and Annie were the couple at the Bay store, the perfect ones who had told him to drop in for dinner.

Oh, but they're young yet, eh?   – A grim and monitory laugh.   – Only in their twenties. I'd like to *uhh!* her! But give her ten years, and she'll be just like my wife.

What about me?

What about you?

That Inuk girl I had that crush on –

Easy enough to get a crush, now, isn't it?

So you really think it would be a mistake to marry her?

Oh definitely,   said Jeremy, pouring himself another drink, it would be a mistake.

22

I feel like I have a spirit inside me like a flame,   his friend Ben once said.   And I have to sleep with my spirit. If someone gives me something that I think is too good for me to accept, then I try to get up my courage to get my spirit to accept it. Because my spirit deserves the best. But my spirit isn't the only thing inside me. There are a lot of different souls.

The husband listened to all the different souls clamoring inside him, his fears piercing the sky with their sharp and dusty backbones . . .

23

The two whores stood in the parking garage, eating the husband's fortune cookies and smiling. Light harshened their teeth and wrapped their bodies in glittering sheets. The husband's whore put the money into her shoe. The photographer's whore put her money into her pants. The husband's whore kept hugging herself. She was a little cold. The garage attendant kept popping out of his office and saying: How long you will be here?

Shut the fuck up, you dirty A-rab,   said the husband's whore. You're gonna get paid, too.

How long you will be here?

Not much longer,   said the husband.   This is such a sentimental spot for us. We're just standing here with our wives remembering the old times. Would you believe we first met here, on a double date?

Okay, okay,   said the attendant.   How long you will be here?

Shut the fuck up, ya dirty A-rab,   said the whore.

She stood fat and beaming with her hands behind her back. The other had her hands in front of her, leaning into a quick and wary smile . . .

Doing this I get the *strangest* feeling,   said the whore. Her upper arms were the size of pumpkins. She had to be over two hundred and fifty pounds. She smelled so bad the husband had to breathe through his mouth.

You must have strange feelings too sometimes,   said the whore, cupping a cigarette in a freckled hand whose puffy flesh reminded him of a cod's or a haddock's, and the match ignited and showered light over her freckles; her hand seemed to glow with its own blood; yawning, she dug her dirty black fingernail under the lacy black bra strap to scratch at her freckled shoulders which quivered with dimples so soft and deep and greasy she didn't really need a cunt; tilting her cigarette-end upward the whore said: I mean, don't you feel strange right now?

I always feel strange,   said the husband.

Well, what are you looking for?

Love, I guess. A new wife.

But does it feel STRANGE?

It feels strange to me that I'm here with you because I don't love you and you don't love me and all I'm here for is some clue.

I'll show ya what you're here for,   crooned the fat whore, suddenly becoming a heavy meaty bomb in action; stinking of urine she streaked for him, the neckless freckled seal-head hurtling for his fly, which she unzipped expertly with her teeth – hey, that was part of the SERVICE! – and now she was pulling him forward by his zipper; she was barefoot against the wall with her head uplifted for the blowjob, coughing and jerking like a red-haired bird;   I have no patience,   she mumbled, her belly jigging with all this effort;   I just wanna make you feel strange is what I think.

After awhile she got up and spat.   – You like my hair this way, Ginny?   she said to the other whore.   I decided to wear it this way just today.

You don't have any kids?   said the other whore after a long pause.

Ten minutes later, when they were in the cab rolling down the brick-flickers, smell of piss in the back, the husband said to himself: Vanna is not this erythrismic whore, that's all I know . . . but I have to love this whore, too, because she tried to be there for me . . . No, I can't love her. I want to, but I can't. She makes me feel lost. Can Vanna be there for me? She's so far away . . .   – and the husband's mind kept flying on steady fever-wings past the replicated squares and Xs of bridge-struts; he flew with a sunny nausea past hot palm trees and low warehouses. There went a nice convention of whores on the corner, in big black boots, bare thighs; one in red rolled her mouth into a kiss –

24

Hello, Sien?
  Yes.
Do you know who this is?
  Yes.
Any news for me from Cambodia?
  Not yet.
Do you think everything's all right?
  I don't think so, sir.

25

Coming back from Battambang they'd stopped for a piss break by one of the half-ruined bridges and he picked a yellow-calyxed white flower, its leaves half eaten by insects; it was studded beneath its bloom with a cluster of pointed buds like bullets. He took it with him when they got back in the car, holding it in his hand and thinking that it might be Vanna. Two ants came out of it, then two flies. Within ten minutes it wilted.

26

Lights whirled around the **CAMPUS** marquee. Dirty ragged men leaned in the darkness. A troll in a skullcap squatted in a doorway on Turk Street.

Uh no you have to go down Hyde, said the transvestite with the pale made-up face. I'll tell you when to turn right. Not this right but the next right.

Not this wife, but the next wife, said the husband.

The transvestite wasn't listening. That was fine with him; he didn't care, either. – I got beat up just last week but I'm too depressed to talk about it, she said.

The high heel twitched. The voice was soulful and whispering like a dead grandmother's.

I couldn't go out for a week, I was so scared, she said.

Water dripped steadily into the fish tank. Blue eyelids, cheek lines. Lips a sideways heart, she blinked disgustedly in the mirror.

I'm not forcing you, he said quickly.

If I'm being forced to that's wrong. But you're not forcing me. You like me, don't you? You don't have to love me. Ready? OK.

Zipper sounds in the sudden dark. And the husband thought: this creature is as strangely and fearfully specialized as a hymenopteran.

The kitten jumped on them in the dark . . .

Stop it, cat! she shouted. I'm sorry about the cat. He's only a baby.

I'll give you a ride back anyhow, he said. You want to go?

Oh it's OK I'll walk.

You don't trust me?

It's not that.

Turning on the light, he saw that she was shaking. She must need her fix.

The TV went on and on. He thought of the different Buddhas made by hand, the faces of Buddha of all sexes, the biggest one with the wheel of enlightenment, six-colored, then the big Buddha standing, the lower Buddha lying on his side dying peacefully, the two Buddhas standing to give birth to a message. She was the Buddha twitching the wig nicely down.

Are we done yet? she said. Please please.

You're really good. You've done this stuff before.

Yes I have. I have. *We're done.* Please.

27

Round the corner, blinking square lights. A thin girl with thin legs twinkled away. A motorcycle cop shone his flashlight into a car. Not as much fun as Phnom Penh. A blonde stood crossing her legs, holding a white purse like some signal while she smoothed her hair. Slowly wandering up the street on tiptoe, she lowered her head, clasping her hands behind her phosphorescent butt. Long lean stockinged legs rubbed against each other. She waggled her cigarette so that the bright pink tip, possibly erogenous, swung through a wide arc of night. She was so perfect at what she did that it seemed inconceivable that someday she would be annihilated, probably not by pickaxe, bulldozer, poison injection or crocodile, but quite likely by some means equally hideous, given how the world regarded her. As he stood watching her from across the street, the husband wondered for a moment why he couldn't simply marry her instead of Vanna. It would be cheaper, in the short run at least, and it would be a lot more convenient. But it gave him joy to acknowledge that his deductions had now marched in single file almost into the grave called transcendent conclusions. He was not lost at all. He had proved to himself that he still loved his new wife, only his new wife. He had divorced his old wife. He had not called the Inuk girl whom he had once considered marrying. He had not called the Peruvian girl, although it is true that he had kissed her. He had disbarred the pronouncements of the wise man and Jeremy from all relevance. He had not been tempted by the fat whore. He had not tried to get to know the transvestite. So he watched the blonde from the shadows, smiling. She jounced her hip at each passing car, flashing her earring, turning her head, doing a quick split, pacing, leaning against cars and streetlights, brushing her hair back until the car stopped. It had a little mobile just above the dashboard, and it had stopped so recently that the mobile was still shaking. The blonde leaned up against the passenger window, negotiating. Finally she opened the back door. Other cars pulled past. The car put on its turn signal and went around the block. After one circuit the man dropped her off. He wouldn't pay enough. She drifted back sadly, brushing her hair, looking both ways. She pulled down her white skirt, her tight skirt; then she pulled it up again like possibilities erumpent. She turned her head smartly, flinging her hair so that she could straighten it. She tap danced and rubbed her crotch. She jiggled her white purse like an instrument, mooning cars with that lovely ass. When the cops drove by, she brushed her hair very seriously.

So time swallowed itself, until at last her pink rainbow blinked. Thus came the emphatic closing of a car door behind a happy whore. The happy couple sped around the corner . . .

Still smiling, the husband wished her prosperity. Although she'd tempted him, he'd been faithful to his new wife. He was a little closer to the orchid, a little farther past the dead grey fronds that hung down in piecemeal walls like tattered birchbark –

28

He dreamed that his former wife had announced that they must move, and he didn't want to move but there was no way around it. They were on the freeway. They came to a shopping mall and she went in while he waited in the car. She never came out. He called her there once and she said she was busy. Finally he decided to drive around the mall and find her. He started the car and made the first turn but that caught him up in a current of speeding traffic that sucked him back on the freeway in the opposite direction and he was getting farther away all the time and there were so many other malls like the one his wife had gone into that he would never find her again.

29

He called an immigration lawyer and she said: How can I help you?

I want to marry a Cambodian girl and bring her back to the States.

Well, that's going to be difficult. Anything else I need to know? Any special skills your fiancée has?

She can't read or write.

I don't think that helps us very much. What does she do?

She's a prostitute.

A *former* prostitute, I take it. If it's been more than ten years there's no problem with the waiver . . .

No, she's a prostitute now.

Hmm. Are you sure you want to marry this person?

How much are your services going to cost me? the husband said. I just want to know if I can do it, is all. It's two thousand just for her passport out of Cambodia, and another two thousand for the baby . . . How much will the whole thing cost me? Can I do it for under ten grand?

I can't tell you how long the waiting period's going to be. I recently did something similar for a gentleman who married someone from the Philippines, but she qualified for the waiver. That made it less expensive. Far less expensive. Immigration's going to drag this one out. A minimum of nine months after they get her application. Possibly two years or longer –

I guess I can always take her to Mexico, the husband said. I can live with her there for a couple of years . . .

30

When he got to England with all the English girls as multitud-inous as English birds (curlews and corncrakes and olivaceous gallinules, water-rails and pratincoles and dunlins and stints), he sat waiting upstairs for his friend Bob in the sitting room's well-lit multicolored grins of book-toothed shelves, book pyramids on the threadbare rug, Bob's folders and manuscripts on the smaller table and the floor about it, his list of Egyptian slides, his atlases, the filecard boxes: CHURCHES DONE, CHURCHES TO DO, CHURCHES NOT USED, then the round table with its pebbles and scissors and pens, and he was so very tired from all the senseless wandering he'd done. Thirty-nine hundred dollars he'd saved up for Vanna now. He sat waiting for Bob with half-closed eyes. Esther was downstairs line-editing a manuscript on Ba'thi Iraq; he heard the manual typewriter's emphatic clicks. Bob was at this moment rattling home in the Tube which went under ever so many English bookshops that looked almost the same as American bookshops except that there was a black and white photo on the cover of *The Temple of the Golden Pavilion* instead of the color drawing, and the paperback of Pound's *Cantos* had a very nice sketch which the husband had never seen before; Bob, who'd lived in England many years now, couldn't care less. The husband sat looking at Bob's art books. It was better than reading the paper, though he'd been quite absorbed by the article about the old man who killed his young Filipina wife for messing around, cut her into pieces, fried her in her own fat and fed her to the cat. (Before half finishing that article, Sherlock Husband had said to himself: I bet she'd been a whore. I smell whores all over that marriage. And sure enough, when he read the fine print, he had cause for deductive self-satisfaction.) As soon as the front door opened and closed, Esther's typewriter stopped, and then Bob came up the stairs and the next thing Bob and the husband were drinking up Bob's whiskey in delight. — Oh, no, that's not the worst hotel in northern France, Bob was saying. I've found a worse one than that. It has a painting of a very dangerous sunset, a quite explosive sunset . . . — You could mention a book to Bob, and chances were that he'd not only read it but had it and could lend it to you immediately; his shelves were like the magic wallet of food in the Saxon fairytale; at that moment the

husband was reading *The Wonderful Adventures of Nils*, which
he'd never finished as a butterfly boy because the girls from
whom he'd borrowed it had moved away, and when he asked
Bob if he knew anything about that other book Lagerlöf had
written, the one for adults, what was it, *Gösta Berling's Saga*, it
just so happened that Bob had a copy, not that he'd been exactly
amazed by it even though it had won the Nobel Prize, but after
more whiskey, beer, wine and whiskey the husband descended
to the privacy of the guest boudoir, spread the covers coaxingly
open, and began to make love to it with his eyes while Bob,
sighing, took the dog out and in, then returned upstairs to grade
a thesis on meaning and metaphor in the sewers of Kensington,
Bob shaking his head over the student's blandishments and
saying: Now isn't that amazing? after which he poured himself
and the husband more whiskey. Scenting this divine beverage,
the husband took respite from his honeymoon to pay another
visit to Bob's observatory of book-space, Bob's disco of book-
wives. The husband loved Bob and believed that he was a wise
man. But Bob did not want to be considered wise. He dispensed
advice only with the most enfrictioned reluctance. So the
husband confined himself to showing him some color prints of
Vanna which the photographer had given him as a gift; he took
them everywhere now because it became increasingly difficult to
visualize her, and Bob said mmm as he flicked through the
photos dreamily. Esther, who was also wise, and this evening
had made a wonderful dinner of cabbage and lamb's neck stew
while the husband and Bob drank down their potations like
magnificent drones, would occasionally give advice upon
request, but she had long since gone to bed by the time that
Gösta Berling was saved from committing suicide in a snowdrift;
God knows how long poor Bob's light bulbs glowed over the
next thesis, about public space and private space in the seven-
teenth-century garden, but Gösta Berling had gone to the ball
by then to undo a friend's girl's engagement to a nasty rich man
and by one of life's weird card tricks ended up wooing her
himself while the wolves howled around the carriage, and the

husband, so desperate to assemble his own wedding kit that he didn't know how to believe in coincidences anymore, was certain that there must be a providential reason why the book had come into his hands, so he was unable to desist from making love to the words like swarming white beads of pollen within red flower-lips; and Gösta Berling jilted the girl and took up with the mad broom-seller, whom he told he'd marry; then he forgot all about her on account of a melancholy Countess, and the broom-seller put sunflowers in her cunt and killed herself in the woods. The Countess didn't even know about it. She was gliding through the disco searching for gold, and when the husband searched for *her*, leaving his broom-seller wife to be hunted for by others who'd never thought her any better than crazy and wouldn't care when they found her at the bottom of the ravine, he found his way blocked by a Cambodian militiaman who was dancing with his fingers spread at eye-level, as if he were calmly clawing at darkness's eyes; the militiaman's eyes were hypnotized; his mouth spread into the tiniest smile of longing and bewilderment. The girl he was dancing with had a red silk flower in her hair. Her hands parted the thick air around her waist as she watched him alertly. Her thighs were as soft as snails. Between her legs was a huge sagging orange-colored blossom, glossy and slimy. When the husband tried to go around her, she gripped his shoulders until the dead broom-seller could claim him, swallowing him up in her desperate Chinese porcelain face. The husband couldn't sleep anymore. He lay in the bed that Esther had made so nicely for him, turning pages in the midnight silence to learn what happened when the Devil went to church, while the cat slept on the husband's sweater, lovely and indifferent to a far from flattering conversation which the husband and Bob had had about her after the husband related to Bob a story that an old Inuk lady in Resolute had told him about a couple in the old days that couldn't get children, so they found a polar bear cub and kept it and treated it like their dear child. Years went by along their wide and wriggly river between snow-ridges; there was usually snow on its flat muddy banks. The bear

grew up, and then a child came. Whenever they had to go away hunting, the bear would babysit and play with the infant. – The old lady said this had happened in her own family less than a hundred years ago. – The husband didn't know what to believe. Bob couldn't believe it. As evidence Bob adduced that the cat had been very affectionate as a kitten, and when she'd been hit by a car and had broken her pelvis Bob had nursed her as tenderly as he could because the vet said that she might not live; and that tenderness caught her like the Royal Palace by night (almost deserted; white columns of kindness deliciously carved, unknown figures leaping out of whiteness, their faces enriched by dark shadows); in Bob's heart the cat glimpsed a huge-eyed face half hidden among the floral works; the topmost layer of a white wedding cake stark against the hot black sky, which was why whenever Bob came in to see her she lifted her head and purred, happy behind her big green eyes, but as soon as she was well she became ALIENATED. So Bob thought that the polar bear would have become ALIENATED, too. Raising himself up on his elbows, the husband watched the cat sleeping and twitching her whiskers and wondered what the key to affection was; behind his weary eyelids there stretched a mathematical sequence of terms which he still couldn't lock into equivalence; the cat was to Bob as the polar bear was to the Inuk child as Gösta Berling was to the Countess as he the husband was to – whom? – He remembered how on the flight to Bangkok the Korean stewardesses in grey skirts and burgundy vests would often pat each other's hips when they went by. They could give love. The polar bear could give love (suddenly he believed that story again). – At around three in the morning, just as he'd gotten to the part about how the saints marched out of the river, dripping and weedy and dull-dark like old dominoes, for they refused to allow the Countess's husband to evict them from the church, there was a faint noise and the cat opened her eyes and he heard Esther coming downstairs, insomniac; she opened the oven door to warm herself at the gas flames while she took her sleeping pill, and the husband dressed and went out to visit her.

Esther said: But you've got to stop fucking around!

and he hung his head and said: I can't help it.

and she said: You don't mean that you have AIDS?

and he said: I don't think so, but I'll probably keep on until I get it.

31

The cool white girl's body had turned away from him, sleeping in his hotel bed, shoulders drawn up like frail bony wings, swellings of breath at her delicious salty armpits (her neck and face smelled like soap) – the Virgin sleeping, too, on a leather thong around her neck (the white girl had said that whenever she fucked, the Virgin turned her back, huddling sadly into the medallion), dark hair on the pillow, thick dark hair between her legs, richer and fleecier and more odorous than the Asian girls'. Something about the way her eyes were closed made the vision-crevices wider and more massive, the darkness within glistening like her eyeball. She'd only let him do her once. But all night she stroked him tenderly. He hugged her, kissed the needlemarks on her veins. In the morning she jerked him off. He lay secure and triumphant against her with the wordless animal happiness which defeated past and future, a new lover to his credit; an hour after he'd left her, he called her on the phone and she said to him: sweetheart.

Instantaneously the disease of love broke out again with all its hideous purpuric spots.

He tried to remember everything about her, everything she'd said and done to him.

Do you want to meet me at the hotel? he'd said.

That would be cool, she'd said.

Do you want to come up?

I don't mind.

Do you want to stay over?

I don't mind.

Do you want to do it?

I don't mind.

When they were done she'd laughed proudly and said: Don't I have a tight cunt?

When she was giving him the hand job she'd said: See how he dances!

In the studio, when he was supposed to be working, he sat thinking about her strange little breasts that he could easily cup in half a palm. She'd always wanted to be a boy, she'd said.

Then suddenly he remembered his new wife and something had imploded so that it was almost impossible to see her when he recalled her; with great effort he dragged out of darkness the

211

rainbow hem of her gauzy dress as she sat enfluffed and red-belted just under the breasts with one hand in her lap, fingers curled against her cheek, her cheekbone very sharp as she sat spilling hair-darkness down the back of her chair in Phnom Penh, her eyebrows plucked into inverted Vs.

32

He felt cold, and he was trembling. He felt that he was going somewhere now, doing something that the necessity of his being nudged him toward (no matter that he must pass through vine-hairs hanging and curling between the knees of roots), so that was good and right, but what was it? It was something secret and spiritual that he could hardly understand yet; he knew only that it must be good; it was the way that he must go.

He remembered a passage he'd read in the memoirs of that German pilot, Hanna Reitsch: *The object was to learn, by repeatedly carrying them out in imagination, how to make the correct movements to control the plane absolutely automatically and without thinking, like a form of reflex action, in order to tide over the dangerous moment when the pilot is uncertain or afraid or for any other reason incapable of swift and lucid thought.*

That was undoubtedly the method. Once he had a definite application for the method, his imagination could go ahead of him, leading him safely to love or death . . .

He was on the # 24 bus on his way to Bob and Esther's for dinner, the Christmas trees already out and lit on the second level of Heal & Son, a baby roaring with unknown anguish, shrilling like an alarm – that irritated him; everything made him tense, in fact: – the red traffic lights that glowed like measles, the start-and-stop of the bus over the pavement whose texture he thought he could feel even through wheels, shocks, floor and seat (the baby cried on); he bore with the nausea as they turned another roundabout like the same old samsara; a blonde with a punk haircut got on just then, and the Op Art herringbone pattern on her sidebag almost made him upchuck; slowly they approached smolder-orange-windowed housing towers ghastly in the drizzly sky and the baby wept   NO! NO!   and they passed **SOLICITORS** and CARPETLAND, the streets more crowded with shops now, which soothed him; maybe there'd be something he could buy . . .   – You gotta shu' up!   the baby's mother kept saying. He looked out at the people skating soundlessly over the bright tiles of the Underground station . . .

33

Better not to try anything than to be wicked! – That's how most people acted, and they were probably right, dying their lumpish lives without collecting more than their share of the general blame; but *he'd* do whatever he was called to do . . .

34

He hadn't drunk enough whiskey at Bob and Esther's. His throat still hurt. The pub down the street was out of onion crisps. And the BBC was going to move him out of his hotel room (this small square grave with diamond-patterned carpet, an adjoining marble tomb of a bathroom on whose black floor he slipped and nearly brained himself every time; the double bed took up most of the room; he lay in it enjoying surcease from his fever and fiddled with the cigarette hole that the white girl had made in the coverlet) because they'd made a mistake putting him there in the first place; it was too good for him or not good enough or something – most likely too good for him; once they moved him out, the white girl wouldn't be able to find him; so he called even though she said she'd probably be out, and he got her mother, who wanted to know who he was, what number he was calling from, how he'd met her daughter, what they'd done together; he told her to have the girl call in the morning. At eleven in the morning he had to go to work and she hadn't called, so when they let him out for lunch at 1:00 he went back to his half made-up room but there was no message from her and he wondered if maybe the desk flunkeys hadn't brought it up yet but he didn't feel like going to see; maybe she didn't want to call him; he tried to call her, but the hotel had closed the line and it was too much effort to make them open it. So he ducked into the pub across the street and had a half pint of Sam Smith's, not the stout but the pale apple-flavored kind. The fat barman reached across every minute to munch peanuts. Muzak played grandiosely; a serious drinker leaned on a crutch; the husband was going to be late to the studio and he felt so sad and rejected that the white girl hadn't called him that he didn't care.

Munching on some cheese crisps (**TRADITIONAL FLAVOUR**), he wandered into the canteen where the producer was supposed to meet him, but the producer wasn't there, so he went down the long hot fire-doored hallways to the studio where the producer was frowning over the script, and he said to the producer: I thought you were going to meet me in the canteen.

I was there,   said the producer.   But then I had to work. Some people have to work.

The producer's friend started to introduce herself, but the producer interrupted and said to him: You mustn't eat crisps. No, I'm serious. They'll dry your voice out.

There are only a few crumbs left,   the husband said. He finished the crisps and went into the other room, which was nicely soundproofed, the producer and technicians now secured in an aquarium where they could frown and gesture and grimace in happy silence behind their window, leaving him free to listen to the second hand going round.

The green light came on. – OK,   the producer said.   Stand by for Seal Hunt III.

214

35

The next morning he had a fever and a sore throat and remembered how the white girl had coughed once or twice; it was 5:00 when he woke up lonely and got up to drink some water but could barely swallow. He lay there until 7:30. Furry bedclothes gnawed at him throughout that long night of sickness. When it started getting light he put on an eyeshade but it seemed to press against his eyes and he could not stop seeing ferocious white dots against the blackness, so he removed the eyeshade, and slowly the albino ants decayed into static. The flicker of his eyelashes, irritatingly magnified, merged with his headache like wet and rusty ferns woven into an unending basketwork of decay. At eight he thought about calling the white girl, but decided to have breakfast first. Maybe the hot tea would help him.

In the Brasserie (why they had to call it that he didn't know) he untwisted his urine-sample-sized jar of breakfast marmalade (NO ADDED COLOUR) and munched his toast, listening to the waitress's shoes squeaking on the parquet floor. The marmalade was good. At long last one other guest came in, a man in a red tie and corduroy suit. Without seeming to see the husband, the man saw him and sat on the other side of the room.

It was 8:20. He got Reception to give him an outside line; then, dreading the thought that he might reach her mother, he called the white girl. The phone rang four times. Hello? said the white girl's mother very anxiously. – Is Samantha there? he said. – No, said the mother, not angrily, not even wearily, only sadly, with such calm and final sadness as to constitute implacability. The mother understood that he and the daughter had done or were doing something that was being kept from her. The mother was never going to pass on his messages or let him see her.

36

Georgette Heyer in uniform green jackets, multiple copies of
Cortázar (grey), Céline (black) and some unknown faraway
writer whose jackets were metallic white like the wrappers of
those Belgian chocolates with the horse picture; these almost
subsumed him, but he kept believing there must be some other
category he longed for but couldn't think of, some special kind
of book that was entirely unfamiliar but very very good . . . –
Yeah, here's *fic-*tion, a lady said. The sound of the escalator
was maddening. A wave of fever drenched him. He swayed and
did not open Mayersberg.

Speak Malay! the green book shouted. A saleslady led him
to an English–Eskimo Eskimo–English dictionary; he looked on
his own for something Khmer but couldn't find anything closer
than *Speak Indonesian!* He stared dull-eyed, open-mouthed, at
Spoken Thai, a Gilbertese–English dictionary, *Da Kine Talk . . .*

Climbing up insecticide-smelling stairs, looking through a
window into another window set among sooty bricks, he saw
other windows with books behind them. Books walled themselves off from him like the Alaskan cemetery fenced with
whalebones. Whether they were books or something else didn't
even matter anymore. He remembered the Polish market in
Omaha with its glass coffin filled with sausage, dried smoked
sausage on top, pickled sausage all around bulkheaded by bags of
beef jerky; one of those sausages and only one was the right
choice, but he hadn't made it. Maybe the English–Eskimo
Eskimo–English dictionary was the right choice. He was starting
not to think so, but it would definitely have been the wrong
choice not to buy it. That's how it would have been with the
white girl, too; if he hadn't made love with her he never would
have known that she wasn't going to pull off her white mask to
be his wife. He was sweating like a mountain-climber. He
thought: I suppose this will be how it is when I get AIDS. –
Then he thought: Maybe I do have AIDS.

37

The marquee said **Cameron Red's Hypnotic Show** and he thought: Well, I don't believe hypnotism is the answer, but who knows? Maybe it'll make all my problems go away.

In the poster, the hypnotist smiled innocuously in black and white like someone on an old record album. But his white fingers reached and clutched; there was a terrifyingly hysterical and concentrated brilliancy in his irises.

38

The hypnotist was smoking a cigarette under a water-stained ceiling in a room wallpapered with a pattern of scarlet orchids shaped like praying mantises. It was evidently his dressing room, since the far door opened directly onto the wings of a stage where chorus girls were rehearsing, stretching their legs upward like soaring tree-ferns even though nobody watched or cared. There was a welding kit under the hypnotist's bed, then the hall to the bathroom door which was stuffed with paper where somebody had kicked or smashed a hole in it (the shower pull was broken off and you had to flush the toilet three times and even then it might not work). The husband said to himself: How do I know that about the toilet? How do I know there's a welding kit under the bed? Why does this place seem so familiar? — and then the hypnotist's eyes bulged out toward him a little more and he got dizzy, the tides of fever carrying him nowhere, only working him back and forth; but for a moment, only for a moment, he was able to remember that this room and hallway and bathroom had existed in the Arctic, which meant that it couldn't exist here, which meant . . . — but now the hypnotist's eyeballs clanged over his own. Just as a sleeping pill's effects begin within the quarter-hour, with numbness behind the eyes, followed by a heaviness in the fingers, these zones of deadness expanding rapidly, so now the hypnotist's thrusts of light oozed down his sore throat until he couldn't feel it anymore; then light curved around and round inside his skull like a turd too big for the toilet bowl, pressing down on his brain, blinking out blood vessels like city lights at curfew, and he forgot everything.

To remember her you MUST forget, said the hypnotist.

He said: I'm searching for something, and I still don't know what it is.

You must FORGET, said the hypnotist.

He said: I married someone, and I don't know who she is.

You must FORGET, said the hypnotist.

He said: I betrayed someone, and I don't know where I am.

The hypnotist said: What about the how and why? You forgot those. Those are the five questions that a good journalist is supposed to ask. Who, what, where, how and why.

You told me to forget.

That's no excuse. What's her name?

Vanna.

What's her name?

Vanna.

What's her name?

I – I forget –

You must FORGET,   said the hypnotist.   What's her name?

Who? What's my name? I don't remember my name.

You must FORGET, FORGET, FORGET, FORGET . . .

He said: I feel that my breast is a closed iron door that I'm standing breast to breast with, and I have to smash it open with my breast or with my head because my heart or my love's heart lies inside.

Something touched him. He didn't know what it was. It was fishy and silverwhite and crewcut-soft like sealskin kamiks.

The hypnotist had brought him out of himself, as when a brook carves rock between scaly trees, slipping ever deeper into its own crack until it can rill out into desire, which is sun and space, white light, then GONE into the bowl of green trees below, sided by rock wall looming and leaning and bending, articulated at its reddish lizard-ledges, cradling that suicidal miracle of a desert waterfall; and it seemed he was going down wide white stairs that led into a lake; and now the lukewarm waters were lapping at his ankles; now they were at his knees and he felt slimy weeds rub against him coolly; now he'd gone waist-deep and his testicles contracted with the cold; the water was getting colder and darker by the time his chest went under and the stairs weren't white anymore; they were black; the hypnotist's pale hand took his and pulled him down three more steps so that the water was at his throat and there was an animal smell; the wife he'd divorced was drowned and rotting there; the hypnotist dragged him down deeper and his face

219

went in, only his hair still floating in that bygone world of breath; he would have floated helplessly but for the iron-dark stairs that clung like leeches to the soles of his feet and sucked the buoyancy out of him as the hypnotist pulled him down; it was all very murky and ripply and bubbly but something was going round him now in nasty circles like a chained mongoose at a snake charmer's and the hypnotist's erection was in his mouth; it was a pink mesa over which hung blue-bellied storm clouds with flickering narrow strings of lightning, and from the hot plateau far away he could see other clouds with stems of rain connecting them to the ground. Then he was speeding through the warm drafty bathroom-tiled vaults of the Tube, seeing lots of slender black-leotarded legs, and the hypnotist was whispering in his ear: When you awake you'll forget all this. You'll FORGET. — He was choking and the hypnotist was suffocating him and chuckling and saying: That's right; now drink your milk . . .

Once he'd paid the price, once he'd done what Vanna was paid to do, then he crossed over and saw her better and more completely than ever before: Vanna not quite smiling in a spangle of darkness, Vanna with her lip-red fingernail glossy against her apple-red lip, looking at him big-eyed with her pupils perfect circles of pure light in her black eyes; yes, she was smiling at him, a slow sad cautious smile out of darkness; there was a glitter of moisture at the corner of her mouth just beyond her finger; he wanted to lick it and get AIDS; Vanna with her shimmering skin gazed smiling gently, accepting him no matter what he did; her chin almost rested on her knuckle but there was darkness in between, the darkness of sunray eyelashes from his strange doomed new wife whom he'd married once and would probably never see again — his wife, his wife, his wife! — he knew now that no answering letter from her would ever come, but if he went back to Cambodia and found her in the disco or in some anonymous rice field whose corpse-mud and bone fragments oozed between her toes, then she'd smile at him in just the same way, so gently and lovingly and trustingly and sadly; and if he went away or didn't come in the first place she'd never think about him again. He saw Vanna striding away with ultraviolet footfalls outside a hotel room . . .

39

Everything jolly now?   said the hypnotist, sitting calm, skinny and brown-skinned beneath the blue dentist's sign with the giant glistening stylized three-pronged tooth, beside which a set of pink-lidded jaws smiled in a light blue circle; quite a sign, really. – Yes, thank you,   the husband said. He went out past all the faces smiling politely, smooth, brown-skinned. A green army truck hooted down the street. A lady sat spoonfeeding custard to her little boy and girl. Two cyclists towed a trailer filled with dark green packages. Another cyclist had dozens of live chickens bundled under him. On the sidewalk in front of her kids a lady was splitting firewood with a cleaver. She had a Chinese-porcelain face. Past her stretched an ocher tunnel of bamboo stalks leaning into one another over a brown creek, and at the far end of its darkness was the place where Vanna was waiting for him after she'd left the hotel room.

40

Everything jolly now?   said the hypnotist. Outside the snow-ledged window, voraciously seeking replication upon the walls of the Quonset huts, the sunrise reflected itself in blackish-yellow necroses of that palest lavender blue sky, and the snow was one shade paler than that, the morning being yellow like the low yellow tunnel with the ladder and then the snow on top; the runway beacons were steady; purple steam moved east. Men in dark coveralls roamed around the terminal, drinking coffee, waiting for more freight on this Sunday morning. Just outside the other window, the master beacon flashed subtly. It flashed on a metal knob and a green door, making the former white, the latter a brilliant greenish-yellow. Sirhan Sirhan, that Kennedy assassin, had insisted in his insanity defense that it was precisely this meaningless winking which triggered his soul's evil trances; so he had no need to employ hypnotists to achieve his desire. The husband saw Sirhan Sirhan on the summit of a mountain of dirty snow; Sirhan Sirhan was the retarded boy whose reddish-purple face was armed with yellow teeth; he turned his hunched head in a series of unblinking spasms, shrieking like a bird. – I'm not afraid of you anymore, the husband said. Because I have someone whose life means more to me than mine. – The fire extinguisher and the two pay phones remained ready to preserve homeostasis, letting people live as if cold and loneliness didn't exist. The orange shimmer of sunlight mounted higher on the dark buildings outside; snowy snow-roofs sprouted confusions of pipes and wires like measures of music. Beyond the work camp lay ice, and more ice, and at the end of the ice the Inuk girl he'd almost married was waiting, and he knew now that she was Vanna.

41

Everything jolly now? said the hypnotist, joining him in holy matrimony to the parking garage whore, the transvestite whore, the streetcorner whore, the English girl whose mother kept crying, and they were all Vanna like dead brown fern leaves on a pillar, like a school of sardines all salted and dried at once, like a grove of trees hung with long brown aerial roots that dangled down like hairs, thick and musty and chocolate colored; he'd reached the end of the tunnel now where a titanic bone-fan of bamboo rose rusty green in the fog. A few stalks had fallen across the creek to spear the other bank, forming high skinny bridges. The vines were like giant guitar strings. She stood in a grove of "textbook" leaves whose veins caught attention as if engraved for beginning students; she picked one and touched her lips to it and gave it to him and then the veins began to crawl and change, first forming his old wife's name, then a semblance of a skull, then an eye, a bullet, a crocodile (the Khmer Rouge had thrown her uncle to the crocodiles).

42

On the whole (not remembering any of this), he was more inclined to trust a pint of Murphy's and some vegetable soup, so he went to the nearest pub. – Cheers. – (The ponytailed old bartender stationed at the taps said that he personally never drank any but bottled beer.) With every swig, the red velvet couch he sat on became more restful. He looked at absurd marine engravings and liked them. – Hey! a regular shouted to himself. I love the sound of broken gloss! – The white taphandles promised unknown flavors more plausible than unknown books or girls because to the husband they really were known; *vis-à-vis* English beverages he was an ignoramus. The last bit of smog-colored foam traveled deliciously down his throat.

43

When you get AIDS, the first thing that happens is you come down with the flu, said one of his wise friends. Then the flu goes away and you think you're fine. And you are, for awhile. It's just that you have AIDS.

So when his fever died after so many days the lucidity was a refreshment as delectable as lemon ice. What a shame to become

223

habituated to that pleasure until it was normalcy, like being addicted to some drug . . .

I feel fine, he said to himself. Of course I don't have AIDS.

44

He stood at the hotel window, looking out between grey ledgestones and tiles at the corner pub's compounded and frosted windows half smoothed by rubbery light, and people's heels struck the pavement like hammers until he thought his ears would bleed. The cold air made him cough. But he stood looking on as if he'd never see those sights again. Certainly he'd never see the white girl again. Two men and a woman stopped in front of the pub for a moment. Then one of the men raised his arm sharply and they went on. Car light flowed across their shoulders. From the Underground he heard a mother say: Keep still. Keep still, will yer. Oi, d'you wa' a smack? — A man and a woman strode across the husband's field of vision and vanished. He'd never see them again. The BBC would pay him any day now. They'd said he'd get the check before he left England, but now that didn't look promising. The husband was a pretty small fish. But they would pay him soon, and once they did he'd have enough to go back to Cambodia for his wife. He was too tired to be properly excited. The right side of his head felt as if it were about to split open. Fluid oozed from his ear. His throat was so swollen that he could barely swallow. Every meaningless detail pierced the senses unbearably, but left no memory. The hypnotist had done that. He stared for a long time at the illuminated orange and blue logos on the Asiana Airlines terminal, a shape between hexagon and oval, comprised of parallelogram tiles of varying luminosities; he couldn't quite parse the shape in his mind, and wondered if the mind must redraw what it sees to comprehend it; closing his eyes he saw plenty of images which his mind was too weary to flush; their vividness reminded him of his childhood; he'd gradually lost the ability to visualize at will as he'd grown older. Korea had seemed to be in dawn time when he came, in keeping with the meaning of its real name, Han-Guk, the Land of the Morning Calm, but then it got dark while he sat in the transit lounge trying to ignore a cartoon starring a growling jellybean and he could now see the whiteness of some of the Asiana tiles; the alien mountains faded into darkness – anyhow, they weren't so alien since he'd seen mountains before but the more one travels the more alien everything is. – Then back in Bangkok: another little table stacked with plates; he had some cow's head or whatever it was, the man pulling it out of the stewpot and chopping it on the half-meter-thick block; the husband didn't ask how much or why; they brought him rice; he uttered *Sprite* over the dull double-heartbeat of the chopper . . . Then Cambodia again, slopping over him like the cold wetness on your belly when you bushwhack up a rainy jungle hillside; he went to the disco, sank knee-deep into the carpet of girl-ferns because the tables were closer together than ever before, trapping him in narrow sharp-edged lanes down which the other prostitutes hunted him, seizing his hand, pulling him down to sticky chairs beside them where he had to buy them a Tiger beer, the darkness hotter and louder as the music blared so pervasively and unintelligibly that he had to breathe it in like all the smoke from the other men's cigarettes that rose in great pillared trunks flanged with leaves that stuck out like shelf-fungus; now the photographer's girl captured him and started screaming at him to buy her for the photographer; then the Chinese-porcelain-faced one clamored silently for his favor, devouring the light before it could reach his eyes so that he couldn't see if Vanna was among the dancers; knowing his poor vision, however, the photographer had printed up a hundred copies of her picture for him to pass out, so he awarded one to the photographer's girl, who began wailing like a mother whose children have been tortured, and he gave one to the Chinese-porcelain girl, who tore it into shreds, smiling, drifting closer and closer like the queen of nightmare pleasures;

225

cautiously he bought her a Sprite, slipped her five hundred riels, but she still wouldn't leave; her arms grew tight about him like skinny lichen-spotted trees; Vanna wasn't there! She wasn't there! He blundered among the dancers, trying to smell her sickly-sweet face powder, hoping for the sheen of her triangular face, but she wasn't there. He went to the temples and the kids crowded around staring, one with a plastic sword, one smiling, one blinking, one leaning, one almost naked, all bashful; they looked down at their sandaled feet as they asked him for money; he was in Wat Korgue – let's see, some Khmer Rouge damage although the altar had retained its stone flower-nipples and concentric curvy polygons like nested frogs' tongues repeated row to row. There were two glazed figurines. One was a woman in lotus position, with only her lips and eyeballs painted. Not Vanna. The other was a man elaborately colored. The husband took out Vanna's photograph and showed it to the kids but they looked blank. He went on to the Wat Svay Popter . . . When he'd been to every temple in Cambodia, he set out for every rice field and she wasn't there though he ducked under every dark ceiling, scanning every hammock and bicycle wheel, studying every pair of sandals on the dirt floor to see if one might be hers, while faces peered in; he searched out whole villages of such houses: displaced people, with chickens underneath (a half-coconut on the platform, a sarong); there was a little boy whose head was shaved to bluish fuzz; the boy held his monkey on a chain so that it wouldn't hurt Vanna's picture and then the boy said: She escaped from place Pol Pot shelled with heavy guns. First time Pol Pot came and attacked her village. Then they shelled with heavy guns for three-four days. She die here malaria. We very sorry, sir. – He thought: If she's dead then maybe she's living on Sailing Boat Mountain. – All he knew about Sailing Boat Mountain was that the Khmer Rouge had killed a few thousand people there, which was all he needed to know. Quite possibly she was the earth-spirit hovering round atrocities, lurking like moisture in the palm trees at the base of that great green rock (they'd thrown the victims off); so he rode

up the muddy jungle road, over barely repaired bridges (the driver flashed his gold tooth in the mirror), past abandoned houses and tree trunks so saturated with wet that he could squeeze them like sponges, past fringed green leaf-awnings slung with cartridge-belts of nuts the reddish hue of a baboon's anus; so he arrived at the white stairs (some garnished with giant snailshells) that the murdered ones had been compelled to climb, their hands already tied behind their backs with wire, and he ascended those green-clad cave-cooled cliffs into the rainy sky; she wasn't there. For an instant he remembered the book he'd seen long ago when he was the little butterfly boy, the book about the five unkillable Chinese brothers, and there was one who was pushed off a precipice and smiled in the air as he fell. – Vanna, Vanna! – He said to himself: Well, no skulls screamed from this mound of jungle over rock despite my dreams when I was sleeping with my other wife; maybe my other wife was warping and torturing my dreams so I couldn't find her but she couldn't have made me dream a dream of perfect untruth; maybe Vanna's sick with malaria in the hospital. – Voilà, another set of yellow concrete buildings chessboard-floored like his foolish ruinous life, the white cross wall-inset (maybe once red plexiglass), fire in the courtyard, smell of jasmine. A girl lay on the bed almost naked, sleeping. Not her. A lady was sweeping the floor very slowly. Some of the tiles were grey; a few were still white. Pale light bled through the blinds, losing itself among the dingy dark wooden cribs, darkness and concrete. A girl's brown feet stuck out from under a blanket. Not her. Three girls lay huddled in colored sheets; ladies stood over the dirty cribs; a dark-skinned woman attached to the intravenous snakes smiled whitely (not her), a nurse put her hand in front of the dark-skinned woman's face; one brown baby began to cry when another cried; a soldier sat beside his child, his feet fidgeting in the sandals; a lady waved a palm-woven fan very gently over her baby; the nurse took her hand away from the dark-skinned woman's face and it was Vanna after all. He rushed to her, bent over her . . . She nodded a little and closed her eyes. She was

burning up with fever. She was his wife, and she was dying! –
He took a vial from his pocket, and began to feed her pills of
pure Arctic ice. He held her hand, which weighed nothing. He
could feel it cooling down as the red fever-flush went away from
her face. – *I wuff you,* she said. – The nurse detached the
intravenous snakes. He put his hand on his wife's heart and kept
it there until the pool of sweat between her breasts evaporated.
She'd been breathing quietly but desperately through her mouth,
and now her lips closed and her sweet eyes opened and she
gestured to her throat until he understood that she needed more
water. He jumped up to fill the pitcher. The water was tepid and
muddy. When he poured it into the cup, he shook in the last
pill of ice, and it turned clear and cold at once; after she'd drunk
it down she smiled at him just as she had when he'd bought her
the gold bracelet, that smile that scorned the world's scorn; then
she sat slowly up and made room for him to sit beside her on the
narrow bed as she put her arm around him and began very
quietly to sing a strange sad song in her lisping voice. He put his
cheek against hers. No fever. She laughed and pinched him.
She pulled him to his feet and they began to dance together,
right there in the hospital, and all the other patients were cured.
She took his hand, and they walked together out of the ward
and through the jasmine-smelling courtyard whose fire had died
down and between the other yellow concrete buildings and past
the white cross and out the gate, and then they were gone from
sad places forever. White swirly mane-ways, down-pods and
foam spilled on the sky-blue sea. He took her where leads
unrolled like grey ribbons too long to have ends, their colors
changing from a cumulus-white with a slight hint of yellow to a
very pale sky-blue. Now she made signs that she was hungry, so
they went caribou hunting with his friends in the summer moss.
Reddish-black racks of seal meat hung on wood frames to dry.
His dear wife felt chilly at first, but when she saw the children
(copper-faced like her) laughing in the icy rocky streams,
catching fish, then she began to forget the spidery green
reflections of palm trees in ricefield water; everyone was good to

her; the old ladies made her sealskin mitts; she learned to enjoy raw meat, to saw off a frozen steak . . . A long low cliff-finger rested lightly on the ice, cushioned by blowing snow, and a dumptruck full of snow left the scatter of houses to discharge its blue-smoking load, which squeaked as it slid out. Pointing at the frozen sea, he laughed and said to her in their secret universal language: Do you remember that wooden stand in Phnom Penh whose only ware was an uneven block of ice, with a rusty sawblade to cut it?   and she said nothing, perhaps because she preferred to remember the ice-pills instead, or perhaps because she never said anything anyhow, only chewed on the piece of caribou fat he'd given her, walking beside him up the low ridge that bordered the sourceless river. Almost noon. The low sun and clear sky held the weird subdued transparency of morning and evening at the same time. In her smooth-soled sealskin kamiks she slipped on one of those strange ovals on the ice swept clean as if by spotlight beams; his arm was around her waist before she could fall. Then he saw that the faint breeze had begun to chill her cheeks. He took her face gently between his mitts and blew on it and she giggled because that tickled. When the color came back, he kissed her in the Cambodian way, inhaling in teasing little sniffs through his nose as he pecked her and she hissed with pleasure; he and she were polar bear twins . . . – He said: Now I'll take you to my house, which I hope you'll like because it's your house, too   (he'd asked the photographer: What do you think Vanna will do when she sees this place?   and the photographer looked around grinning and said: She'll shit in her pants, man! She's gonna love you so fucking much! By her standards you're a millionaire! Once she sees this place she'll never *ever* leave you!) – So the Twin Otter taxied in the snow; steam puffed from a tomato-red Quonset hut; a raven flapped; sunrise over blue clouds; past the wires the Twin took off at a sedate angle, leaving the velour hills alone. He'd given her the window seat and she couldn't take her face away from the glass; it was so beautiful. They were going from one heaven to another, by the scenic route because he wanted to draw it out as much as he could before that first time when he'd give her the key to the house and take her to the bedroom and they'd fall asleep side by side. (It was a little strange, the way he almost always imagined her sleeping as he fell asleep. Making love with her, taking her into a supermarket for the first time, giving her her first elevator ride, letting her try ice cream, buying her dresses, gold rings, a new red motorbike to ride up San Francisco's steep hills (her name pricked out in gold on the bar between her legs), these were all things that gave him joy to look forward to, but somehow sleep was the real tree whose trunk was a hundred roots, each root, as big around as an arm, one of these other happinesses, all intertwined like pipes, wrapped with vines of sleep which bore white flowers and blackish-blue berries. He was tired. He felt unwell. He wanted to sleep.) So the plane landed in the desert. The floor of the canyon was entirely river, cool, green and shallow, with the usual surprises in the lowest overhang: grey ferns downheaded like stalactites. In that shadow was the last coolness. After that, slanting rock-sides burned to touch, although there was another shelf at an angle of forty-five degrees from which huge trees jutted, both evergreens and pale green virgins leaning into space as if to drink the vapor, at least, of the river they could not reach. A man and a woman were wading up the stream slowly, knees apart. The woman was soaked and muddy, and evidently had lost her gauzy butterfly hairclip. But she seemed tranquilly happy. A wake formed from her like a shadow. From time to time she stumbled, and then the man would give her his arm, and she'd smile. Her rainbow prostitute dress shimmered like a glorious rage of dragonflies; the drops of river-water that danced up from her knees reflected every color like crystals: the pinkish-red that formerly looked so dramatic in the Cambodian night when she came walking down stenchy greasy pitchblack alleyways, the yellow splash, that hue of streetlights which Cambodia didn't have yet; the electric bluish-green that once shocked its way down breast and belly in the darkness, now a summer riverwater color, a little mournful as artificial glows always are

231

in daylight . . . She was smiling shyly and holding her husband's hand. Her earrings sparkled rhythmically as she walked through the water; they glittered like sunlight on mica. He took her slender arm and steadied her when he saw an eddy; he slipped his hand round her narrow waist. (Of course she actually would have hated all this; in Cambodia she always had to go by motorbike even if it was only two blocks, and she wouldn't even ride the same motorbike he did.) The upside-down Vs of her eyebrows glowed blackish-gold in the strong sunlight; the sunlight glistened on her cheeks. – Yellow glare of mustard fields, then phosphorescent white of cottonwoods, then grey-pink and greyer green ridges studded with little blue tree-buttons; he was taking her to their new house hidden beyond a tall slit in the sand ridge so narrow he could barely lead her through. She got tired, and he carried her across the blue desert of Utah, the yellow desert of Nevada, the grey desert of California, so grateful to be able to ease her way. He showed her everything, led her safely between the skyscrapers too aloof and alien even to accept each other's shadows, brought her under the red struts of the Golden Gate Bridge to marvel with him at the fog-colored bay and Marin headlands; on his shoulders he carried his darling wife up the steep slopes knit-sweatered with buttercups, ferns, grasses and raspberries; she stopped to weave him baskets from the windy grasses shaking alertly like sentient porcupine quills and antennae-forests while cars swirled and flickered overhead, bridge-shadow on the water . . . Now before sleep Scarlatti's sonata K. 95, the thrilling happy feminine hurrying beats of that bridal march which no one else would ever want to make a bridal march out of because it wasn't sedate; he thought it simply glorious, brief and glorious, like a girl hurrying to her sweetheart; she was rushing to him in that church filled with all his relatives and everyone else he'd ever known so that she wouldn't have come to his distant land believing that he was ashamed of her; he wanted the whole world to see her and love her as she came down the aisle to him on no one's arm, the clavicord pounding like a million angels' hearts, nothing but joy . . . He closed the window. Then he opened it once more to look upon the steeply slanting awnings and triangularly-crowned windows of that London street. – Everything jolly now? said the hypnotist.

45

Where are you coming from? the US customs woman said.

London.

OK. Wait a minute. No other baggage?

Nope.

On his card she scribbled "C.E.T."

This code will get you right through, she said. Otherwise they'll be suspicious about the absence of luggage.

Thanks, he said.

Don't mention it.

At the exit, the lady who took cards read "C.E.T.," stopped dead, and sent him to the special agent's desk.

Where you coming from?

London.

How long were you there?

A week.

Purpose of trip?

Business.

What kind of business?

Journalism.

I see you were in Bangkok, said the customs man, flipping through his passport very lazily. Earlier this year?

Yep.

You like it there? I bet you really liked it there.

It was all right.

I lived there ten years, the customs man said.

What part of Bangkok?

You wouldn't know if I told you. I bet the only places you know are Pat Pong and the shopping mall.

What shopping mall? said the husband defiantly.

The customs man had unzipped his backpack and was turning it inside out. The husband almost admired him, because he was impervious to the husband's dirty underwear, squeezing every wrinkle so gracefully, looking for contraband . . .

And the husband thought: Have I only lately become a sleaze to them, or did they always think I was a sleaze?

He stood in a dream until the agent let him go.

46

Hello, Sien. I hear you wanted me to call.

Yes, sir. I have some news for you. You know sir we contact Cambodia go disco show picture your taxi girl they say no one like that is working there now. They say no one like that ever worked there.

She's not there anymore?

No, sir. When she working there? Long time ago?

September.

September is not long time. I don't know why, sir. I think maybe your letter was too heavy. We enclose the four photos of you and the four photos of her. When it got Phnom Penh my contact say only one picture of her and one picture of you in there. Letter was too heavy.

You think she's dead?

I don't know, sir. I think maybe no news is insufficient news. We must try another way.

47

By now, through the weird and inverse pointillism of so many other influences, Vanna's image had disintegrated and dispersed in the blackness of his mind like the dust of a losing protostar.

That night in a dream he saw a woman he hadn't seen for many years, a white woman with a beautiful face whom he'd always loved and who had never loved him. In his vision she wasn't saying anything to him, only gazing lovingly into him, which was enough and more. In real life this woman was dying or had already died.

the answer

William T. Vollmann

It is by the activity of our passions, that our
reason improves . . . The passions, in turn,
owe their origin to our needs, and their
increase to our progress in science.

J.-J. ROUSSEAU, *Discourse on
Inequality* (1755)

The phlebotomist rolled on white rubber gloves before
she stuck him. When she asked questions for the case
record, she looked right through him. When she was finished
the doctor came in. The doctor was tall and muscular like a gym
teacher. He didn't bother to shut the door.

Drop your trousers, said the doctor.

He looked at the door.

Drop your trousers, I said.

He dropped his trousers.

The doctor rolled on white gloves with an angry and disgusted
face.

Doctor, do you see anything?

Take a deep breath, said the doctor.

The doctor slammed the culture probe up his urethra. He
grunted with the sudden stunning pain. The doctor almost
smiled.

Doctor, what do you think my chances are of having the
virus?

How would I know? I don't know how you've been spending
your life. What's more, I don't want to know.

Do you think I have a fifty-fifty chance?

239

You've been doing a lot of stupid things,   said the doctor, writing something onto the chart.

He rose and flipped a box contemptuously down.   – Have some condoms,   he said.   Maybe your wife can still be saved.

He knew and sensed that everything was going
according to timetable. There was no need to
interfere. They knew everything themselves.
It would only make people nervous. They were
good lads.

YAROSLAV GOLOVANOV, *Sergei
Korolev: The Apprenticeship of a
Space Pioneer* (1975)

1

As small black vermin-birds fluttered through the air
of the Greyhound platforms, which then whirred
behind picket by picket through the scratched windows, he
thought: Well, in a few hours my life will be different.

Rolling down the concrete tube fringed by stalled buses, they
proceeded across the Bay Bridge, whose replicated girders sick-
ened him through the windows. Pale shining bluish-whitish-grey
water gazed at him. He was so tired.

He got to the clinic and they kept him waiting for an hour
and said: You see that the numbers match.

I see that,   he said.

Well, it says right here: **HIV ANTIBODIES PRESENT**.
You have the virus.

So I finally won the lottery,   he said.   That's good. That's
very good.

I wouldn't be smiling like that if I were you.

No, he said, I'm sure you wouldn't. But I'd be smiling if you were me. I'd really like to see how you coped with that.

Here are some brochures on AIDS resources which you might like to look over . . .

Oh, I have all the resources I need if I want to get AIDS.

You certainly are upbeat about it.

Then why aren't you? the husband laughed. He went out smiling.

2

You can notch the fish's fin, harden the removed bit of tissue with epoxy, and then slice it with a diamond saw, slice it thin for the microscope. Now turn the brass knob on the stem, your eye gazing passionlessly into that other world that used to be a fish; when it comes into focus you'll see the fish's age straight-away; it's just like counting tree-rings; it's no different than half-listening to the interpreter explaining the difference between Soviet pistols (he never did learn the difference between the K-54 and the K-59) while gazing out the car window at the houses on stilts over the squishy river, houses connected by gangplanks; you can see the people inside looking out; there is no privacy. That's how it must be for those mercilessly illuminated fish-cells. When he was six or seven his parents told him that he was a big boy, but he got sick and then he was little; they wouldn't use the oral thermometer. They made him pull down his pants on the bed and then the anal thermometer went in, cool and greasy. The whole world saw. He lay still. When they pulled it out and told him that he could move, he continued to lie there with his face in the pillow. He'd gone out of himself; the worst thing now would be if anyone saw him coming back into himself; then that would prove that this thing had happened. But you do it; you look, see, stare, observe, count, measure and categorize. You have to do it! You suck into your eyes the naked children squatting in the mud, coffee-colored puddles in the muddy road, grass-roofed wooden booths in the mud. You match the num-bers, my dear technicians. **HIV ANTIBODIES PRESENT**. Then you continue on down the wide almost empty mud road so beset with puddles that the driver must snake along on brown ridges between them while whitish-pale beggar children hold out their hands screaming. But you do it; you undress it. The fish has been caught; that is the end for the fish there between tall lush pale green trees.

Vanna's husband didn't believe any of it yet. He remembered so many other false alarms.

There had been that night outside the hotel when a cyclo driver came to him and said that he and the photographer were in danger. So he had to buy the cyclo driver orange juice.

What sort of danger are we in? said the husband. I haven't noticed any danger.

So much the worse for you, Monsieur. Pardon me, but I speak frankly; excuse me, Monsieur, but so much the worse for you.

Well, what do you want, exactly? I'm only a poor stupid American. We Americans cannot understand mysteries.

Ah, tomorrow I will bring you a souvenir, Monsieur. No obligation, but I am a very poor man. Five sons. My situation is intolerable.

That is sad; I'm sorry, but I can't save the world. What is this souvenir? You say you speak frankly; then speak frankly. I give you five more minutes.

The situation is grave, Monsieur. Very grave for you. What do you do tomorrow?

I go to work.

With the Ministry of Foreign Affairs?

Yes.

I would not get in the car, Monsieur.

Why? This is very fatiguing for me, complained the husband. Your French is full of obfuscations . . .

You quit me now?

Yes.

So much the worse for you.

I think I've heard that before.

The husband went back to the hotel and told the photographer. The photographer agreed with him that it was probably nonsense but wondered where he could hide his film. The next morning they stood on the hotel balcony together, watching bright-green uniformed police gathering on the sidewalk. The official car did not come on time. It was the first instance of the car not coming on time. The husband went and called the Ministry and they said they knew nothing about it. Then the car came and nothing had happened and everything was fine . . .

3

He had a sore throat.

THE BORDELLO OF PAIN

WILLIAM T. VOLLMANN

This is a libation to Jupiter the Liberator.
Look, young man! For you have been born
(may heaven avert the omen!) into an age
when examples of fortitude may be a useful
support.

CLAUDIUS THRASEA PAETUS,
upon opening his veins (AD 66)

1

In the empty house silent within the night winds he scraped a can of dinner into the saucepan and stood waiting for it to cook while his hands held one another on the white enamel coolness of the stove not far from the burner, and he wondered how the stove could stay so cool when the chili was already boiling. He swallowed his pill, in much the same spirit of obedience as when at the board table restaurant in Phnom Penh he'd drunk a fruit shake because that was religious food. He ate dinner, and put the saucepan in the sink to wash later. He picked up the newspaper and read **Khmer Rouge sees opening in Cambodia chaos** and he thought of the place where they'd suffocated babies by the hundreds, hanging them from the branches to choke inside plastic bags. He thought of the scars on Vanna's back.

2

On the marriage bureau wall, dozens of green lizards waited, light green with silver legs. They waited for him because he'd married her.

3

He was so alone! With his other wife he'd been resentful when he did what she wanted and guilty when he didn't, and after either failure, once she'd driven off into the night screaming and weeping so that in the middle of his anger he was terrified that she might get into an accident, then he'd lie down on his stomach on their double bed, waiting for the trembling and the sickening stabs in his guts to go away, and then when he felt a little better he'd go into his study to find his address book – he had to find someone who could help him; he had to! – it was the infatuation with wise men all over again – and he'd lie back on the double bed with his heartbeats almost shattering his chest; he was speeding through the pages like an addict: his two best friends in San Francisco didn't answer; in New York it was too late now; he devoured the numbers for Arizona and Nebraska but there was nobody anywhere; *he was so alone!* – that was the worst part of those arguments, the dread in the middle of the shouting that afterward, no matter what, he'd be so alone . . .

4

But something had changed in him. He knew now what he wanted. The other girls had helped him; the hypnotist had revivified his desires; the disease had given him a directness and urgency which he'd never had before in his life. He loved Vanna and no one else. One way or another he was going to be with her.

5

The reception room at CBS on that slow summer Friday was like some dream too stuporous to be affected by doom, the security guard's martyred face personifying the hum of lights, the black leather swivel chairs waiting for buttocks, the old reception man shaking his head in weary amazement, saying: I tell ya, George!,   while ladies with legal pads and sodas wandered in past the metal detector and messengers trudged out bearing big square boxes of disbelief on their shoulders. A man whose slacks were composed of some spongy effete material leaned over the reception desk, offering an almost alarming view of his fat ass. Grizzled cameramen strolled out yawning, their scuffed leather shoulderbags resting easy in place now that continued use had worn a hollow in each scapulum.

I tell ya, George!   the reception man said again.   All right, she says you can go up now. Second floor, first right. What's that you said, George? 'Scuse me but I got *interrupted.*

You don't look well,   Padgett said to him.   You've got to get over it. I've been divorced twice, and the second one was just as hard as the first, but I got over it. I hate to say this to you, but your work is slipping.

I'm fine,   he said.   Maybe a little tired is all. So you can't use me?

I hate to have you put it to me like that,   Padgett said, neatening papers on her desk.   I really thought you understood.

I understand now. Do you have any advice for me? Seems like lately I've been asking everyone for advice . . .

I know how it is,   Padgett said.   It's hard to be alone again, isn't it?

I'm not alone. I just got married.

Well, congratulations. Who's the lucky lady?

Someone I met in Cambodia.

That's fabulous, Padgett said. Why didn't you send me an invitation? Listen, I've got a meeting I have to go to. Thank you so much for dropping by –

6

He picked up the newspaper and read **Khmer Rouge officials return to Phnom Penh** and there was a photo of someplace blurry; he thought he recognized the place where the English teacher's friend, another fatherless boy, said that his girlfriend, who died of a headache in 1989, was cremated.

He said to himself: For me to get through this, I'm going to have to stop reading the papers.

He said to himself: I'll be a fine one then. A journalist who doesn't read the papers.

7

He picked up the newspaper and read **More rioting in Phnom Penh.**

8

He picked up the newspaper and read **Bloody clash in Cambodia.**

9

It was lunch hour at the Time-Life Plaza and he lurked among the people squeezing balls of aluminum foil in their hands, sitting on the edge of the pool whose row of fountain-foams resembled the heads of asparagus. He was waiting for an editor from *Asia Today* to come outside. Maybe the editor would give him a job. Businessmen in amazing shoes strode past cigarette butts, and golden monograms glittered on their heels. The businesswomen in "burgundy" dress suits – the standard color – dangled their high heels. Then the editor from *Asia Today* came out, and he looked into the editor's face while the editor looked into his face and he saw that there was no sense in even asking.

10

The funny thing was that he couldn't feel anything wrong inside him yet. He thought he looked great. The doctor said that right now he was only HIV positive. It would be two to six years before he developed ARC, which was to say an AIDS-related condition, which was to say being sick, and then once he got sick enough they would be able to note down in his medical records that he had AIDS. It was easy to believe that the virus wasn't doing anything yet, but of course it had already begun wearing him down moment by moment, like a river undercutting its banks. When he was in Phnom Penh the Tonlé Sap had been rising, so people were laying down mounds of fresh dirt with shovels, walking on them, smoothing them out. A little boy was swimming beside his porch. It happened every monsoon season, they said. The air smelled like fish. There were crowds. A woman was wading from one house to the next. Serious crowds with spades tamped down the levee.

11

The photographer called him and said: Well, I just heard from your friend Sien. That disco's finished. They closed it down.

What happened to the girls?

The girls? Probably in some fucking concentration camp. I'd say you better kiss off any chance you had of finding Vanna again. Sien's out of it. He doesn't want to get involved anymore. You better go to Thailand and shop around. There are thousands like her. It's too bad, though. That disco was GREAT! And I feel sorry for those poor girls . . .

What do you think Vanna would have done if I'd been able to get her home? What would she have done when I first took her through my front door?

Remember when you asked me that before? I told you she would shit in her pants, man! She would have loved you so much for your money! She would have never ever left you . . .

Well, thanks for saying that.

Oh, that's all right, the photographer said.

12

He woke up and had a sore throat.

13

He picked up the newspaper and read **Cambodia** and did not read anymore. He went to bed in the night-sodden house and dreamed that Vanna was screaming with terror, stretching out her arms to him, waiting for him to come and get her while she was still alive . . .*

14

Berkeley was like Seattle, the same white fog, hills of trees, angry-looking boys and girls storming into the record store, people in rainbow-colored backpacks clicking cassette cases restlessly, skateboarders, students ambling and loitering, girls wandering in a dream of ice cream, boys and girls coming out of the record store exchanging complicitous looks, as if they'd just jerked each other off, because they'd BOUGHT things, hairy-legged wiry boys in shorts, daypacks, luna-green bike helmets, a ponytailed man in earth shoes wiggling his butt against the railing, a professor grinning like Fu Manchu as he strolled, arms behind his back, discoursing to his prettiest pupil, black boys in backwards hats walking and eating pizza, then of course the long-haired fathers who carried their babies on their backs.

Well, I don't know,   the editor was saying.   I'm not really familiar with your politics. I guess we could maybe work something out. I'd have to put it up to the group. The fact that you're a white male kind of makes me uneasy.

Tell the group that my grandmother was a Seneca Indian, the husband lied cunningly.

Oh, now *that's* cool. Actually I can kind of see the resemblance.

In the end they commissioned him to do an article on the AIDS ward. The group had even chosen the title: "The Bordello of Pain."   – Because the *outrage* that we feel for these victims is

---

* Witness's testimony: "In the society built up by the Pol Pot–Ieng Sary clique there was no prostitution (a good mark to their credit). There a man was not allowed to have two wives. If a married man or married woman had a lover, the couple would incur death."

the *same* outrage that we feel for women whose bodies are exploited by unmediated prostitution! a girl explained.

The husband didn't care. It was five hundred bucks. Like any prostitute, he had to get along somehow.

15

Armed with his myriad press cards, he entered the Bordello of Pain. Skeletons that had not yet died surrounded him like a traffic jam in an afternoon thunderstorm, glistening cars creeping all the way to the horizon; a long crooked verticality of lightning, then thunder close enough to make the car jump . . . Five hundred bucks. He asked them each what drugs they were taking, how they'd contracted the disease, what message they wanted to give the world. Five hundred bucks. Some were calm and one was happy and all the rest were angry fearful people who wanted to blame someone because they were dying. The one who was happy chuckled and beckoned him and whispered: I see the same death in your eyes. – Skinny arms and legs thinned second by second in front of him. A lady coughed. She couldn't eat anymore. How skinny she was! A skeleton scuttled screaming underneath a bed; a lady said: That's where she always goes to cry. – A lady smiled at him and whispered: Thank you so much for coming here. You're so patient and quiet with me that I almost feel that you're one of us . . . – A lady said to him: I guess what I want to tell the world is that when you know you're dying your choices seem to fall away. There's only one thing left to do. Whatever's the most important thing, that's what you do. That's all you have time for . . .

Vanna's husband whirled upon her. – And for you, he said to her in a very low voice, what's the most important thing?

She smiled and took his hand. – Love, she said.

William T. Vollmann

BRIDAL MINES

Death isn't sad; it's Being itself. Death is the
founder of consciousness, and therefore of
political awareness.

PAUL VIRILIO and SYLVÈRE
LOTRINGER, *Pure War* (1983)

1

In foggy grassless moon-dips of gloom under spreading
trees, he made up his mind to defy the embargoes on
wife and life that had been set upon him; clambering down to
grey smooth-packed dirt gashed deep by the fingernails of floods,
he ducked under the last tree and came out onto the hill-swollen
coast that was wild with grass and poison oak and weed pods
and the last blue flowers of the season. Fog horns blew ragged
and strange against the chilly breeze. Digging in his heels, he
descended a wall of eroded dirt headlong to the beach, riding
down the raking wounds his haste scored in the earth, rushing
down like the powdered soil that crumbled out of his tracks.
The sand was wet. Between waves he climbed up a boulder that
became an island every minute or two; he stood watching the
sea-lurch, chalk-grey and cold, come to cover the other bird-
dunged rocks. Masses of foam near shore highlighted the dark
stone teeth. Farther out, there was nothing to see but grey grey
sea, grey sky; he breathed the smell of rotten kelp . . . All doubt
was scoured away as he swore to himself that he'd find her. He

dreamed of the jungle almost every night now. He was going to her. That was what he promised himself. And as soon as he became his own witness – impossible to unoath anything now – he felt relief and exaltation, standing on that bemusseled black boulder, ocean foaming around him like beer, slapping up and spraying him . . . A white and grey gull perched beside him, seemingly one-legged. Rocks jutted up tirelessly in the surf.

2

He stood on a steep slope of scree and broken glass in worn-out shoes, fog scudding and rippling down the low waves of sage and Scotch broom (poison oak a warning among them with its bright red leaves). Suddenly the fog turned blue. It must be thinning, he thought. The bluish-greyish-white purity of fog caressed the hill's rounded swelling; the grass-tips wove gently; the flower-stalks whipped back and forth as if on strings; the bushes shuddered . . .

3

He was back at the Hotel 38. The ragged chain of light that hung down the door-edge kept flickering whenever someone passed by. Sometimes it flickered quickly, sometimes slowly. Sometimes the light changed to darkness, and then he knew that someone was standing outside listening.

4

He washed his clothes, and the next morning they were still wet. He had to travel. He packed them in a plastic bag and they got hot and steamy. That evening he hung them out to dry. In the morning they were still wet. He packed them into the plastic bag. In the evening they were mildewed. He thought: Is that how people smell when they're dead?

5

At the restaurant where the pigtailed girl in the green T-shirt that said   HONEY   stood cleaning her knife, the proprietor chopped meat and then the girl took her knife outside to talk with a girl who wore a gold chain around her neck, and a man wheeled a cart slowly down the alley and blue smoke drifted from three passing motorcycles and a wide white car rolled gently by. Peering down his nose into thick spectacles, the proprietor, bulging his chest out, put a hand on his hip and gazed placidly at the world. The girl came in, wiping her nose with the back of her hand, and cleared away a table. A couple sat at another table. The woman slid her foot easily out of the sandals, bent like a bird, and sucked up Coke through her straw. The man reached into the dish and put more on his plate. The proprietor crossed his hands against his back and jiggled his buttocks to the radio song. Vanna's husband ate pork. The girl was pretty, but he remembered his wife in the reddish-brown luminescence of everything, the old teak woodwork in the hotel room glossy reddish-brown like the back of some beetle, the cabinet a redder shade of brown, some different wood maybe or just the light, then her standing there with slightly raised shoulders against the cabinet not quite smiling at him in the crimson dress and blouse with the long gold stripes down it; her arms and hands and gentle slender fingers were more chocolaty

265

like the puddles on the Battambang road, so thick-brown they were almost orange, but her face, though partaking of brown, was much paler with a moony lemony delicacy especially where the sunlight was touching her on cheekbones and chin and sweet soft throat and between her eyes where he used to nose-kiss her to make her laugh; and her dark hair and eyes were much more intense than the brownish-black cabinet-darkness just behind her, her hair and eyes a positive negativity of perfect black! She stood with her fingers half-open and her face turned almost completely toward him, not quite, and this was his wife now and forever, her belly not entirely flat as with the younger girls, her cheekbones a little too sharp for easy beauty. A single earring caught light like a maddening crystal; she seemed to wear somebody's soul from her ear. No other soul, though; the other ear was hidden by her unguent-sweetened hair . . . And he thought: Soon she'll take her shower and I'll take my shower and we'll lie side by side in the blessed darkness and I'll put my arm around her and put my head on her heart as she cradles my head and I'll listen to her heart getting slower and slower and slower . . .

6

As the hot night faded, Joy and Oy and Noi and Pukki now probably faking their last orgasm, he sat in second class, waiting for the train to take him to the border. On the far side of the tracks, where sarongs hung over cubicles made of corrugated siding, a young woman with long black hair prayed her hands down her face. Beside her, an old lady got to her feet and hobbled barefoot, bent half over under a burden of water. A third woman, whose age seemed in between that of the other two, began to prepare rice. When it was steaming, the young woman began to chop or massage something unknown behind the metal wall, and all at once the black night sky turned morning grey, the train honked sourly, and they began to slide into the new day whose trains and buildings, still cool, mysterious, almost pure, would not fail soon to set about their own solitary routines. His window passed wet grey walls to which laundry clung like spiderwebs. Fire cans seethed orange beside a brown canal; siding-roofed houses crowded under a gracious tree, sweating a smell of smoke. An illuminated train shot by the other window, occluding the morning-clouded sky. In the dark leaf-roofed alleys, boys bicycled out, balancing ice sacks on their handlebars.

7

The almost empty train pulsed open-windowed past fishy-smelling palm fields, fat lady vendeuses singsonging up and down the aisle with Coke, dried fish, satay, rice . . . He bought an orange peacock's fan of chicken that was wired between two halves of a bamboo stick. It was very fresh and gingery and good.

8

The silver-blue backs of metaled houses formed a plain interrupted by shadow-crevices, a canal, an occasional tall palm . . . then these ended suddenly in grass as high as the window. A silver-fogged river flashed on him like relapsing fever. Silver fog lived on the grassheads like an aura. He saw a woman with four gold rings on her finger; she pressed her hand to her nose, looking in the window at him, and then the train was past. Bushy islands undercut by silver water-ribbons gave way to housecubes open and shuttered, grey walls. The train breasted the walled river of grass . . .

9

Again they passed another train, through whose windows he saw other heads and then windows, cutout palm foliage. Trains seemed to him like destinies. He wondered what kind of person he'd be becoming if he were on that other train.

10

The conductor approached in his olive-green uniform, a pad of mysterious forms under his arm like birth control calendars. He punched four and gave them to Vanna's husband. He put a pen in his mouth when he punched them. The golden star and double arrowhead on his shoulder, the golden medallion on his lapel, the grand golden lozenge-emblem just above the slick black visor of his cap, these tokens gave indisputable proof of his majesty. He leaned against the seat, almost erect, writing, saying something with a gentle smile, the long tendons vibrating in his arms. His pockmarked face was lowered, his pants creased to fresh knife-edges. After he was gone, all the passengers had to explain to one another the various forms he'd assigned them. Suddenly, Vanna's husband remembered a maxim he'd heard: In Cambodia you can give every official a gift; in fact, you'd better give every official a gift; in Thailand you'd better not give them a gift unless you know them.

11

At midday the train stopped for an hour. He went out and sat under the platform canopy, staring at a giant yellow Buddha whose topknot was just a little higher than the highest tree. Two skinny old monks, their once orange robes brown, leaned forward on a bench, patiently. There was a stand with glass-fronted triple shelves on narrow legs, puffed full of white balls with something red hiding inside. – He thought: I wonder if that's how my balls are now, with AIDS inside them . . .

12

Now they rattled through the heart of Thailand, plains of yellow-green, wet rice fields steaming like cunts, the underside of another green tree, white birds on the narrow rivers, a horizon-line of grey-green trees. The bridges were all grand (in Cambodia, each one having been meticulously blown up by the Khmer Rouge, the Hun Sen government rebuilt the only way it could, just twin metal tracks on the rusty trestles, good enough for military vehicles, the river waiting in between, so don't wobble right or left; and every bridge was guarded by soldiers); they were all painted, window-high; no soldiers stood there looking down on green rice-stubble in water . . . But in the middle of a rice field he saw a stick-bridge with its sticks projecting like crazy darning needles.

Yotaka. The flagman held out the dark green banner to send the train on; the red cloth hung sleepy in his other hand.

Vanna's husband gave a kid one of his apricot cookies, and the kid prayed thank you. His mother kept her money between her breasts. She had to reach up there to pay the conductor.

Prachinari. The rice fields ended, and then there was jungle with mountains ahead, and that Cambodian sandalwood smell. Sometimes they came out again into rice-lakes, but those were now bayed by trees and mountains. Houses stood on stilts among the big tree-ferns; and between the houses' legs lived colonies of birds in baskets.

Aranyaprathet. Last stop. All day the fan had been slowly dipping and turning overhead; now it went off and Vanna's husband felt his stomach begin to coil . . .

13

He passed an open-doored place that said **COFFEE SHOP –
RESTAURANT** and inside it was all girls kneeling before a
smoking Buddha; all the chairs faced Buddha, and beyond
Buddha was only the bar. The owner had died. It would be
closed for nine days.

14

He thought: Aside from this, what do I have left to accomplish?
– Nothing, really. I don't care if I never screw another whore.

He thought: Crossing the border isn't really worth it.

He thought: The reality is that these trips are getting harder
for me physically, emotionally, morally and maybe mentally.
There is nothing out here that I really want.

15

He thought: How many of my sweaty twilights has God seen?

16

He remembered how one night he'd sat up in bed beside her,
kissed the medallion of Catherine Tekakwitha which he wore
on the homemade loop of parachute cord now stained greyish-
green by years of feversweat and sleepwax and the fumes of
happiness, and he prayed for Vanna. She was watching him. For
the first time he slipped the medallion off. Then he hung it
round her neck. After that, he gave her the medallion every

night, and in the morning she gave it back to him. On their last night he kissed it and gave it to her to keep, and she confided to him her own most precious thing, a snapshot of her baby . . .

17

Far away on a sidewalk corner, a boy bounced a ball. He was many zones of light away. That sidewalk might as well be the whole empty world. Dresses hung in an open bay of light. A yellow traffic light opened and closed like a mouth. People were sitting at sidewalk tables by a parked wheel-stand that sold nothing. Their bent backs gave off aquarium colors as they ate.

18

You want to cross the border with Khmer Rouge? But that is illegal; that is very dangerous!

Well,　he told the translator,　it's all *Esquire's* fault. *Esquire* said I had to. Otherwise, I'll lose my job.

I know some people without legs,　said the translator. Because they try to cross the border. Why you want to do that?

Oh, to meet the Khmer Rouge –

The translator laughed incredulously.

Staring into the square black stagnant pool in the center of town (a squiggly white-cube reflection weighing down one corner of it), he tried to screw up his courage to ask a cyclo to take him to the border. The translator had said that they had checkpoints on the road at night. It was all so pointless, and so much effort, and nothing but a nightmare to reward him at the end of it, if he got anywhere at all. Why didn't he just drown himself in that filthy pool? – He felt very much alone. Outside the fence, the cyclo drivers sat in their vehicles in a row. The lighted markets with their piles of red and yellow fruit seemed to balance the leaves that hung over him like some scaly underbelly of the night. A barefoot boy passed through the tube of green light that spilled on the street. He was carrying a basket. Vanna's husband felt sad.

The man gladly accepted fifty bhat. On this kind of cyclo the driver sat ahead, towing the passenger in the wheeled booth. Seeing those sturdy brown legs pedaling him into the palmtree darkness, Vanna's husband felt inexpressibly lonely and sad. The man pedaled him down back ways, smoking a cigarette as he went. No one else was on the road. He saw people eating inside, and they were laughing loudly at something that one of them had done or said. On the sidewalk he passed three children, a boy and two girls. The boy gripped one of the girls' knees.

On the main road Vanna's husband kept his head down every time a car or motorbike passed. The sound of crickets and the smell of hemp were overpowering. The man pedaled on very slowly and serenely, like a distance swimmer. After a short time they reached the first bridge.

Ahead were white and red lights (very still and bright).

The lights were getting closer now and he wondered if that was when the trouble would start. They were very still and steady.

So they came to that first checkpoint, a triangle of incandescent tubes in the road, swarming with insects. A giant beetle crawled slowly up one of the bulbs, seeking something it would never find or understand. Then it slid to the ground.

There were three Thai policemen. They turned Vanna's husband back, and he beamed like an idiot and went. But he'd noticed that the car and motorbike drivers did not stop at that first checkpoint unless they wanted to. On his next attempt he'd lie down in the back of a car.

A firefly winked low in the grass. A motorbike shot by. A reflected light shone upon another stagnant pool.

In the car he made it to the second checkpoint before they

were stopped. The soldiers returned him to the first checkpoint, and this time the three policemen shouted and shook him. Again he grinned as stupidly as he could. Astonishingly, they did not arrest him or take his passport. After they had driven him back to town he sat trying to decide what to do. He could walk (it was only six kilometers) but what then? If he evaded the glares of checkpoint light, if he succeeded in clambering over the rolls of barbed wire at the end, then he'd be in a jungle filled with land mines. The best thing that could happen to him would be losing a leg –

19

There she was in the dimdark hotel room sitting side-saddle on the bed with one arm resting on his back while she touched her widely smiling mouth (though it was not exactly a smile since her eyes didn't change; it was just sweet and incomprehensible) with her forefinger – a pose she must have considered endearing or photogenic, since she did it all the time for the photographer; her husband didn't remember her doing it much for him; perhaps it was a trick she'd learned from some actress; anyway, she lounged in her waspdark-and-goldstriped dress, her elbows bent like wings, her face a little elongated by her "smile" in the mysterious blue air-conditioned quiet of the hotel darkness, no one able to see them because he or she had closed the shutters; her hand patted him very softly through the towel that entubed his waist; that was all he had on; he lay resting so beautifully, resting, happy with her weight on top of him, her butt against his side; he patted it; he wanted her to take her shower and lie down next to him so that he could hold her very tight and sleep (did she sleep when he slept or did she just lie there patient and close-eyed? he'd never wondered that before). He lay down and slept for an hour. Then he went out to try again.

20

This time he went on foot, ducking down into the feculent ditch whenever he saw or heard a vehicle. He neared the checkpoint of incandescent lights and veered left, crawling slowly. When he was even with the checkpoint, the white brightness grabbed and blinded him even as he tried to inch away from being seen. They did not see him. He felt a cold itch between his shoulderblades until he was in the darkness again. He waited for his sight to come back. Then he crawled for a long time. Vines cut tensely across his vision. The moss felt like a wet dog's sides. Already the bugs were crawling over him. He glanced back at the checkpoint and was shocked by its hellish brightness and proximity. Suddenly the soldiers began talking in agitated voices. He flung himself down onto his belly. There was a splash. His heart was pounding so fiercely that he thought he might vomit. Something soft and cold crawled across his neck in a series of rapid spasms. He lay very still until the talking stopped, and then he waited some more, until at last he heard a truck grinding loudly toward him from the town. That noise would surely cover him as well as any mask of leaves. He began to worm his way closer to Cambodia. When the truck drew abreast of him, he lay down again. Silent mosquitoes bit his face and neck. His chest ached from his heartbeat. He passed the second checkpoint, glimpsing in its outreach of alarm-glare many giant brown leathery leaf-cups like radar ears hanging dead in the dripping shadows, listening to life, and then that choice of surrender too was behind him, and there was only one more. It would be dawn soon. The mosquitoes were not so thick now. He began to allow himself hope that after all he'd be fully embraced by the jungle body. The darkness was bleeding in the east by the time he reached the place where the road turned left to the cleared zone where they had an open-air border market in the mornings and early afternoons, and it was bleak and far too bright but the soldiers were busy bellying themselves into prostitute-laughs. The lanes of barbed wire made him despair for

a moment, but he followed the nearest wall, going away from the soldiers and the light, and after a half-mile there was jungle instead of packed-down dirt, and at dawn the barbed wire wavered, pressed heavily by brown limbs and creepers, and so he found a hole; he knew from the Pat Pong girls that there'd always be a hole if he wanted one badly enough . . .

21

Skinny boys were shouting at him. They tied his wrists behind his back with wire. – Are you imperialist lackey of traitor? a boy shouted. – Yes, he beamed. I am a traitor.

They were very happy then. They'd finally found someone who was guilty.

They led him along the edge of a luminous brownish-green creek that smelled like muck. A huge crab dandled its claws in the middle, clutching at unripe twigs. It was not a beetle-shaped crab like the ones in the markets, but broad, flat and brown. Leaves and garbage were everywhere. The view vanished into stinking greenness. The trees were not especially tall or leafy, but they were everywhere. Weird structures of roots and intersecting vines like musical instruments played chords upon his heart. They led him through turnstiles of latticework roots the hue of ginger-bulbs, and it got darker and so did the stench of the creek. There was another crab, even bigger than the last, and it was eating someone's face half-sunk in the reddish-brown ooze. There was a crowd of toiling crabs, and then more barbed wire and they were there where they were supposed to be. She was looking on him full at last with that sweet soft pale smooth delicate face of hers, open and trusting, smiling – really smiling! – a pouty little smile like a kiss, her gold chain necklace coming shooting out of chin-shadow with the heart lying on her thin bluish-white blouse just above her breasts, inverted-V eyebrows seeming to question him a little as she smiled; the recognition of him took up her whole face as she sat waiting for him with that sad smile; he was hers; soon he'd be sleeping beside her forever.

Epigraphs and Sources

The Butterfly Boy

Epigraph – G. W. Leibniz, preface to *The New Essays* (1703–5) in *Philosophical Essays*, ed. and trans. Roger Arlew and Daniel Garber (Indianapolis: Hackett Publishing Company, 1989), p. 293.

Ulrich and the Doctor

Epigraph – Chuck Taylor, *The Complete Book of Combat Handgunning* (Cornville, Arizona: Desert Publications, 1982), p. 63.

More Benadryl, Whined the Journalist

Epigraph – Bert Hölldobler and Edward O. Wilson, *The Ants* (Cambridge, Mass.: The Belknap Press of Harvard University Press, 1990), p. 154.

The New Wife

Epigraph – N. Sanmugathasan, General Secretary, Ceylon Communist Party, "Enver Hoxha Refuted," in *A World to Win: International Marxist Leninist Journal*, no. 1, May 1981, p. 8.

Quotation in sec. 32 – Hanna Reitsch, *The Sky My Kingdom* (London: Greenhill Books, Lionel Levanthal Ltd., 1991), p. 81.

The Answer

Epigraph – Jean-Jacques Rousseau, *The Social Contract* and *Discourse on the Origin of Inequality*, rev. anon. trans. (New York: Washington Square Press, 1967), p. 188.

I Wouldn't Be Smiling That Way If I Were You

Epigraph – Yaroslav Golovanov, *Sergei Korolev: The Apprenticeship of a Space Pioneer*, trans. M. M. Samokhvalov and H. C. Creighton (Moscow: Mir Publishers, 1975 rev.), p. 7.

The Bordello of Pain

Epigraph – Tacitus, *The Annals of Imperial Rome*, trans. Michael Grant (New York: Penguin, 1975 rev.), p. 396.

Witness testimony footnote – "A group of Cambodian jurists," *People's Revolutionary Tribunal Held in Phnom Penh for the Trial of the Genocide Crime of the Pol Pot–Ieng Sary Clique: Documents (August 1979)* (Phnom Penh: Foreign Languages Publishing House, 1990), p. II–60.

Bridal Mines

Epigraph – Paul Virilio and Sylvère Lotringer, *Pure War*, trans. Mark Polizzotti (New York: Semiotext(e) Foreign Agents Series, 1983), p. 125.

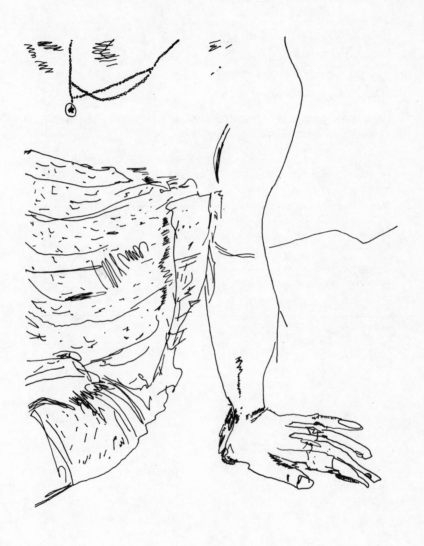